Vengeance Unbound

Gary Wayne Walker

HBE PUBLISHING

DEDICATION

To the Memory of my Mother, with Love

ACKNOWLEDGMENTS

This story is a work of fiction and all dialogue and action involving any of the characters portrayed are entirely the result of the author's imagination.

This book would not be possible without the help and encouragement of the Central Valley Writers and Artists group headed by our able instructor, Janice Stevens. Along with Janice, I am especially indebted to fellow-members Tom Morton, Gayle Taylor Davis and Anne Biggs.

I also want to express my gratitude and appreciation to my dear friend of more than half a century, Lynn Collings, who did a superb job of line editing much of the manuscript. My thanks also goes to my editor, Dan Dunklee, for his patience and his thoughtful suggestions intended to make the final product more consistent and coherent.

Finally, this book could never have been written without the loving and unconditional support of my wife, Lonna, who read every word of every draft over a period of nearly three years. A retired high school English teacher, Lonna's support and valuable contributions were indispensable to the writing and completion of this work.

G.W.W.

Chapter 1

Panorama City, Monday, March 10th, 1975

The house in Panorama City was located in a neighborhood that was no longer middle class. It had once been a street where people were proud to live, but nearby industrialization on Van Nuys Boulevard, especially the construction of the GMC plant, had changed all that. Many of the houses were rentals in need of fresh paint. Their yards dying of neglect, dilapidated sofas serving as porch furniture.

The life insurance agent parked at the curb and gazed at the house through the passenger window.

He had seen it before, of course. He had been inside the aging, frame stucco dwelling for more than an hour the day he wrote the application on Tommy Baldwin, the thirty-year-old truck driver who lived here with his wife and two small children. He was staring at the house because he was suffering from a bad case of nerves. He didn't want to go to the front door. He didn't want to deliver the contract.

Arnold Taylor felt a sense of foreboding. Something awful would happen if this policy took effect. While the calamity he feared may never play out, the fear was no less real.

Maybe he was just being paranoid. After all, he had been a compulsive worrier since junior high, when a multitude of catastrophes enveloped his family. The larceny, economic hardships and violence, along with the subsequent front page headlines created a stigma that had etched itself like an ugly scar onto his psyche. The yearlong drama had ended in 1955 with his father's sudden, violent death.

This was the first time in his twelve-year career selling life insurance that he feared a contract would be accepted rather than rejected. It had nothing to do with the fact that he disliked Tommy Baldwin. Nor was he unhappy about the $210 commission for three hours work.

There was no denying the one truth that had him so tied up in knots was a number. FORTY-FIVE.

It had been forty-five days since one of his clients was murdered arriving home from work. Forty-five days before that, the same thing had happened. And forty-five days before that.

While life insurance is always a matter of life and death, the 'death' part of it had never seemed so imminent. Today, the number, forty-five, suggested catastrophe.

When it came to Arnold Taylor's clientele, the Baldwin family was pretty much at the bottom of the economic scale. If Tommy Baldwin was ever targeted, his wife and kids would face far more hardship than any family in his client files. Taylor took a deep breath, then rang the doorbell.

"Come on in, Arnie, and thanks for always being so prompt. It's exactly four o' clock," said Helen Baldwin, a demure brunette with worried eyes.

"Can I get you a beer?"

"No thanks. I'm not much of a beer drinker, especially when I'm on the clock."

"Suit yourself," said Tommy, a six foot two inch truck driver with curly black hair. He pulled at his white sleeveless undershirt to scratch himself, exposing a massive hairy chest. Baldwin could have passed for a professional wrestler, or perhaps a bouncer in a topless bar.

"I suppose you prefer something more sophisticated, like martinis, right?"

"No, Sir. I'm not old enough to drink martinis. I like gin and tonics," Arnie jested as he sat at the kitchen table in the chair opposite Tommy and to the right of Helen. Whenever he returned for second or subsequent visits to prospects or clients, he almost always sat in the same seat. It was a comfort zone kind of thing.

Arnie tried his best to conceal his negative feelings toward Tommy. It wasn't the thirty-year-old man's condescending manner, it was the way he treated Helen. During the second interview, when the application had been written up, Arnie had advised against the $15,000 whole life policy he had wanted from the outset. Instead, he urged him to start off with a minimum of $150,000 annual renewable term contract, a less expensive policy that would increase in premium in small amounts over the years and could be converted to permanent insurance in increments as Baldwin's wages increased.

"Why in the world would I want to leave a hundred and fifty grand to my wife?" he bellowed. "You know what she'd do with all that money? You know what she'd do? She'd turn right around and marry some Robert Redford look-alike and they'd spend all their time together partying on my dime."

Arnie had heard this one before. A lot of men seemed to think their wives would be sleeping with another guy before the check from the life insurance company even arrived. To Arnie, Helen Baldwin didn't fit that profile. At twenty-six, she was personable and pleasant enough to look at, but she had no marketable job skills and two little girls to raise, the oldest only five.

Taylor pointed out that a little more than $40,000 was owed on the mortgage, that their $800 in savings wouldn't even cover the funeral. They had a $138 a month car payment on a '72 Ford Pinto, and other factors that suggested a need for a greater amount of coverage. But it was to no avail. Tommy wouldn't budge. Helen would get $15,000 if Tommy 'croaked', and not one damn cent more.

Ten minutes later, after Arnie had gone over the essentials of the contract, Tommy gave his life insurance agent a curt "thanks" and "good-bye," and took the policy to the back of the house. Helen was wiping her eyes with a handkerchief and shaking her head.

"Fifteen thousand dollars is better than nothing," said Arnie, "a whole lot better. It will give you a little breathing room until you decide what you want to do. Anyway, chances are good you won't need it until you're both very old."

After he opened the front door, Arnie turned around and observed Helen still sitting at the table, her tears now a quiet downpour. "Listen, I appreciate your business very much, and I want you to feel free to call me anytime. Take it easy now."

At four twenty-five, he pulled away from the Baldwin home in his '73 red Gran Torino. He turned right off of Lanark and onto Van Nuys, where the massive Panorama Towers could be seen ahead on the left.

The twelve-story building housed the Bear Republic Life Insurance Company on the sixth floor. Thirty-seven agents, including Arnold Taylor. Though he sensed he should stop at the office before going home, he continued north to Granada Hills, where he would turn left and drive a couple of dozen more blocks to his home in the Knoll Wood section of the foothills. He would call the office when he got home. There was no doubt in his mind his anxiety was warranted.

This was day number forty-five.

Arnie sat in the car for a couple of minutes as if in an trance, then got out and entered the house. Inside, he heard the familiar sound of Merv Griffin's voice emanating from the television, as Sandi sat on the sofa knitting an afghan. She mumbled a greeting, but he walked by in silence on his way to the kitchen wall phone. He dialed the Bear Republic phone number and, as soon as he said 'Hi' to Angie, the switchboard operator, she shouted:

"Arnie, Mr. Amalfitano wants you to get in here as fast as you can. He said to tell you we're now at number four, whatever that means . . . "

Arnold Taylor ran out of the house and headed back to the office. He hadn't uttered a word to Sandi, who sat there smiling.

It was her turn to use the phone.

Chapter 2

After glancing through the front window to be certain her husband's car was gone, Sandi Taylor got up, turned off the TV, walked to the phone. She dialed her favorite number and waited for the familiar voice.

"Hi Stan, it's Sandi. Is Dan Turner there?

"Hi! It's me. The jackass got home a couple of minutes ago and flew out of here like a bat outta hell, five seconds after a phone call to his office.

"No, he didn't say a word, either coming or going, which means he's still pissed off about last night.

"Like I told you at lunch today, it's not what we were arguing about that has him in such a tizzy. It's that I told him, 'Well if you're so angry, why don't you get a gun and shoot me? Isn't that what people do in your family?'

"I know, I know, I shouldn't have said it, but he shouldn't have slapped me. I just couldn't help myself. I had to say it. Knowing how sensitive he is about his father, I knew there was nothing else that would set him off like bringing up his stupid-ass family's sordid past.

"Yeah, I'm positive it was the office. I heard him say the name, 'Angie.' She's the switchboard operator. You know, the one whose son was shot down over Hanoi.

"Anyway, I'm pretty sure I know what the big hubbub is all about. I'm sure you do, too.

"Okay, I'll meet you at the Holiday Inn in about a half an hour. He won't be back for a while, we can pick up where we left off this afternoon. I love you."

Twenty minutes later, after applying a modicum of makeup and changing into a short skirt that showed off her legs, Sandra Ann Taylor backed her '69 Mustang out of the garage and drove the same route her husband of twelve years had taken not a half hour earlier. South on the

405 to the Roscoe Boulevard exit. The Holiday Inn was a few blocks from the Panorama Towers, but she and Dan both felt it was safe meeting place. The bar was frequented mainly by tourists and out of town businessmen.

They had met on the tennis courts of North Hollywood High. She was a high school junior and he was a freshman at Occidental. They sat on a bench and visited for a while, and she gave him her phone number. By the time she was a freshman at Cal State Northridge, they were having sex a couple of times a week. He said he was going to law school after finishing at Occidental, and wouldn't be able to get married until he passed the bar. She liked the thought of being married to a lawyer.

There was also a great physical attraction between them. She told him she was taking the pill, but that was not true. She wanted to get pregnant, the only sure way he would marry her before graduation. He didn't believe in abortion.

During the spring of Arnie's senior year, she got pregnant. While in her third month, the two were married in a small ceremony at the Congregational church in Glendale. Shortly after, she had an abortion and had her tubes tied. All without his knowledge. She didn't consider herself the nurturing type and had no interest in being a mother. She simply told her new husband she had miscarried and would never be able to have children. Arnie was disappointed – very disappointed, as he had always hoped for children.

Then Arnie gave her a jolt, one she could never get over. He decided not to go to law school. He felt he needed to get out in the business world and make money. He realized he didn't have the temperament to be a trial lawyer; always at war with someone. Furthermore, Arnie didn't want to be compared to his father. Instead, he became a life insurance agent, a good one. He brought home a decent paycheck, and enjoyed the freedom that came with the job. But his wife was embarrassed to be married to someone who sold insurance. She often told him so.

Sandi parked her car in the back lot of the Holiday Inn, opened the door and got out, and stood there for a moment before heading toward the back entrance. After taking a deep breath, she exhaled, smiled, and started walking.

The time had come for Dan to make good on his promise. If he's ready to grant her request, Sandi's reason for dating him in the first place, would be fulfilled. She would be able to get on with her life.

Chapter 3

Arnie got out of his car and looked around the parking lot. He was surprised there wasn't a police car in sight. Then he realized that if Dom had called the police, whoever came would likely be a detective driving an unmarked car. Perhaps Lieutenant Columbo was inside, cigar in hand, his beat-up old Renault parked out on Titus somewhere. Unfortunately, this wasn't TV, but the real world. He would have bet a thousand bucks someone from the LAPD was upstairs in the boss's office waiting for him.

Dominic Amalfitano was agency manager of the Bear Republic's San Fernando Valley office. A Vietnam veteran, he left the giant insurance company after four years to join the Marines when LBJ escalated the war in the summer of 1965. Discharged as a sergeant after serving two of his three years of service in combat in Southeast Asia, Amalfitano had been awarded two purple hearts and a Marine Corps citation for exceptional bravery under fire.

A soft-spoken Italian American with an unmistakable New York accent, Dom, as everyone called him, was widely recognized as an excellent manager. Many agents thought he could move up to the home office in San Francisco if he wanted to, or to one of the company's premier agencies on Wilshire Boulevard in LA, or 42nd Street in Manhattan. He had taken over the Panorama City office in 1970, and in a little over four years, had grown it from eleven agents to thirty-seven. At thirty-eight years of age, Amalfitano had earned a hefty ninety thousand dollars in 1974.

Arnie had become a life insurance agent in 1964, after graduating from Occidental and serving a six-month tour of duty at Fort Ord in Monterey as a member of the US Army Reserve. He had completed his six-year obligation as an enlisted man in army intelligence in 1970, having never been called to active duty. He opposed the war, but had never demonstrated against it, written letters to the editor, or made any kind of a public fuss. Arnie made no bones about his position, however, whenever the subject of Vietnam came up. He was against it. The war was the only subject he and his boss could not discuss. They had tried once, while having lunch in a nearby restaurant. The agency manager had gotten up in the middle of the meal and stormed out. It was several days before the two spoke again.

After exiting on the 6th floor, Arnie, unsmiling and feeling flushed, nodded at Angie as he walked past the switchboard and turned right to enter the manager's office. Upon closing the door behind him, a black-haired man in a gray suit stood to greet the beleaguered agent.

"Arnie, this is Lieutenant Frank Hogan of the LAPD," said Amalfitano. "For the past half hour or so, I've given him a broad outline of the problem we're facing."

Handsome, maybe '5,"10," a little pudgy, graying at the temples, Arnie judged him to be somewhere south of fifty.

After Lieutenant Hogan and Taylor took the two seats at the front of the desk, Arnie asked, "Who's number four?"

"Don Watson--"

"Oh my God." he said, then dropped his head and stared at the floor, silent and dumbfounded.

Dom continued. "He was shot around two this afternoon while getting out of his car when he arrived home early from work. It's like the first three murders—each policyholder was shot before he could even get to his front door."

"Who called to report the claim?" asked Arnie.

"His son, Jeff," said Amalfitano, his voice barely audible. "About an hour ago. The file's right here. I've shared its contents with Lieutenant Hogan. The contract was issued about five years ago. Watson's wife, Cheryl, is the beneficiary."

Hogan turned to his right to face Arnold Taylor. "How old is Jeff?"

"Oh, twenty or twenty-one—something like that. I met him briefly a year or so ago. He's a student at UCLA."

Arnie paused for a moment, then grabbed a handkerchief from his pocket and wiped the sweat off his face. "The face amount is $50,000 and . . . "

"We know all that, Arnie," Amalfitano said. "And I've also informed the lieutenant that in all four cases, the wife's the beneficiary. He already knew, of course, that the killings are all forty-five days apart. What he didn't know is that all four victims had the same life insurance agent."

"Until now, this was the missing piece," said the lieutenant, "the fact that all four of these victims bought their life insurance from the same agent. We suspected there must be some link that tied them together, but we just didn't know what it was. We didn't even notice they were all Bear Republic policyholders. Even if we had, I'm not sure it would have gotten our attention. After all, Bear Republic is a very large company. Millions of people are insured by you guys, right?"

Amalfitano nodded. "That's correct. We're the ninth largest life insurance company in America, and since we're based in California, we have a disproportionate market share here in the Valley and, for that matter, throughout the state."

"Anyway," said Hogan, "we normally get interested in the life insurance only when there is some reason to expect foul play on the part of the beneficiary. You know, the *Double Indemnity* kind of thing."

Arnie understood the lieutenant's reference, as would most life insurance agents, at least the older ones. He had seen "Double Indemnity" on TV as a kid. Fred MacMurray, the agent, had conspired with Barbara Stanwyck, the wife, to kill her husband so that she could collect the life insurance and split it with MacMurray.

Frank Hogan rose and looked at Arnie. "I hope you don't mind, Mr. Taylor, but I'm going to have to ask you some questions. I realize this is a terrible shock and that you might need some space for a little while, but I must get information from you right away. This is the first real break we've had in this case, and I'm anxious that our homicide folks get on this immediately."

"What Lieutenant Hogan has not told you, Arnie," said Amalfitano, "is that he's angry that it's gone on this long before the police were told about the life insurance. He told me that we should have reported this immediately after the second murder; that a lot of valuable time has been wasted and, maybe, and it's a big 'maybe,' the last two killings could have been avoided."

"That's right," said Hogan. "The important clue here is not the fact that they're all Bear Republic policyholders, but that all four of them bought their policies from you. This could be an important link in solving the crime."

Arnie shot a quick glance at the lieutenant and then looked down at the floor.

"I knew Dom would have to call the police if there was one more murder," he said, "that this couldn't be just an unfortunate coincidence. Until now, I was just hoping against hope–even praying – that it's just plain old bad luck." Hogan looked over at Amalfitano, frowned, and then back at Arnie.

"Your boss didn't call anyone, Arnie. I'm here strictly as a result of an anonymous tip. Some guy called around 3:30 this afternoon. He gave us your name, and said he was calling the newspapers."

"I have another appointment in a few minutes," Amalfitano said. "Can you take this to Arnie's office? He's really the one you came to see."

Chapter 4

Arnie ushered Lieutenant Hogan into his office, closed the door, and sat behind his desk while the police officer took one of the two chairs normally occupied by clients.

"I just remembered something," said Arnie, "I think I heard that Don Watson was critically, maybe even terminally, ill. Pancreatic Cancer. Oh well, I can look that up in the file later. Anyway, it doesn't matter now."

Hogan grimaced without comment, then took a quick look at Arnie's office. An uncluttered desk, a couple of framed photographs of his wife and mother, and four four-drawer file cabinets.

"This may take a little while, Mr. Taylor," said the lieutenant. "I need to ask you a number of questions to get more of a handle on what's going on."

"Fair enough, but first I want to ask you a question, Lieutenant. Did the man who called in identify me by name?"

"Yes, he did. He said Arnold Wayne Taylor," said Hogan.

Arnie paused for a moment. "That's very interesting. I only use my first and last name in business. I'm sure most of my clients, as well as most business associates here at the office, don't even know I have a middle name. If they do, they don't know what it is."

"While you don't use all three names professionally, your middle name is really not a secret," said Hogan. "Is that correct?"

"No, it's not a secret," said Arnie, "but the use of all three names makes me wonder whether the caller knows me personally. He seems to know more about me than most people. Anyway, I can't help but feel that it's not good news that the caller knows that much about me."

"Let's move forward, Arnie. We're looking for the killer, not the caller. Whether or not it's the same person is a moot point." Hogan opened a small notebook and pulled a pen from his inside pocket.

"Do you mind if I take off my jacket?" asked the Lieutenant. Arnie motioned for him to go right ahead.

"For starters, I'd like to make one thing perfectly clear —everyone in this office is a suspect at this point, including you. I'm starting with the assumption that either the killer works in this office, or someone is feeding him information about your clients. Of course, this assumption could change. We need to begin by learning as much as possible about everyone who works here. Everyone. That includes the janitor who picks up the trash every night, the agency manager, the management staff, the girls in the office, secretaries and agents. Anyone who has anything to do with the office."

"Amalfitano a suspect? He has as much to lose as I do. More, why, they could shut down the entire office if these killings continue. My good friend, Michael Wong, is a suspect simply because he works out of this building? This is getting crazier by the minute."

"I sympathize with your frustration, Mr. Taylor. Please understand, investigating murders is our job, it's what we do. We start by assuming everyone is a suspect. Then we narrow the list until maybe, two or three remain. Eventually. . .bingo, we've got him. Or her." Lieutenant Hogan continued. "Now, does everyone in the office know someone is killing your clients?"

"I suppose so," said Arnie, "since the girls in our GSO all know. They talk back and forth while working all the time, of course, and to the agents as well. No information is sacred around here. For example, one of the girls is currently sleeping with one of the agents, a married man I might add, and there's not a soul in this office that doesn't know about it. There's always plenty of talk going around. You know, office gossip, that sort of thing ."

"GSO?"

"I'm sorry, Lieutenant. That's how we refer to our General Services Office, which is staffed by three clerical people, all female, and a GSO manager, Judy Isenberg. All life insurance applications are submitted to this unit, where the apps are reviewed and then forwarded to the home office in San Francisco. When the medical exams are completed and underwriting requirements satisfied, the home office issues the policies and mails the contracts back to our GSO, where they are checked for accuracy, and given to the agents for delivery to the clients."

"And death claims are also submitted through this GSO unit?"

"Yes," said Arnie, noting the large circles under Hogan's eyes. The man looked as if he hadn't slept for a week. His large, sorrowful eyes reflected the appearance of one who had been through the wringer more than a couple of times. Arnie assumed the lieutenant was the lead investigator on this bizarre case, and that his disheveled appearance and hunched shoulders reflected his fatigue and sense of futility, which had been going on for six months.

"Do you get along well with other agents and staff here in the office?" asked the lieutenant. "Let me put it another way. Do you have any reason to believe someone has it in for you for some reason or other?"

Arnie took a deep breath and looked down at his desk while rubbing his right earlobe. The question made him uncomfortable. "Well, I'm probably not the most popular guy in the office, but I don't think anyone despises me enough to kill my clients. Besides, what motive could somebody possibly have? Once it comes out that all of the victims bought policies from this office, it's not only bad for me but for every agent and employee in this office. That's horrible publicity. The part I don't get, if someone is that angry with me, why don't they just greet me with a .38 revolver when I get out of my car some day after work? It's almost a Chinese water torture going on out there."

"You're certainly right about that, Mr. Taylor, which brings us to the key of solving any crime. . .motive. Who in this office could possibly have a motive to go after your clients? A motive so strong, that every time there is a new victim, it acts as a curse for every agent peddling Bear Republic products?"

Arnie, incensed by Hogan's language, expelled an audible breath of air. "We don't 'peddle' anything around here, Lieutenant. Most of us are professionals who do a thorough analysis of the client's needs before making recommendations. Every agent in this office has attended college, at least junior college. Many of us have bachelor's degrees from first-rate four-year colleges, and at least three have MBAs, one of them from Stanford. One is even a CPA, which says a lot about how professional our organization is."

"I'm sorry, Mr. Taylor. That was a poor choice of words."

"The truth is," said Arnie," I'm especially sensitive about degrading comments like that. I live with that same bullshit every day at home." For a moment he was sorry he had brought Sandi into the conversation, but upon reflection, he didn't regret it at all. The two sat in silence for a moment.

"Do you mind if I smoke?" asked the Lieutenant.

"Go right ahead," said Arnie. Hogan reached in to his pocket and pulled out a pack of Salems. While the lieutenant lit up, Arnie was conscious of the barely audible commuter traffic on Van Nuys Boulevard six floors below.

"You made a couple of comments I would like to explore, Mr. Taylor. First, what do you mean when you say you're probably not the most popular guy in the office"?

"Don't get me wrong, I have lots of friends here, including a couple of very good ones, I've just never really been 'one of the boys,' if you know what I mean, and I never will."

Arnie noticed a look of incredulity on Hogan's face, signaled by a wrinkled brow, which narrowed as he tossed Taylor a long, pensive look. He took a deep drag from the cigarette and nodded for Taylor to continue.

"Well, for starters, a good eight or ten of our senior agents, our leading producers, are gamblers. I'm not talking about betting on Super Bowl games or the World Series. I'm talking about contacts with book-ies, frequent trips to Lake Tahoe and Vegas, that sort of thing. A year or so ago, ten of us were seated in a nice restaurant a block from the home office in San Francisco, and after everyone's lunch order had been taken, someone suggested that each of us write down our estimation of what the total bill would be. Whoever missed by the largest margin, would then be stuck with the entire tab."

"Wow," said the lieutenant, "So what happened?"

"I quoted Sam Goldwyn's famous line, 'include me out.' I was the only one not willing to play. I got the usual rolling eyes and stares like I'm so tight I squeak. Or worse yet, I'm a goody-goody who is above engaging in such trivial pastimes as gambling. The truth is, I have noth-ing against gambling. It's just not in my blood. For me, it's like scratch-ing something that doesn't itch."

"Are there other examples of you being something of an outsider?"

"Yes, and strange as it may sound, it's all centered around politics," said Arnie. The lieutenant took another drag of his cigarette, and stared at the agent in silence. Arnie pulled a desk drawer open, retrieved an ashtray, and pushed it across the desk to Hogan.

"I'm a Democrat, though I did vote for Nixon in '72, a vote I've come to regret, I might add. The fact is, I grew up a staunch Repub-lican, a great admirer of Eisenhower and Earl Warren and Senator Tom Kuchel. But I became unhappy when the party of Lincoln turned against Civil Rights, and downright angry when Nixon widened the war in Vietnam after promising he had a plan to end it."

"This is actually a problem for you in the office?" asked the lieu-tenant as he shook his head. "It's hard to believe."

"Well, believe it," said Arnie. "This is a very conservative busi-ness. You know, personal initiative, all that sort of thing. Almost all the agents come from Republican families, and they're Rotarians and Kiwanis members. Many of them attend conservative fundamentalist churches, some fought in Vietnam, and all of them are scared to death the federal government will eventually put us out of business."

Lieutenant Hogan smiled. "And you don't think so?"

"No, I don't. More life insurance is being sold today than ever before, and the same is true of health insurance, which, ten years after Medicare came along, has actually helped the business rather than hurt it."

Arnie noted Lieutenant Hogan shifting uneasily in his chair. The agent knew most police officers were Republicans. They saw the seamier side of life on a daily basis and had little patience with so-called "bleeding heart" liberals.

"Tomorrow, I'd like to meet with you at your home, if that's okay," said the lieutenant." I want you to be real specific about anybody who you believe really has it in for you. I'm not talking about gambling issues or conservative versus liberal stuff, that's pretty commonplace, what with Civil Rights, Vietnam and Watergate. I want to know about anyone who really stands out for his dislike of Arnold Taylor, whatever the reasons. Someone you would never want on your blind side."

"If you don't mind, I'd rather not meet at my house," said Arnie. "As I indicated earlier, my wife and I are not getting along well these days. I don't want her to be privy to the information I will be sharing with you. I only want her to know what the rest of Southern California will know after they read it in tomorrow morning's *LA Times*."

"Fair enough," said the Lieutenant. "How about Bob's Big Boy in Toluca Lake for breakfast?"

"That's fine, I love Bob's. I used to take dates there, good memories."

"Seven o'clock? I need to get going on this as early as possible."

"I'll be there. Before you leave, I need to give you some background on my family. You'll discover it soon enough anyway, since I'm certain you're going to be digging in to my past. You might as well hear it from me."

A little more than an hour later, as the two were headed out the front door, Dom Amalfitano walked out of his office to shake hands with Lieutenant Hogan and pledge his complete cooperation with the LAPD, no matter where the investigation led.

The agency manager then tossed a cold stare at Arnie and asked him to step into his office for a moment. Dom said there was a new development he needed to share right away.

When Taylor left the office a couple of minutes later, he wasn't just emotionally exhausted, he was angry. Very angry.

16

Chapter 5

The Red Barn was located in the heart of Panorama City, a couple of blocks north of the Towers at the corner of Parthenia and Van Nuys. The owner, Bill Castle, a popular figure in the area, never forgot a name, and was always kind and generous to the help. The busy restaurant was known for its great steaks, and a good, old-fashioned '50s style jukebox that always seemed to be playing Rock and Roll. Entering the restaurant, customers were greeted by the smell of sawdust and the voice of Elvis, Buddy Holly, or other music legends of the era.

Ricki Wright had driven past the Red Barn a hundred times, but had never walked through the door.

"Would you like to start with something from the bar?" asked the waitress as Ricki was being seated.

"Yes, a gin and tonic with a twist of lime, please."

"Do you have a preference for the gin, or would you like the house brand?"

"Bombay Safire," said Ricki.

Blessed with a face that reminded people of Jacqueline Bisset, Ricki had a figure that would have made a perfect model for Botticelli, had she been around five hundred years earlier. She always had the last laugh on those who thought what they saw was the whole package. Behind those sparkling green eyes, there was a first-class brain, an intense curiosity and relentless ambition.

Seated at a small table in a dark corner, Ricki saw a man with a familiar face walk into the main dining room. Arnold Taylor stood perhaps thirty feet away, slowly glancing from one side of the room to the other. He had given her a quick glance, but had not shown any sign of recognition. She noticed he looked disconsolate. The hostess approached and led Taylor to a booth located diagonally about twenty feet from where Ricki sat. He sat on the left, meaning he would have a clear view of her whenever he looked in her direction.

Ricki and Arnie shared a history that went all the way back to the fall of 1951, when her family settled in North Hollywood. They were both assigned to Mrs. Kirkman's fifth-grade class at Colfax Avenue School.

When Arnie obtained a paper route delivering the afternoon Herald-Express, she would often help him fold newspapers and then ride along the route, the two jabbering about everything from television's Dragnet to Jackie Robinson to General Eisenhower. Something of a tomboy, he always treated her as a pal, one of the guys.

Then, at a most inopportune time, everything changed. She became curvy and pretty. No longer one of the guys. She waited for him to ask her to school dances at North Hollywood Junior High, to go out on real dates.

But Arnie's world was imploding. The family lost their house as a result of malfeasance on the part of his lawyer-father and Arnie's mother initiated a divorce. It was very bitter. Eventually, his father riddled his mother and a male friend with bullets and fled to Mexico.

During this period, from the fall of 1953 to April of 1955, Arnie's self-confidence plummeted as he suffered a loss of pride manifested by a lack of interest in school, girls, sports and world events. His days of passion for the world around him were over. Arnie shut himself off from her and everyone else. He became a loner, a frail, youthful version of one of television's more popular characters, Jackie Gleason's 'Poor Soul.' After the Taylor family tragedy had passed, Ricki's hopes for a teenage romance were dashed forever when he was awarded a four-year scholarship to Black-Foxe Military Institute in Hollywood. He was now living in another world. Out of necessity, she put Arnold Taylor behind her and got on with her life.

Ricki took a sip of her drink and casually glanced in Arnie's direction. He was staring at her. He smiled, got up and headed toward her table as she rose to greet him. He hugged her and after planting a big kiss on her cheek, asked, "Mind if I join you?"

"Not at all. In fact, I'd love it," she replied. "When I saw you walk in, a couple of minutes ago, I assumed your wife would be joining you, or perhaps a business client?"

"Nope, I'm all alone tonight, or was until I was fortunate enough to run into you. This has probably been the longest day . . ."

"Before you go any further, Arnie, do you remember how long its been since we've seen each other?"

He paused for a moment, looked directly into her eyes, "Yes, I do. It was August, 1962, and we were in the same beer line at Dodger Stadium. Thirteen years ago."

"Do you remember who was playing that day?" she asked, while tossing him her prettiest smile.

"Yes, it was a double-header and the Dodgers were playing the Cubs. Koufax beat Dick Ellsworth in game one, but I don't remember anything about the second game other than that we won."

Ricki smiled. "Okay, I was just checking your memory. I see it's as good as ever. I don't remember anything at all about the double-header except that we chatted for a good ten minutes while waiting to get to the front of the line. You were about to start your senior year at Occidental, and I was getting ready to return to NYU to finish my undergraduate work in marine biology. Now, please continue with what you were saying before I so rudely interrupted."

"That's okay, it's fun to reflect on the last time we ran into each other. I was about to say that this has been one of the longest days of my life and, as you well know, I had already had more than my share of long days before I even left home back in '63."

Ricki got the waiter's attention, who approached and asked Arnie what he would like to drink.

"I'll have a gin and tonic," he said. "Bombay Safire, and a twist of lime."

"Funny," she said. "That's what I'm drinking. Good to see we still have some things in common." For the first time since he had walked into the Red Barn, Ricki noticed Arnie wearing a grin.

"I was just about to say the same thing. We've been apart for more than twenty years, even living on opposite ends of the country, and it's like nothing has changed. Before I go any further, are you aware that I'm a life insurance agent representing Bear Republic?"

"Yes, I've heard that," she said. "I was surprised. Really surprised. I was sure you were a lawyer since that was always what you said you were going to be."

"Well, I'll tell you all about that, but first I have a couple of questions for you. I know you went back east for college and I heard somewhere that you got married, and a couple of years later, divorced. And that's the extent of my knowledge on Ricki Wright other than that you're obviously back in town, pretty as ever, and sitting across from me at a nice restaurant."

"Actually, I'm twice divorced. I have two children, a boy and a girl. My dad died a couple of years ago and left my mother a nice little bundle of cash. She's now home, still in North Hollywood, watching my kids, Peter and Laurie, while I attend public administration classes at Cal State Northridge."

He shook his head in disbelief. "I'm so sorry, Ricki," he said, "I had no idea you've had such a rough go of it."

"Oh, please, don't feel sorry for me. I don't have any complaints. I've decided that, life is one long roller coaster ride, with ups and downs and in-betweens. I wouldn't trade the last dozen years for anything. In fact, I can't wait to find out what my next adventure will be. You only go around once, and I'm determined to live life to the fullest."

Arnie said that his life had been a roller coaster, too, but it had not been of his choosing. He related to the Kingston Trio hit of the late '50s, where that guy couldn't get off the Boston MTA and was doomed 'to ride forever neath the streets of Boston . . .'

Over dinner, Arnie told Ricki about the four murders of his clients, and the precarious position it put him with Bear Republic.

The first victim owned a small printing shop; the second, an engineer at North American Rockwell; the third, a music arranger for The Rockford Files; and today, an air-conditioning and refrigeration mechanic. They lived in diverse places; Glendale, Northridge, Chatsworth and Tujunga; the engineer was Japanese, the printer a Mexican, and the other two, Caucasian.

"This is so weird," said Ricki. "The thing that doesn't make sense, is the motive. Serial killers usually go after a certain type, like homeless people or prostitutes, or homosexuals. But none were connected other than the life insurance. You."

"Oh, there's something I failed to mention," said Arnie. "There is a method to this madness. All murders have occurred exactly forty-five days apart, a span of exactly six months as of today and each have been shot as they arrived home from work.

"And finally," said Arnie, "after spending a couple of hours with Lieutenant Hogan, my boss, called me into his office and said I'm suspended as a Bear Republic agent. No sales. Of course, he's right; by tomorrow it will be all over the newspapers that I'm the link in these murders. Even I wouldn't buy a policy from me.

"More than anything, it was Dom's attitude that upset me. He said that we can expect hundreds of cancelations. That it's going to cost the company a ton of money, and it's my fault. He intimated that I must have been pretty damn obnoxious to have annoyed someone to the point where he goes out and commits murder to bring me down."

"My God, Arnie, what are you going to do if you can't sell insurance? You've been doing it for a long time now. I'm sure you've built up quite a business. I suspect you'd have a hell of a time getting on with Prudential or Equitable or New York Life or any other major company given what's happened."

"I really haven't had time to think about it, Ricki. "Dom says he will pay me $2,500 a month to put on training classes in-house for new agents, but I'm not interested. For one thing, I have a respectable renewal account, minus whoever leaves me as a result of the scandal. Besides, if I'd wanted to be a teacher, I would have gone to grad school and would be in a college classroom expounding on Shakespearean tragedy, which, come to think of it, I seem to be living. Anyway, my financial status is the last thing on my mind at the moment. I'll get by, somehow. As you know, I'm a survivor."

After the waiter had cleared their table and they had enjoyed a third drink, Arnie looked at his watch and said it was time for him to go home. As he rose from his chair, he said, "May I walk you to your car?"

"No thank-you, Arnie. I'm going to have one more."

"Are you sure? It'll be your fourth and you have to drive all the way to North Hollywood."

"I'll be fine," she said. "Whenever I stay late in this part of the Valley, I always check in to the Holiday Inn on Roscoe."

Arnie gave her his mother's phone number, and Michael Wong's, as a means of contacting him and she gave him her mother's. After giving her a quick kiss on the cheek, he walked out of the Red Barn without looking back.

Ricki downed half her drink while watching him walk to the door. She experienced ambivalent feelings about this fortuitous meeting. On the one hand, Arnie was a dear friend. In fact, the oldest she had outside of her family. Given their past, she felt a strong emotional tie to him.

On the other, this had been more than two old friends getting together to catch up on their respective lives. She had been truthful in as far as what she told him, but she had not told him everything. She did not mention the fact that she had been watching him for months and knew everything he told her, all but his link to the recent murders. This was all news to her. If her suspicions were correct, she would soon become the biggest star in the department.

Ricki Wright was an undercover cop in the LAPD. Arnold Taylor was her number-one target.

Chapter 6

Tuesday, March 11, Toluca Lake

At 6:35 on Tuesday morning, Arnie turned right off of Rinaldi and headed south on the 405, the San Diego Freeway. People were beginning to refer to freeways by the numbers. Arnie thought this was an absurdity. His head was filled with enough numbers: birthdays, anniversaries, Zip Codes, area codes, phone numbers, his Social Security number, dates of historical interest. There was no end.

Arnie failed to notice a late-model green Plymouth Fury turn off Woodley onto Rinaldi near the on-ramp. It was a car length behind him as he got on the busy freeway.

He was on the San Diego Freeway, not the 405, until, he would exit east to the Ventura Freeway, not the 101, and drive to the Cahuenga exit. Names not numbers.

Why was he focused on something so trivial? So many problems. Life, death, divorce, career. All he can think of is numbers.

The green Plymouth remained behind him, but the driver had dropped back a couple of car-lengths and moved to the far-right lane to allow more distance. The vehicle remained in that lane and continued to follow Arnie's Gran Torino onto the Ventura Freeway, heading east all the way through the Cahuenga off-ramp, where, the driver watched and drove past Bob's on Riverside Drive, as the Torino pulled into the coffee shop's back parking lot.

When Arnie walked from the parking lot to the Bob's Big Boy entrance in front, he passed the news racks.

The *LA Times* had the story in the upper right-hand corner of the front page.

VALLEY SERIAL KILLER STRIKES FOR FOURTH TIME.

Below, in smaller font,

"Bear Republic Acknowledges All Four Victims Bought Life Insurance from Same Agent."

The headline of the *Valley News and Greensheet* took up the entire top of the page;

VALLEY SERIAL KILLER LINKED TO

GIANT INSURANCE COMPANY.

Arnie was relieved that his picture did not appear on the front page of either paper. He put some change in the rack, grabbed both papers, and walked into the lobby where Lieutenant Hogan stood waiting.

****

The lieutenant felt rested for the first time in weeks. He finally got that good night's sleep he so badly needed. The link with the four murders was weak. It begged more questions that it answered, but it was something, and it allowed him a small respite.

Also, his wife, Gail, was not only sober when he got home, but had dinner on the table in fifteen minutes. Meatballs and spaghetti, a cold beer, and a store-bought apple pie for dessert.

The Hogans were married in 1952, the year he joined the Los Angeles Police Department. For the first couple of years, they were very happy. But after the birth of their daughter Michelle, Gail became depressed, and never really recovered. What was first believed to be postpartum anxiety became something long-lasting, more severe. She went through a series of psychiatrists and psychologists, but none were able to help her. She was given Miltown, Librium and finally, Valium. She was hospitalized twice, once after a suicide attempt during which she drank an entire bottle of Johnnie Walker Red, her favorite form of escape.

Frank Hogan, a good Irish-Catholic boy, was in an unhappy marriage. He stuck it out as long as Michelle was at home. But she was now nineteen and living in San Diego while attending junior college. Hogan became a workaholic, spending as little time at home as possible. Gail was a person who sought solitude. She was happiest alone with her two best friends, Beefeaters and Johnnie Walker. At some point, he just might have to move out and file for divorce, Church or no Church.

Hogan greeted Arnie, and escorted him to a booth in the rear of the restaurant.

"I was watching when you grabbed the papers off the rack," Hogan said.

"Yeah, I was curious to see how the media handles the situation. Whether or not they name me. But I'll read them later. Have you read *The Times* this morning?"

"Yes," said the lieutenant, "At home while having coffee. For your information, you have been identified as the agent for all four victims. I wouldn't spend much time worrying about it, Arnie. Your identity would eventually become public anyway. Besides, common sense dictates you'll probably appear to be a victim rather than an assassin."

"Do you really agree with that, Lieutenant? You told me yesterday that everyone's a suspect, including me."

"Well, yes, that's theoretically true," said Hogan as he glanced at a darkhaired, rotund man being seated at a table about twenty feet away. "But let's get real—some suspects are more likely to be the killer than others."

The waitress appeared, pad and pencil in hand. "Have you two decided what you would like to order?"

"I'll have bacon and eggs with a side of toast and some orange juice," said Arnie. "The eggs over easy, bacon crisp, and coffee. Could you bring some coffee right away?" The lieutenant shook his head and ordered waffles.

"Let's keep our voices down. We certainly don't want to be overheard, this being such a sensitive matter. Ah, also, nothing personal, Arnie, but you look like shit. Did you get any sleep at all last night?"

"A couple of hours I guess. It was a night of alternate restlessness and apprehension, with brief periods of sleep in between. Sandi never came home so, I had that to worry about, too. That is, worry that she might show up."

Arnie shifted his body, trying to get comfortable. "The truth is, I'm certain I would have slept even less had she been there, so it probably was a blessing she never came home."

"Aren't you concerned that maybe something bad happened to her? Has this ever happened before, her not coming home without letting you know in advance?"

"No, it hasn't," said Arnie, "but she's fine. Either she was with that guy she's been seeing the last six or eight months or she stayed with her parents' in Chatsworth. She's always been daddy's little girl."

"Let's talk about your wife," said Hogan, "since you've just said something very interesting. You say Sandi has had a boyfriend for six or eight months? That's exactly the time frame of the four murders.

"Yes, that's true, but I'm not certain when he started seeing her. Hell, it might have been a year, or more, for all I know."

"How did you discover she was cheating on you?" asked Hogan.

"Well, this isn't her first fling. I can tell when she's sleeping with someone else because she always smells like soap when we have sex. You know, like she had cleaned herself up more thoroughly. She'd usually be in the shower a couple of minutes before we went to bed, but then I'd notice she was in there a good ten minutes, sometimes longer."

"And that's how you know she's seeing someone else? You're convinced your wife's cheating on you because she smells like soap?"

"Well, there is another reason. An agent at the office, someone she doesn't know, told me he's seen her in the bar at the Holiday Inn over on Roscoe Boulevard a couple of times. He said she's always with the same guy. He recognized her from the awards banquet last year."

"He recognized her, but she didn't recognize him? That seems odd," said the lieutenant.

"Not really," said Arnie. "my source is not someone I'm close to, so we've never socialized. He's a nondescript sort of guy whom she would not likely remember. Plus, my freind says she only has eyes for her boyfriend."

Arnie yawned and picked up his coffee cup, took a deep swallow, then stared directly into Hogan's eyes.

"Did your fellow-agent say what this guy looks like?" asked the lieutenant.

"Yes, he said the man looks Italian, or something similar. And he's overweight, around 250 pounds."

"I want to know the name of your source, Arnie. Mr. Amalfitano is going to have a dozen or so agents for me to talk to this afternoon, and

I'd like to ask him some additional questions."

"His name is Whit Payne. He'll tell you anything you need to know."

The two sat in silence for a minute or so while Hogan removed a small notebook from his inside coat pocket, then shot another glance at the heavyset man seated nearby.

Arnie took in a deep breath, and exhaled an audible sigh. "Everything I've told you is correct, Lieutenant, but I still don't see a motive."

Arnie's early comment on how he was happy Sandi hadn't come home last night had given Hogan a great segue into focusing this meeting on their marriage. At this moment, Sandi Taylor was suspect number one in the four murders.

They spent a good forty-five minutes talking about Sandi, how Arnie met her, and when and why the marriage started to go south. How Arnie decided a couple of years ago that the marriage was over, but just hadn't taken the time to deal with it head-on. Frank Hogan then picked up the tab and said he had to get going.

"I have a meeting scheduled with Captain Coogan downtown at ten o'clock, and then grab a bite and be back in Panorama City at one o'clock for the first of three scheduled interviews with your agent friends."

Chapter 7

Tuesday, March 11, Burbank

When Arnie left Bob's Big Boy, he went to see his mother. She lived only a couple of miles from Bob's, on Pass Avenue in Burbank. Arnie knew she always got up around seven and read the newspaper while having her first cup of coffee. He thought she must have been terrified when she saw this morning's *Times*.

Gladys Doleshal had been Gladys Taylor for twenty-two years, including the period when her sons Danny and Arnie were born in 1938 and 1941, respectively. Her son from her first marriage, Robbie, had died of cancer just two years ago. Gladys and Ray Doleshal, a lighting fixture salesman, had been happily married since 1967. Arnie and his mother had always been close. She knew her son was unhappy, and that a divorce was in his future.

After opening the front door, Gladys threw her arms around him and said, "What in the world is going on?" She held on tightly before letting him go.

"I wish I knew," he replied.

"I'm disappointed, Arnie. To learn this terrible news by reading about it in the paper? Surely you've known about it for a while," her voice revealing a combination of anger and frustration.

"Yes, of course I have, but why worry you?"

"Because, I'm your mother."

She gestured for Arnie to take a seat on the living room sofa and asked him if he wanted coffee. He told her no.

"I didn't realize what was going on until the second murder," he said. "Even then, I was sure it was a coincidence."

"So what did you do then, report it to Bear Republic?"

"Yes, after the second murder, I told Dom Amalfitano, the agency manager, but he sat on the information, until some big shot in the claims department in San Francisco called him. It's not often they pay a death claim for a murder victim, but two involving the same agent just forty-five days apart? Now there are two more?"

"You must have been worried to death these past six months," said his mother, "I feel awful. You deserve all the love and support you can get. I'm sure you're not getting it from Sandi."

"I appreciate your concern, Mother. But there was nothing you could do. Besides, you've had enough grief for ten lifetimes. Why burden you with my problems."

"Are you sure you don't want any coffee?" asked his mother, her tone now more congenial. "It's barely eight thirty, and you're a morning coffee drinker."

"Okay," said Arnie. "I've already had my quota while spending an hour with a detective, but, sure, I'll have another one. Can you put a little bourbon in it?" After a brief pause, he added, "Just kidding."

"It would be fine with me if you weren't. I could use a shot or two myself," she said.

Gladys returned to the living room, set her cup on the table next to her recliner, and handed the second cup to her son on the sofa.

"I think you underestimate your mother, Arnie."

He threw her a quizzical look, then said, "How's that?"

"Well, ever since I read about this mess in the *Times*, I've been thinking we ought to contact an old friend."

"Really? Who?" Arnie asked.

"Mike."

"Mike? Mike Slovak?"

"If anyone can find this killer, he can. You know it as well as I do."

Arnie took in a deep breath, sighed, and thought for a moment.

"That's probably true, Mother, but we're playing with fire here. He's been on the lam for more than twenty years. How could we ask him to find the killer, then give the information to us, so that we can inform the police? Before they make an arrest, won't they want to know the identity of our source? What would we tell them? By the way, what's Mike doing these days?"

"I told you some time ago he's back with the mob. It's the only way he can survive. He's been on the 'most wanted' list for so long, it's impossible for him to get a normal job. They'd catch him sooner or later."

"So he survives by being a hit-man for the old Cohen gang?" asked Arnie.

"Yes. But remember, his job is to eliminate rival gangsters, not ordinary folks."

"Eliminate. That's a nice way of putting it, Mother. You mean executing them. How often do you see him?"

"I saw him a couple of years ago. We met at Mike's favorite pizza place, Villa Sorrento, you know, on Magnolia in North Hollywood? Ray was with me."

"I still don't get why you met with him," said Arnie. "It seems, well, bizarre, given our family history, in which he played no small part."

"He wanted to know how everybody was, whether or not you and Danny were married. . .had any children. Stuff like that. He also wanted to know if I'd ever noticed anyone following me. I told him the same thing I'd told him the last time we met. Someone followed me for five or six months after the shooting, probably to see if I could lead them to him, but twenty years has gone by. Mike and Ray talked like old friends."

"I agree that he's probably our best chance of finding the killer, but we need time to think this through. There are definitely some problems."

"Like what?" She asked.

"Well, the police and Amalfitano seem to think this is an inside job, that it's very likely someone who has access to my files, and I agree with that, at least as a working hypothesis."

"Don't you always keep your office door locked?" Asked his mother.

"I do, but that doesn't mean someone couldn't have gotten a hold of the key somehow, or made a copy. But, I can't believe anybody in the agency is that crazy."

"Well, we don't have a lot of time to think this over. Do you want me to call Mike or not? What do we have to lose?"

Arnie looked down, and stared out the front window.

"You're right, Mother. We have nothing to lose. The worst that can happen, is that he can't find the killer. But, back to my earlier question. What if he does, then what?

"It's obvious, Arnie. The police receive an anonymous phone call. It could be Mike, or anybody. The information would have to name of the killer, some evidence of his guilt, and his location. What else would they need?"

Gladys Doleshal smiled and said, "You won't believe it when you see him. He's gained about fifty pounds, doesn't wear glasses anymore. He has contacts, and his head is shaved like Yule Brenner. Why, Sherlock Holmes wouldn't recognize him."

After ten minutes of idle chit-chat, Arnie got up to leave, though he wasn't sure just where he was going. His mother gave him another big hug,

"Don't worry, Honey," she said. "It's only temporary."

"You always say that, when there's a crisis. 'It's only temporary.'"

"So is life, Arnie," she said, as she stood watching him walk to his Gran Torino.

Chapter 8

Wednesday, March 12, Chatsworth

Hans and Lenore Schwartz were from the upper Midwest. Hans, a University of Wisconsin graduate, served as Superintendent of Parks and Recreation for the County of Los Angeles prior to his retirement in 1974. Lenore had quit teaching when their daughter was born, and eventually became active in their local Lutheran church and Republican politics.

Hans was a sturdy, confident type, wise and distinguished looking. An immaculate dresser with streaked gray hair and a neatly trimmed mustache. He was of medium height and weight. Lenore, a soft-spoken woman with a slight German accent, doted on her husband and seldom disagreed with him about anything. Thin, with frosted, blonde hair that resembled her daughter's natural blonde. Lenore's high-boned face got in the way of her being pretty.

Sandi had called her parents around nine Tuesday evening and asked if she could spend the night. She told her father her marriage was over, and she didn't want to go home.

Hans and Lenore were not surprised. Their daughter had been complaining for years about Arnie, and what a mistake it had been to marry him in the first place.

It was nearly 8:30 the next morning, when Sandi, barefoot, headed from her bedroom to the dinette where her parents were having breakfast. She heard them talking about her and saw their faces from the hallway before entering the kitchen. She was dumbfounded by their low voices and look of gloom. After all, getting a divorce couldn't be a surprise. It had been coming for years.

"It's bad enough, Lenore, when the only issue is whether or not to leave Arnie," said Hans." Now, everything's changed. It's a much more complicated."

"I'm here," Sandi said, "so you might as well stop whispering." She took a seat, and stared at her father.

"What do you mean, 'more complicated?'" asked Sandi, while fidgeting with her ponytail.

"Surely you're aware there's a serial killer here in the Valley who is going after your husband's clients," said her father.

"Well, sort of," said Sandi. "He told me a couple of months ago that two of his clients had been killed. Then Monday he came home around 4:30, called his office, and ran out of the house without saying a word. But, what does all this have to do with the fact I've decided to leave the jackass?"

"You obviously don't understand the seriousness of what's going on, Sandi," said her father, pointing at the paper. The situation is now worse, much worse."

"You must be hungry," said her mother, forcing a smile. "Let me get you some breakfast."

"Thanks, but the last thing I want to do is eat. I'll have some coffee, though."

"Get it yourself," said her father. "The pot's where its always been." Sandi started to get up, but her mother already had the pot in her hand.

"Where did you go after Arnie ran out Monday afternoon?" Asked her father.

"I didn't go anywhere. I stayed home waiting for Arnie to show up, or at least call. I finally left around eight after calling Susan."

"You were home until eight o'clock? That's a lie, Sandi, and you know it." Her father's voice got louder, his face reddened. "Your mother started calling you around five to invite the two of you over for dinner. She never did get you. Then last night, you finally call us. We were worried about you, but now you have a much bigger problem than we ever imagined."

"What do Arnie's problems at work have to do with my leaving him and filing for divorce? I still don't get it," said Sandi.

"Haven't you heard any news the past couple of days? Well, read yesterday's paper, and then maybe, **maybe**, you'll realize your leaving him right now, is a stupid idea."

"I don't agree, Hans," said Lenore. "If she's going to leave him, I say this is the perfect time. If she makes the break now, she's out of the picture. It will be his problem, not theirs."

"I'm afraid it's not quite that simple, my dear," said Hans. He glanced at his wife, pursed his lips, then stared at Sandi again.

"If you leave him now while the killer is still out there, you will receive as much unfavorable publicity as Arnie. Go ahead, look at yesterday's Times. You'll see what I mean. You can't leave your husband when he's in this much trouble. You must stand by him. If you don't, it could be disastrous for Arnie, and a major problem for you, too. In fact, you could immediately become a suspect, perhaps the prime suspect. It could appear that you set him up, hoping he spends the rest of his life in prison—or worse."

"That's crazy," said Sandi. "No matter how many times I've referred to him as an asshole to my friends, which he is, what motive could I possibly have to kill his clients? If I hated my husband that much, why wouldn't I just hire someone to take him out? Not that I haven't considered it."

Sandi laughed, but Hans and Lenore looked at her in shock. "You're kidding, of course," said her father.

"Of course I am," she said, still smiling.

"I'd still like to know where you were Monday night when I kept calling," said Lenore. "This story about you staying home and sitting by the phone is ridiculous."

"It's not just ridiculous, Lenore," said her husband, "it's total bullshit." Hans' voice was louder than ever, while Lenore sat, her hands clasped together, and looked down at the table.

Sandi ignored her mother's question and started reading the article in Tuesday's *Times*." Total silence engulfed the room until she finished. Then, with tears rolling down her cheeks, she finally looked up.

"Where was I Monday night? Are you sure you want to know?" Her father nodded.

"For a couple of hours I was with my boyfriend in the lounge at the Holiday Inn," said Sandi.

Her mother shouted, "I don't believe it."

"Jesus Christ," mumbled Hans.

"Who is he, and how in the world did you meet him?" asked Lenore.

"His name is Dan Turner. I met him in the bar at the Holiday Inn several months ago."

"What? The Holiday Inn? I don't believe you."

"He's handsome, charming, and very sweet. He has beautiful black, curly hair and a sense of humor that won't quit. One of the funniest guys I've ever known.

"By the way, I really did stay with Susan Monday night, and all of yesterday, but only because Dan got a phone call around 6:00 that evening and had to leave."

"What's this character do for a living?" asked her father.

"He and a couple of family members are in commercial real estate. I think he's pretty well off. He doesn't seem to work much, that's for sure."

"So what's the attraction, Sandi?" asked her mother.

"One thing I like about him is that he's not so serious like Arnie, nor does he have an opinion about everything. But best of all, he's not a robot spitting out useless information. You know Arnie, always quoting some book or movie, or reliving some conversation he had twenty-five years ago. I told him he's boring. I tune him out 70% of the time."

"Sandi, that's a terrible thing to say to anyone, let alone your husband," said her mother, now sobbing. "Maybe he's the one who should be having an affair."

"He's not," said Sandi. "There's a lot of things wrong with Arnie, but that's not one of them. And damned if I care if I hurt his feelings. Remember the *Twilight Zone* episode about the guy whose talking annoyed people so much, he made a bet that he could remain quiet? Then cut his vocal cords so that he couldn't talk? Well, that's what I wish Arnie would do. Just shut the fuck up."

Her parents both shook their heads. Hans asked, in a calmer voice, "And since when did my daughter start hanging out in bars?"

"The afternoon I met Dan. I was with Carol Lohman. As far as I know, she's the only one who knows I'm having an affair. And it's not what you think, Daddy. I only go to one bar, the Holiday Inn, and that's to be with Dan."

"I don't want to hear anything more about this Dan Turner." Said her mother. "Arnie may not be perfect, and yes he's a talker, but he has lots of friends, is well-educated. He's a good insurance agent, and he does have a sense of humor. It's just different from yours."

"But you and Daddy. . ."

"It's the petty disagreements with him over politics, sports teams, television shows, movies, and just about everything else that annoy us so much.

"I still disagree with your father about the timing of your leaving him. Since you despise Arnie so much, and even worse, have become an adulteress, I think you need to get a divorce right away."

"Not now, Lenore," bellowed her husband, "not while he's smack in the middle of this serial killer business." Hans pushed his chair back, stood up, poured another cup of coffee

Sandi picked up the Wednesday paper, slipped off the rubber band, and looked at the front page.

"I don't believe it," she stammered. "That's Dan Turner."

"Who?" asked her mother.

"Dan Turner, my boyfriend." She raised her voice. "Who in the hell do you think we've been talking about?"

Sandi placed her hands on both sides of her face, ran out of the dinette to her bedroom, slamming the door.

Hans and Lenore exchanged glances, and looked at the picture. The individual was identified as Frankie Crosetti, a mobster. He had been shot to death yesterday morning in the parking lot behind Bob's Big Boy in Toluca Lake. The caption read,

"Police are certain it was a gangland killing, but have no suspect."

Chapter 9

Wednesday, March 12, Granada Hills

It was a little after eight o'clock when Arnie awoke, feeling rested for the first time in a couple of days. He had thought about staying at his mother's, but what the hell, the house was just as much his as Sandi's. If she wanted to show up and sleep there, so be it. She could sleep in the guest room. No, he would do the right thing and let her have the master bedroom. Anyway, it didn't matter. She didn't come home, which was fine with him.

Arnie brought in his morning *Times,* went into the kitchen, turned on Mr. Coffee, and smiled. Those endless television commercials featuring Joe DiMaggio were right. Mr. Coffee was the best, and it was so easy to use.

While the coffee was brewing, Arnie sat at the kitchen table and opened the morning paper. Relieved that the front page didn't have anything about the serial killer, he picked up the phone and dialed his office. After Angie asked how he was doing, she transferred him to Michael Wong.

"Michael, it's Arnie, at another period of woe in my life."

"Excuse me? Woe?"

"I can't stop thinking about that poem I read as a freshman at Occidental by Blake.

> *Man was made for Joy and Woe*
> *And when this we rightly know*
> *Thro' the world we safely go*
> *Joy and Woe are woven fine*
> *A clothing for the soul to bind*

"Wow!" said Michael. The guy who wrote that sounds more like a philosopher than a poet. And even though I was a math major in college who hated poetry, I not only like it, I get it."

"William Blake was an English poet during the Romantic Period, around the time of our American Revolution. Anyway, I had forgotten the last two lines and had to look it up. Reading it again actually cheered me up a bit," said Arnie.

"Susan and I have been worried about you," said Michael. "We were wondering if you'd like to spend a couple of nights at our place. We could shoot the bull, have a couple of drinks. You know, just hang out and relax. You need to get all this shit out of your mind, and we're just the ones to help."

"Thanks, Michael. Tell Susan I really appreciate it, but I'm okay, all things considered. I try to remember that life can always be worse.

"Hey, tell me what's going on in the office. How did it go yesterday afternoon when Lieutenant Hogan came in for the interviews?"

"The lieutenant canceled," said Michael. "He called and told Rolene something had come up that needed his immediate attention and would be back in touch."

"He canceled? I can't believe it. How did Amalfitano react?" asked Arnie.

"He wasn't here either. That's why the lieutenant talked to Rolene."

"You're kidding—Hogan didn't come in, and Dom wouldn't have been there if he had. Damn."

"Michael, is Whit Payne in the office?

"I'll have to check," said Michael. "I haven't seen him yet, but I've only been here about twenty minutes. Why?"

"He has some information about Sandi, which I shared with Hogan yesterday morning at the Big Boy in Toluca Lake. I think the lieutenant considers my wife a suspect, which I find rather odd, even comical."

"Well, I'm not surprised," said Michael. "After all, you're not exactly Sandi's favorite person and, besides, it's my understanding everyone's a suspect, even me. Even you."

"Yeah, I know, Michael. But let's get real. Sandi's a termagant, but she's not Bonnie Parker."

"Termagant? What in the hell is that?"

"I'm tired of calling her a bitch," said Arnie, "so I'm mixing in words like 'termagant' and 'vixen' once in a while out of boredom. The one term I won't use is 'shrew,' since Shakespeare's classic is a lie. Shrews are never tamed.

"Anyway, is Whit there?"

"Hold on a minute, I'll check."

While Arnie waited, he glanced at the sports section. The Dodgers were now at spring training in Vero Beach, Florida. Manager Walt Alston was predicting another pennant.

Michael returned to the phone. "No, he's not in, and no one's seen him yet."

"Damn. I really want to talk to him."

Michael's tone changed, his voice softer, his telephone manner more serious.

"Arnie, did you say you were with the lieutenant yesterday morning at Bob's restaurant in Toluca Lake?"

"Yeah, we met for about an hour and a half."

"Could you be a little more specific?" asked Michael. "Like, when did you get there, and when did you leave?"

"Oh, I was there from 7:00 until, well, maybe 8:45 or so. Why?"

"Why? Because a mobster was shot to death in the back parking lot a little before 9:00? It's the headline story in this morning's paper."

"I saw something in *The Times* about a gangland murder," said Arnie, "but I didn't take the time to read it. The back parking lot?"

"Yeah. And surprise, surprise—the victim had an Italian name, Crosetti, Crossenti—something like that."

Arnie felt his heart racing, and took a deep breath. "Jesus," he said. "Never a dull moment. I cannot believe all the violence out there right now, whether it has anything to do with me or not."

Arnie hung up and started thinking about Lieutenant Hogan as a no-show at yesterday's scheduled meeting with agents. He was annoyed—he had been assured Hogan's number-one priority was to find the serial killer. And after only two and a half days, he had more important things to do? How could Hogan now be so detached from the business at hand given the situation? Then it dawned on him that maybe the lieutenant was still at Bob's when the shooting occurred. That was the reason he never made it to the office. Maybe he witnessed it. Hell, maybe he did it.

Arnie picked up the phone again, glanced at the lieutenant's business card on the table, and dialed the number. Hogan was out, so he left a message that he would be home for a while, and to please call him at his earliest convenience. Arnie sat there a couple of minutes, growing angrier, when the phone rang.

"Hello."

"Mr. Taylor, this is Lieutenant Hogan."

"You certainly don't let any grass grow under your feet, do you, Lieutenant. It hasn't been two minutes since I called."

"I didn't know you called, Mr. Taylor. I'm at our office in the Van Nuys City Hall. My purpose in calling is to ask if you know how I can get a hold of Whit Payne. He's not at the agency this morning."

"Well," said Arnie, "my guess is, he's either out on an appointment, or he's home. I just called the office myself and asked for him, so I know he's not there. Why the urgency?"

Hogan ignored the question, and continued. "I got his phone number from the lady at the switchboard, and I've already called his house, but no one answered."

"He's divorced, Lieutenant, and lives alone. Somewhere in Mission Hills, not far from the office. I can give you his address if you like."

Arnie went into his small home office at the end of a hallway. He retrieved a list of all agents at the agency, including addresses, phone numbers, names of wives or girlfriends, etc. He read the information to the lieutenant, and was about to ask another question when Hogan cut him off.

"I don't mean to be rude, Arnie, but I don't have time to talk. Where can I reach you during the next couple of hours?"

"Try me at home first, then the agency, then my mother's, and last, call Michael Wong, at the agency or his house."

The lieutenant already had the first three numbers, so Arnie gave him Wong's home number in the event he wasn't in the office. He also gave him the number of the Chinese restaurant Michael's father owned in Van Nuys, the Phoenix West. Wong eats lunch there a couple of times a week, and he and as many as a dozen agents, including Arnie, could usually be found in the bar there on Friday afternoons for an hour or two beginning around four or four thirty.

Arnie got up from the kitchen table, and poured himself another mug of coffee. He walked out to his backyard and stared at his palm tree, deep in thought. All he wanted was to ask Whit if he had been at the Holiday Inn Monday night and, if so, was Sandi there with her boyfriend.

Why was Hogan in such a hurry to get a hold of him, now? Not twenty-four hours earlier, Arnie had told the Lieutenant everything that Whit had told him, and all he did was jot down a quick note. Why was this suddenly such a big deal?

Arnie sensed something was going on. He had no idea what it was, he just knew it wasn't good.

Chapter 10

Wednesday, March 12, Panorama City

At 12:20 that afternoon, Arnie exited the sixth floor elevator of the Towers and walked into the Bear Republic Agency. He nodded and smiled at Angie, and walked past the switchboard to the desk occupied by Rolene Ward, the boss's secretary.

Rolene, a pretty brunette, divorced, in her late thirties, had been the manager's secretary for ten years, having been hired by Amalfitano's predecessor, Gene Rupert. Efficient and, equally important, able to get along well with the agents, Dom saw no reason to replace her. One of her most important assets was the ability to guard carefully all the confidential information that crossed her desk, which was considerable. Some agents thought her a bit stuck-up, but they were a small minority. She was merely reserved and businesslike. Michael Wong and Arnie were especially fond of her, and she liked them, too, mainly because they were always friendly without crossing the line. Even Sandi liked her. The previous summer, Rolene had come to the Taylor home one evening to watch a Dodger game on television while enjoying one of Arnie's famous barbecued rib eye steaks and a couple of beers.

"How are you doing, Arnie? I can't imagine what you must be going through right now."

"I don't think anyone believes me when I answer that question, but, all things considered, I'm all right. It's funny, though. I knew that being a success in the life insurance business was no cakewalk, but nobody prepared me for this shit." He lowered his voice when he spoke the last word, then continued.

"My dilemma brings to mind a story Lincoln used to tell. When asked how it felt to be president during our nation's great Civil War, he said it reminded him of the man who had been tarred and feathered and run out of town on a rail. When the poor fella was asked how he felt about it, he replied, 'Except for the honor of the thing, I'd have just as soon passed.'"

Rolene laughed. "Well, of all the agents, I can't think of anyone better equipped to handle this than you. And your story makes my point even stronger."

Arnie wondered if there was a double meaning in her comment. Did she know his family history? If Dominick Amalfitano knew, then she probably did, and it was under lock and key in his personnel file. One thing for sure, Rolene, one of the nicest people he had ever known, wouldn't hold it against him.

"Do you know when Dom is coming back into the office?" he asked. "I understand he was in yesterday only for an hour or two, and now I see he's not here today either."

"He was in for a couple of hours yesterday morning, but then said he had to catch a plane to New York. His sister passed away—you know, Sarah, the one who's been suffering from breast cancer for the past three or four years."

"Gosh, I'm sorry to hear that. Did he say when he would be returning?"

"Yes," she said. "He should be back in the office Monday morning."

"I feel bad about Sarah," Arnie said. "I really do, but, my God, of all times for him to have to be away."

Arnie sat at his desk and received an update from Maria regarding pending business items. An immigrant from Mexico, the twenty-six-year-old, good-natured woman was a single mom with a husky, eight-year-old boy at home. A Giants fan, she liked to kid Arnie whenever the Dodgers went on a losing streak. Some agents were amazed he even hired her, since everyone knew he claimed to have nightmares about orange and black, the Giants' colors.

During the past two years, Maria worked mornings for Michael Wong, and afternoons for Arnie. She originally worked full-time for Bill Kaiser, but he didn't like Mexicans much. Bill never complained about Maria's work, though, so Arnie and Michael were happy to get her. Maria was happy, too.

Without question the most eccentric character in the office, Kaiser also didn't like Negroes, Jews, women life insurance agents, or liberals. Especially liberals. Arnie thought it funny that the only female agent in the office, Eli Lieb, was Jewish and a liberal. "Three strikes and you're out" didn't apply here, not with her substantial production and the pressure on Amalfitano from home office to recruit more women agents.

Kaiser, thirty-four, at 5'9, was only an inch taller than Arnie, but more on the thin side. With blue eyes, blonde hair, and Germanic features, Arnie thought Kaiser could easily play a Nazi in a Hollywood movie. His loud voice and overbearing manner made him intimidating at times, but, because of his humor, he was one of the most popular agents in the office. Bill often showed up on a motorcycle for a couple of drinks at the Phoenix West on Fridays. He never failed to regale everyone with his off-color jokes and tough-guy demeanor. Arnie liked him, in spite of their being so different.

A John Bircher back in the '60s, and currently a rising star in the local National Rifle Association chapter, Bill thought Eisenhower a socialist, maybe even a communist. Arnie was more amused than annoyed by Bill's political and racial views, but it was clear the two could never be close because of such diverse political philosophies and personalities.

Arnie wanted Maria to return some phone calls for him, and suggested she use his office. He would sit at her desk, trying to figure out what to do next.

Maria's phone rang and he picked it up.

"Arnie, it's Angie." He looked toward the front entrance, about thirty feet away, and noticed the switchboard operator staring at him without her usual smile.

"Rolene needs to see you right away. She's in Mr. Amalfitano's office with the door closed."

Upon entering the large office, Rolene stood in front of the boss's desk with the phone to her ear. She motioned for him to close the door.

"Here he is, Lieutenant," she said, handing the phone to Arnie. As she started to leave, he cupped his hand over the receiver and said in a soft voice, "Rolene, stay here. Please." She sat down next to where Arnie stood holding the phone.

"Hello, Lieutenant Hogan. This is Arnie."

"Are you alone?" asked Hogan.

"Yes," he replied, glancing at Rolene.

"I'm sorry, Arnie, but I have more bad news. Your friend, Whit Payne, is dead. Shot more than a day ago, probably Monday night, while eating dinner alone at home. Police discovered his body early this afternoon."

Silent for a moment, Arnie teared up, started to speak, and stopped. Then, in a soft voice, the words finally came.

"No! I don't believe it. Are you kidding me? Why in the world would anyone want to kill Whit Payne? Jesus! What next."

46

"No! I don't believe it. Are you kidding me? Why in the world would anyone want to kill Whit Payne? Jesus! What next."

Chapter 11

March 12, Wednesday afternoon, San Fernando Valley

After telling Arnie about Whit Payne, Lieutenant Hogan set the phone down and wiped his brow with a handkerchief. He then walked to the door of his office, opened it, and called in three newly assigned police officers to the case who had waited outside for twenty minutes.

Hogan already knew George Porter, who'd assisted him on several cases over the years, including a front-page armed robbery case a couple of years ago that took a good nine months to resolve.

A bachelor who loved to party, George pretty much had his pick of available females, and he made the most of it. Handsome, debonair, standing six foot four with wavy brown hair, he would have made a perfect Apollo for a Greek sculptor.

When there were annual formal dinners for those who worked in the homicide division, other officers and their wives always speculated over which babe he would show up with. While it was never the same one, they all shared one common trait. They looked like a Playmate of the Month.

The other two, officers Gary Merrill and Jim Grant, were casual acquaintances, but Hogan had never worked with them. They sat on the three chairs already arranged in a semicircle in front of the lieutenant's desk.

"Only Captain Coogin, Inspector Lewis, and Deputy Chief Fleming, know what I know, but since you're all now part of my team, you will, too. We have reason to believe a Mafia informant operates inside our department, so keep your damn mouths shut. All of you. Not a word to anyone, inside or outside the department about this case. Is that clear?"

The three officers nodded.

"Why do we think there's an informant?" asked Officer Merrill.

"Never mind, that's not your concern, Gary. I repeat, don't mention it to anyone either. Just keep your mouth shut."

The phone rang and the lieutenant immediately picked up the receiver. Captain Coogin was on the other end.

"Are you kidding me, Captain? Don't I get a say in this?

"Okay, but for the record, I'm not one bit happy about this. In fact, I think it stinks."

Hogan slammed the phone down, rolled his eyes, and said, "They've assigned a goddamned woman to our unit. One experienced in undercover activities, so they say. Shit, that's all we need. She'll be joining us in about five minutes, so we'll wait until she gets here before getting started."

"I hope it's Angie Dickinson," quipped Jim Grant.

Hogan knew the Hollywood beauty played the lead in a popular TV series about the LAPD, *Police Story*, but never watched it. He had heard enough about it, though, to know she played a character named Pepper Anderson. All this women's rights stuff is a bunch of bullshit. Gloria Steinem, Betty Friedan, Germaine Greer. What next? A woman chief of police? A woman president? Jesus Christ. There would be no end to this nonsense.

Following a knock on the door, a lady opened it and entered. The three officers stood and stared, speechless, their faces frozen.

"I'm sorry, but the inspector failed to tell me your name," said Lieutenant Hogan.

"Wright. Officer Ricki Wright," she said.

After introducing Ricki to the other three officers, Lieutenant Hogan asked her to pull up a chair and join them for a briefing on the current status of the serial-killer investigation.

The officers pulled out notepads and pens and looked at Hogan, with occasional side-glances at their new colleague.

"As all of you know, there have been four murders to date, going back six months, and have two common threads. First, all four victims had been shot after parking their cars in their driveways, then exiting their vehicles to walk to their front doors. They've all been shot twice, once in the head and once in the area around the heart. All with the same weapon, a .38, which so far, we have been unable to track.

"Secondly, and this has all of us baffled, all four purchased Bear Republic life insurance policies from the same guy, Arnold Taylor, an experienced agent who works out of the company's Panorama City office. He lives in Granada Hills, a short distance away, and is having serious marital problems, which may or may not be relevant to what's going on. There's no known motive since, in all cases, the insurance proceeds were left to their wives. And from all appearances, there's no connection among the four victims or their families."

Lieutenant Hogan noticed that Ricki was writing nonstop, while the three men made occasional notes.

"May I ask a question?" said George Porter.

"I'm only taking questions if they refer to something I've just said. There are other pieces to the puzzle, which will be explained as we move along. So, do you still have a question, George?"

"Yes, I do. Based on what we've heard so far, it sounds like you're thinking the missing piece has to do with Arnold Taylor. If that's the case, isn't it true that there are coincidences in this world and this might just be one of them?"

"Yes, coincidences do happen, but stop and think for a minute. There are over two million people in the San Fernando Valley. What are the odds that, from a population that large, along with a couple of thousand life insurance agents, four murders would be committed by the same guy, and all of his victims bought their policies from the same agent?"

Porter shifted in his chair, but had no response.

"May I ask a question?" asked Ricki Wright.

The lieutenant nodded and mumbled, "Go ahead."

"What are the odds," she said, "of Thomas Jefferson and John Adams, our second and third presidents, dying on the same day, and that day being July 4th, 1826, the 50th anniversary of the signing of the Declaration of Independence, a document written by Jefferson, with assistance from Adams?"

Lieutenant Hogan tossed her a cold stare while the other three officers tried, without success, to suppress smiles. An awkward silence enveloped the room.

"Or," Ricki continued, "what are the odds of Shakespeare and Cervantes, the greatest writers in the history of their respective countries, England and Spain, dying on the same day?"

"You've made your point, Ms. Wright," replied Hogan, his voice raised and his eyes focused on all four officers.

Hogan continued, "As I've said, coincidences do happen, but, for the present, we're going to assume that Taylor has something to do with this mess. That's not to say he's responsible for the murders, only that there must be some connection with him."

Ricki raised her hand again. "How certain are we that the four victims were not in some way connected, perhaps in some illegal venture their families know nothing about, like dealing drugs? You used phrases like, 'as far as we can tell, there is no connection,' which takes us back to Arnie as the common thread. Is anyone looking into this?"

Hogan sat up straight, narrowed his eyes, and focused on this very pretty woman who not only had a nice ass, but was a smart-ass as well.

"Did I hear you say 'Arnie,' Ms. Wright? How do you know he goes by that name? Do you know him personally?"

"Yes, I do," she replied, "and Lieutenant, please call me Ricki like all my friends, including my associates here in the LAPD."

"Okay, Ricki, I'll try my best to remember. Please be mindful that I'm not accustomed to working with female officers, so this is kind of an adjustment for me. In fact, for all of us."

Before continuing, Hogan took a deep breath and internalized that both of her questions had merit and, that while he resented her even being in the room, she might very well prove to be an excellent addition to the team. In any event, acrimonious camaraderie must be avoided at all costs. There was too much at stake to expend energy over turf, petty issues, and modern cultural trends he could do nothing about.

"I'll do my best to address your question, Ricki. Now, please go on with your bombshell information that you actually know Arnold Taylor personally."

"Arnie and I both grew up in North Hollywood and were in school together from the fifth through the eighth grade. Actually, he was my first boyfriend, though that didn't seem to go both ways. We were, well, pals, and spent a lot of time together talking, riding our bikes, stuff like that. I even used to go with him on his paper route.

"He left North Hollywood Junior High at the beginning of ninth grade to attend Black-Foxe Military Institute in Hollywood. I've only seen him three times since. He was my grad night date when I graduated from junior high in 1956. We ran into each other at Dodger Stadium in the early '60s, and, get this, I had dinner with him at the Red Barn in Panorama City Monday night. He had just learned of the fourth murder. Talk about coincidences, I had barely been seated when he walked in, looking forlorn and exhausted."

"Did you tell him you're a police officer?" asked the Lieutenant.

"Of course not, he thinks I'm attending grad school at Cal State, Northridge."

****

Ricki knew before she came to this meeting she would have to level with the police department about her relationship with Arnie, or risk losing her job.

She decided she wouldn't lie about anything material to the case, nor would she volunteer information that could get her recused from this investigation. Maybe, just maybe, she would find herself in a position to resolve the issue that had her watching Arnie in the first place.

"Okay," said Hogan, "let's get on with this review. There's work to be done and we have to get moving as soon as possible.

"So, the morning after Monday's murder of the fourth victim, which was yesterday, Mr. Taylor and I met for breakfast at Bob's in Toluca Lake. About five minutes after we were seated, a man entered the back room where we were the only customers and ordered breakfast. When Mr. Taylor gave me a brief description of the man his wife was presumably having an affair with, I noticed that it matched the profile of the customer seated about twenty-five feet away. I concluded that he had followed Mr. Taylor to the restaurant.

"The man's name was Crosetti, an underworld figure, who, as you know, was shot to death in the parking lot upon leaving Bob's. I had remained behind when Taylor left, to see how long it would take for our visitor to leave—to see if it appeared he was following Taylor. I now think he was waiting for me to leave, so as not to be so obvious. Anyway, I ordered another cup of coffee and waited out the stranger, who left about ten minutes later and was murdered as he opened his car door in the back lot."

"How did Taylor know what his wife's boyfriend looked like, and did he notice Crosetti?" asked Officer Merrill.

Lieutenant Hogan shifted in his chair, straightened his tie, and looked at Merrill.

"I'm not sure Taylor noticed him. As far as I know, he had never seen the man before. The description he gave me was given to him by another agent in the office who had seen Sandi—Taylor's wife—with her boyfriend in the bar at the Panorama City Holiday Inn a couple of times.

"Now here is where this already complicated case becomes a first-class puzzle. Taylor's informant, so to speak, was an agent by the name of Whit Payne and. . ."

"That's the man who was found dead earlier today," said Officer Jim Grant. Hogan nodded affirmatively.

"So," continued the lieutenant, "we have Crosetti murdered in the parking lot behind Bob's yesterday morning, and now Whit Payne dead, apparently a good thirty-six hours—probably at least forty—before being discovered. Anybody think there's a connection here? Too many coincidences. This puzzle has to fit together somehow, and we're going to solve it.

"Merrill, I want you to make arrangements to get over to the Bear Republic office and spend some time with every agent there. There might be something that comes up that will help us. Be careful not to discuss the case with anyone, including Amalfitano, if he's there today. You're the one asking the questions, not them. I had planned to handle this myself, but I was too tied up after Crosetti's murder to go yesterday. You're merely going to ask each agent, individually, about Arnold Taylor's general reputation, and whether or not anyone had a particular grudge against him. If so, for what reason. You can leave right now."

As Gary Merrill got up to leave, he glanced at the other officers, then looked at Hogan. "This will take more than one visit, maybe two or three. At any given time, many of the agents are out of the office."

"I understand," said Hogan. "The main thing is to get started right away."

Hogan stood and stretched, then looked at officers Jim Grant and George Porter.

"Jim, I want you to be at the Holiday Inn by three o'clock."

Hogan looked at his watch. "That's about forty-five minutes from now. That's when the bartender starts his shift. His name is Stan Bryant. Take the photograph from today's paper, have him identify Crosetti, and ask about him being in there with Sandi Taylor, but don't mention her last name. Just say Sandi. Better yet, don't give him a name at all. Ask him who Crosetti was with when he was in there. Find out all you can about the two of them. Oh, and ask if Crosetti went by an alias. I doubt that he used his real name. "One more thing, Jim," said the lieutenant. "Before you go, call Rolene Ward at Bear Republic and ask if you can pick up a photograph of Whit Payne. The phone number is 781-7800. I'm pretty sure the office has a file containing pictures of all their agents. Tell her it's very important and that you will return it. After your discussion with Bryant about Crosetti and Sandi, show him the picture of Payne and watch how he reacts. If all he says is that he's seen the guy in there, that's fine. But I'd like to know if he's ever seen Payne visit with Sandi or Crosetti. If so, that might shed a different light on this whole matter. In any event, call me here at the office as soon as you leave the Holiday Inn."

Next, he turned to Officer Porter.

"George, I want you to come with me. We're going to have a little talk with Sandi Taylor, but not until Jim Grant reports back to me regarding what he learns this afternoon at the Holiday Inn. I'll call Taylor first, to find out how to locate her. Based on an earlier discussion, I'm assuming she's either at her home, or her parents house in Chatsworth. One thing for sure—she's not with her boyfriend."

Hogan smiled with that last comment, as did Porter.

Ricki, the only remaining officer without an assignment, knew she wouldn't be left without anything to do. Not after she had sat through the entire briefing. She stared at the lieutenant, waiting for him to continue.

"You just might be given what turns out to be the best assignment of all, Ricki," said Hogan.

"You're the one who suggested that the four victims might have something in common that has nothing to do with their life insurance agent, and you just might be onto something. I want you to investigate those four people and see if you can find a common thread. But this must be done quietly, behind the scenes. The last thing we need is for your old grade school sweetheart to know you're an undercover officer assigned to a case that revolves around him."

Ricki looked relieved. "I'll get right on it," she said. Hogan looked away as she shot him a beautiful smile.

The lieutenant was going over a couple of loose ends with Officer Porter, following the briefing with the four officers when his phone rang.

"Frank, this is Roy Pinkerton in the crime lab. I've discovered three very interesting details regarding the corpses of Frankie Crosetti and Whit Payne. Can you come over to the lab right away?"

"I'm at our office in Van Nuys, Roy, and I really don't have time to make a trip downtown. Can you just give me the basics over the phone? I never understand what you're showing me anyway, so just spell it out, okay?"

"Okay. First, the .38 revolver found on Crosetti is the one we've been trying to trace for six months. It's the weapon used in the murders of those four men who have the same insurance agent."

Hogan leaned forward in his chair, his mouth wide open, and pounded his right fist on his desk.

"Well, I'll be a son-of-a bitch. This means he's the likely killer, though it's possible the weapon was planted by the guy who killed him. In any event, this is a real break in the case. Thanks mucho, Roy, this…"

"Wait a minute, Frank. That's only the first one. There are two more," said Pinkerton.

"Yes, you did say that. Are the next two as important as the first one?"

"That's for you to decide.

"Crosetti also killed Whit Payne. The bullets found in the four victims of the insurance company-related murders, and the two found in Whit Payne, were all fired from the weapon found on Frankie Crosetti."

Before Lieutenant Hogan could respond, Pinkerton continued:

"Finally, Frank, the .38 revolver that killed Crosetti belongs to Mike Slovak. We're positive the three gangland murders tied to Slovak over the last year or so all involved the weapon that killed Crosseti."

Chapter 12

March 12, Wednesday, Holiday Inn, Panorama City

Officer Jim Grant entered the Holiday Inn cocktail lounge at 3:15 after stopping at the Bear Republic office to pick up a photograph of Whit Payne from Rolene Ward.

A blonde-haired, blue-eyed man of medium height and build, Grant could easily have passed for a game-show host. At thirty-eight, he was a happily married, proud father of three, all under the age of ten. A fifteen-year veteran of the LAPD, Grant had spent most of his career working in the homicide division. The only customer at this early hour was an older, heavyset man with a Gabby Hayes beard seated at the far end of the bar.

"I'm here to see Stan Bryant," said Grant as he flashed his badge at the bartender.

"You're talking to the right man, Officer Grant. What took you so long to get here? I've been on the job for at least fifteen minutes," he said with a smile, glancing at his watch.

"Then you obviously know why I'm here," said Grant.

"You betcha I do. You're here on account of my customer, or former customer, that is, Dan Turner, who got murdered yesterday over in Toluca Lake. It turns out, he was really Frankie Crosetti, a mafioso. And dumb me—ever since I was a baseball fanatic as a kid, I thought Frankie Crosetti was one of those wops who played for the Yankees prior to DiMaggio, Phil Rizzuto and, my favorite of all, Yogi Berra."

"That's correct, Mr. Bryant, that's why I'm here, but you got me on the baseball connection."

"I'll forgive you, Officer, but only if you call me Stan. I'm 'Stan' to everyone around here, 'Stan the Man.' I don't even know who Mr. Bryant is."

"Fair enough, Stan. I'd like to ask you some questions, but if you would first get me a Coke, I'd appreciate it very much, especially if you would put a cherry in it."

The bartender set the Coke on the bar, dropped three cherries into the glass, and looked at Grant. "I don't know very much, Officer, but I'll answer any questions I can. Fire away."

"For starters, Stan, how long has Crosetti been coming in here?"

"Oh, I guess a year or so, maybe nine or ten months. I'm not really sure. But I will never forget the first time he came in because of what happened that afternoon."

Grant took a big swallow of Coke, glanced around the room for a moment, then asked the bartender to continue.

"Well, a good-looking blonde had sat down at the bar with a red-haired girlfriend about five minutes before Turner arrived. Do you mind if I call him Turner? That's the name I knew him by, and habits are hard for me to break."

The officer nodded.

"Anyway, the bar was pretty crowded that day, it being around 4:30 or 5:00. Seated a good half-dozen or more stools away from the two ladies, Turner asked me who the blonde was.

"'Never seen her before in my life,' I told him. He asked me what she and her friend were drinking, and I told him vodka gimlets. Then, he told me to send them two more gimlets and tell them it was on him. When I set the drinks on the bar and told them who was picking up the tab, they both turned and smiled at Turner, and lifted their glasses toward him, ya know, like a toast."

Stan excused himself for a couple of minutes to greet two new customers who had just sat down. Grant glanced over at Gabby Hayes, who appeared not to have moved a muscle since the officer had come in. The old guy looked comatose.

The bartender returned and continued his narrative "Well the two ladies finished their second round of drinks, and Turner asked me to send them two more gimlets. I don't mean to say they had a lot of drinks, maybe three or four at the most, but Turner always paid for the drinks."

"So, did he finally join them?" asked Officer Grant.

"Yeah, after an hour or so the crowd began to thin out, and he moved over and sat next to the blonde. Now, this is where the story gets interesting, and it's the reason I remember it so well. Whoops—three more customers. Back in a jiffy."

While Officer Grant collected his thoughts, he thirsted for a Coors, but there was no way he'd order one. No drinking on the job. The cocktail lounge was now full, all of the barstools occupied, the aroma and sight of smoke unmistakable and annoying to nonsmoker Jim Grant, and the noise level up a few decibels. A good ten minutes later the bartender returned.

"Before you continue," said the officer, "had Crosetti introduced himself to you as Dan Turner yet, and did you know the name of the blonde?"

"Yes and no," replied Stan. "He had introduced himself as Dan Turner as soon as he sat down that day, but it wasn't until later on that I learned the woman's name was Sandra."

"Did you ever find out her last name?" asked the officer.

"No. Only Sandra."

"Do you happen to remember the name of the redhead?"

"Well, I didn't learn it that first day they came in, which was the only time I saw her, but a couple of weeks later I asked Sandra whatever happened to her girlfriend, the redhead. She said, 'Oh, you mean Carol. I don't bring her anymore because I'm only here to see Dan, and we don't need any company, if you know what I mean.' As she said that, she turned and looked at Turner as if he were Paul Newman or Robert Redford, which he wasn't neither one of them."

"Okay," said Officer Grant, "Please continue with your story of their first meeting."

"Well, what happened was that the redhead, Carol, left, but Turner and Sandra sat there and talked and drank for at least another hour. Then he excused himself while she remained behind, and I later learned he went to the front desk and got a room for the night. I only found that out when I asked about it after seeing them getting on the elevator a little later. Before that, they'd had a bite to eat in the dining room."

"I have only a couple of more questions, Stan, but first I want to tell you how much I appreciate how helpful you've been."

"Hey, I have nothing to hide," said the bartender. "Like I said when you walked in, I'll tell you everything I know. Of course, what I know is limited to this cocktail lounge, the best bar in town, thanks to Stan the Man himself. Oh, and a little credit goes to my friends Jack Daniels and Johnnie Walker."

Jim Grant smiled. This bartender was quite a character. He made a mental note to return here sometime strictly for a drink, and the entertainment provided along with it for free.

"Did you happen to notice whether or not Sandra was wearing a wedding ring?"

"Not the first time, I didn't, but when they met here a couple of days later, I did notice she was wearing a ring."

"So, they continued to meet here on a regular basis, is that right?" asked the officer.

"Yes," said Stan. "At least a couple of times a week and, before you ask the question I know is coming, yes, they did continue to go up the elevator to a room he rented."

Officer Grant then pulled a photograph from his inside coat pocket and showed it to Stan.

"Ever seen this man before?" asked the officer.

"Yeah, I have. A nice guy, always alone. Whit something. He came in once or twice a week. Whenever I saw him I thought of 'nitwit,' but he actually seemed like a pretty smart fella."

"Did he ever converse with Sandra and Crosseti?"

"Not that I ever noticed."

"One last question." said Officer Grant. "Is there anything else about the two of them you'd like to say that hasn't come up in our conversation?"

The bartender held up his hand for Grant to wait, fulfilled more requests for drinks, rang up the cash register a couple of times, and spoke briefly on the phone.

"One more thing," he said upon returning about five minutes later. "One afternoon, when Sandra got here a couple of minutes before Turner, I asked her how she was. Ya know, the 'how ya doin' kind of thing? I guess her answer shouldn't have surprised me, given the fact she and Turner were having an affair hotter than a firecracker up Faye Dunaway's ass, but it did."

Stan looked around the room at the customers for a moment, then glanced at his watch.

"What did she say?" Asked Officer Grant.

"She said that life was good now, but once her current husband was history, life would be wonderful. "Did she say what she meant by 'history?'" asked Officer Grant.

"No, she didn't, but I was about to ask her that question when she repeated the word by spelling it out, H I S T O R Y."

"Then what happened," asked Jim Grant.

"She gave me a big smile and a wink, then turned and greeted Dan with a sloppy, wet kiss.

Chapter 13

March 12, Wednesday, Panorama Towers,

Gary Merrill arrived at the Bear Republic office in the Panorama Towers a couple of minutes before 3:00. At 6'2, with a slim build, the 30-year-old Merrill had a shock of hair that reminded people of John F. Kennedy.

Divorced and the father of two young sons, he had a certain intensity about him that stood out from most of the cops working Homicide. Some of his friends in the department referred to him as Sergeant Friday, which he considered a compliment.

Lieutenant Hogan had called Rolene Ward, so she knew Merrill would be there around three. After the officer introduced himself, she told him that about twenty minutes earlier, word had gotten around the agency about Whit Payne. Within the next ten minutes or so, there had been a mass exodus from the office of all but three agents. Two of them were in their first month on the job and hadn't even heard of Whit. The third was a retired agent who came in occasionally to call a couple of old clients and visit with friends. As she gave Officer Merrill this information, the older man walked past them. He said good-bye to Rolene and went out the front door.

Merrill took a quick look at the large room filled with workstations, which Rolene referred to as 'cubby holes,' and, along three sides, private offices with windows facing the outside. The two new agents were apparently somewhere inside the maze of workstations. He saw a good halfdozen female secretaries at their desks outside of some individual offices, others speaking quietly in small groups, but not a single male anywhere. The threat and fear of death that had inundated this office was as thick as early-morning fog in Santa Monica.

A strong smell of tobacco was evident. The officer asked if anyone in the office smoked cigars.

"Yes," Rolene said. "Four or five do, but they're only supposed to smoke inside their private offices with the door closed. The rule is seldom observed, however, since Mr. Amalfitano himself occasionally walks around with a cigar hanging out of his mouth, or as he calls it, 'a Cuban.'"

"Boy, and I thought cops smoked a lot. This place could pass for a chimney," said Merrill, who smoked a couple of cigars a week. "Now, tell me more about the reaction when they learned of Whit Payne's murder."

"Well, the news spread through the office like wildfire," she said. "Our agents are not only depressed, but in shock. They're convinced the killer is the same one who shot Arnie's clients. They think he's moved from targeting clients to Bear Republic agents."

"Lieutenant Hogan called Taylor in confidence, Ms. Ward. How did the others learn of it?" Merrill said, with more than a hint of irritation in his voice. "Unless the press somehow got wind of it."

"He told Arnie, who told me because, well, I guess he felt he needed to tell someone. He knew I wouldn't say a word, and I didn't. And I don't think Arnie said anything either, since he left immediately after the lieutenant talked with him."

Officer Merrill nodded for her to continue. "Someone said they heard about it on the radio. The news said that Whit Payne worked in the same office as Arnold Taylor. Another agent came in and said the same thing. Almost immediately, some agents were huddling in small groups while others picked up their briefcases and walked out the door. What's left is what you see. No one but secretaries and administrative personnel, all female. Staff who can't just walk out when they feel like it. You can be sure Angie and I will be here until closing time at 5:00," she said as she gestured toward the switchboard, which was now on overload. Angie could be overheard telling one caller after another to hold until she could get back to them.

Merrill wondered if the situation might have been calmer if Amalfitano had been here rather than at his sister's funeral. Upon reflection, he decided it wouldn't have made any difference. A dead comrade is a dead comrade, whether in war, or here at home where no one even knows who the enemy is.

"Do you think there's a connection between Whit's murder and the other four killings?" she asked. The detective, deep in thought, ignored the question.

"May I please use a phone, Ms. Ward?" asked Merrill.

"Of course," she replied. "Mr. Amalfitano's office, so you'll have some privacy. And Officer Merrill, please call me Rolene." He noticed her face redden in an innocent blush, then smiled and nodded his assent.

About ten minutes later, Gary Merrill came out of the agency manager's office, expressed his regrets about the ongoing situation, and left the office without further comment.

****

Officer Merrill had called Lieutenant Hogan and explained the present situation in the Bear Republic office. Hogan told him not to be concerned about interviewing agents at this time, given the frenzy resulting from Payne's death. Conducting interviews is not presently appropriate and should be delayed.

Besides, Officer Grant had just called regarding his visit with the bartender. Hogan ordered Grant back to the office, for another team meeting at 4:00, to bring everyone up to speed. A lot had transpired in the past couple of hours.

Hogan was now using his temporary office in the Van Nuys City Hall full-time. It was much closer to the ongoing activity than headquarters downtown. Officers Grant and Merrill could be there from their present locations in ten or fifteen minutes. Wright was already there, just a couple of doors down.

Grant and Merrill both arrived at the Van Nuys office around 3:55, so Officers Porter and Wright were summoned, and the meeting began.

"As you all know, we now have evidence that Frank Crosetti murdered all four Bear Republic victims and Whit Payne. We're also pretty sure Crosetti was killed by Mike Slovak. Ballistics match several of his other hits.

"Porter and I have not visited Taylor's wife, yet. I had a feeling we should wait until you got back to me. That way, we might learn something important. Something that might make our visit with Sandi Taylor more productive.

"Guess what?" continued the lieutenant, "Grant turned up some information that could be crucial in solving this case. Who put Crosetti up to it, and why."

Hogan noticed two hands go up. "You first, George, and then Ricki."

"Will the public be informed that Crosetti is the serial killer?"

"Good question. Within the hour, headquarters will be issuing a statement that evidence points to him as the serial killer. Originally, I was opposed to the information getting out so fast, thinking that we might learn more if the news was suppressed for a while, but I was overruled. It's probably the right thing to do as far as the public is concerned, not to mention the Bear Republic agents, especially Taylor. Everyone out there can now breathe a little easier, except us. There's much more we need to learn before this case is closed.

"For starters, we still need to know why the four victims were singled out in the first place. Who gave the information to Crosetti, why Payne was killed, and why Monday night, the same day the fourth victim was killed."

"What about Slovak?" asked George Porter. "Will the public be informed he killed Crosetti? It's already been in the news that it was a gangland slaying."

"Your question's right on target," said Lieutenant Hogan. Our official line is, we're still investigating who murdered Crosseti, but we're certain it was a gangland slaying."

Hogan looked at Ricki, but Gary Merrill jumped in with a quick question.

"Do you mind if I smoke a cigar?" he asked, as he looked at Hogan.

"Only if you open the window and give me one."

"I have one for each of us, including Ricki." Giving her a side-glance.

"I'll tell ya what, fellas," said Ricki, "not only will I smoke one with you now, but when this case is wrapped up, we'll all go to my favorite bar at the Smoke House, and I'll light up in front of God and the LAPD Get it? THE SMOKE HOUSE."

There were groans, rolling eyes, and from Lieutenant Hogan, laughter and the thought that this babe was beginning to fit in real well. She was just like one of the boys, except for a few more-than-ample curves here and there, and a face pretty enough to stop traffic.

After each of the guys had inhaled at least once and made flattering comments about the brand, Bolivar, from Havana, Hogan gestured for Wright to get on with her comment or question.

"Am I the only one here who thinks it rather interesting that Amalfitano went AWOL just when all this stuff started? First, the murder of Whit Payne, then the murder of Crosetti by Slovak. How do we know Amalfitano's in New York at his sister's funeral? How do we know he even has a sister?"

"Those are valid questions, Ricki, and eventually we'll have the answers. Remember, though, nobody has more to lose than Amalfitano, including Arnie Taylor. I hope the fact that the agency manager is Italian does not factor into your concern."

"It certainly does, Lieutenant Hogan, but the difference between you and me is, I admit it, and you won't."

She was right, but this was no time to acknowledge it. Without responding, the Lieutenant asked Grant to give a rundown on what happened at the Holiday Inn with the bartender.

Grant answered a number of questions, followed by an announcement by Hogan. He wanted the group to know that he and Porter would be calling on Sandi Taylor the next day.

"I'm surprised no one has said anything about Carol, the Redhead," said Ricki Wright. "I think knowledge of her being with Sandi when she met Crosetti might prove invaluable. If one of you guys could call Arnie's contact information, I bet I could find out a whole lot about Sandi Taylor."

The lieutenant quickly agreed. He told Officer Merrill to call Arnie and find out who the redhead is without telling him the reason. Ricki would take over, cozy up with Carol, and obtain information about Sandi Taylor that Stan the Man himself couldn't possibly know.

At this point, something else entered Hogan's mind. "I'm surprised that none of you have brought up the fact that with Slovak involved, we have a rare opportunity. It's possible, of course, that he's the killer of the four Bear Republic clients, and merely planted the murder weapon on Crosetti. But I don't believe it. Slovak has never been known to take out anyone who wasn't a gangster. As far as we know, none of the four were involved with the underworld, but Wright is looking into the situation.

"If, in resolving this case we also apprehend Slovak, imagine what a coup that would be—and I mean for all of us. He's been on the 'most wanted' list for at least twenty-five years."

There was a knock at the door followed by Hogan's secretary sticking her head in the room to inform the lieutenant that his boss, Captain Coogin, was on the phone and insisted on speaking to him now.

"Yes, Captain, this is Frank Hogan."

"Frank, are you sitting down? I've just learned something from the assistant publisher of the *Valley Green-Sheet* that adds a whole new twist to the insurance company case."

"Well, Captain, your call couldn't be more timely. We're just about to wrap up a meeting about this nightmare, but fortunately everyone on my team is still here."

"Do you remember the case around twenty years ago that involved a Hollywood lawyer who got into some serious trouble, and after shooting his wife and a male companion, disappeared for a while, then—?"

"Yes, I do," said Hogan, "but I was only a rookie then and other than what you've just said, I really don't remember much about it."

"Well, Arnold Taylor is the youngest son of Everett Taylor, the attorney, and, as a kid he lived with Mike Slovak for five years. As far as anyone knows, the boys and their mother got along very well with him."

"And Slovak killed Frankie Crosetti, who killed four of Arnie's clients," said Lieutenant Hogan.

"Exactly," said Captain Coogin, who then hung up.

Lieutenant Hogan's face reddened. He smiled, pounded his fist on the table. "Well I'll be a son-of-a-bitch."

Chapter 14

Van Nuys City Hall, Wednesday Evening, March 12,

Lieutenant Hogan already knew about Arnie's tempestuous family life as a young boy. Including the fact Slovak lived with the Taylors for five years. He just hadn't made the connection. Arnie had told Hogan the whole story at their meeting Monday evening. A couple of days later, the lieutenant learned that Whit Payne was murdered that same night, probably during the time Arnie and Ricki were enjoying a reunion of sorts over gin and tonics at the Red Barn.

Another thought entered Hogan's mind as he pondered the course of events that were unfolding. He grabbed his phone a couple of minutes after 6:00 and dialed Ricki's number, hoping she hadn't left the office yet. She hadn't, and a couple of minutes later, she walked into her boss's office, smiled, and sat down.

"I have good news, Lieutenant," she beamed, but he held up his right hand, cutting her off.

"Why didn't you mention Arnie's family history when you told us the two of you spent a lot of time together during the years, 1951-1955. That period coincided exactly with the time frame his father was in a hell of a lot of trouble with the law. Trouble everyone knew about, right?"

She started to respond, but he cut her off again.

"Your involvement with our investigation is a risky venture, one that I had serious doubts about the moment I learned you and Arnie were pals when you were kids. I should have recused you from this case immediately."

Ricki displayed no emotion whatsoever, but remained silent while her boss continued.

"And here we are, Wright, just a couple of hours later, and it's clear you withheld vital information about his youth from the moment you revealed to us that you knew him. That, in fact, you've known him most of your life."

Hogan's tough-guy demeanor, reflected by his thundering tone of voice and solemn frown, was mostly an act. After all, he had momentarily forgotten about it himself, but that had been an honest oversight on his part. In her case, he was certain it was a deliberate act of deception. There was no way she could have forgotten about Arnold Taylor's father.

The lieutenant paused to relight the cigar he got from Officer Merrill two hours earlier. After exhaling, he remained silent and stared at her, simultaneously astonished and impressed with her composure and self-confidence.

"Why didn't you say something before our meeting broke up, when we learned that Mike Slovak, Arnie's old friend, had murdered the hoodlum who assassinated four of his clients? Why are you protecting him?"

Ricki hesitated before answering. She wanted to be certain he had finished his role as the Grand Inquisitor, at least for the moment.

"There are two things I would like to say, Lieutenant, that might shed some light on the nature of my relationship, past and present, with Arnie Taylor.

"First, yes, I'm trying to protect him, but only insofar as it relates to his family history. He suffered enough for the sins of his father at an age when everything hurts. He experienced a deep loss of self-worth as a result of the way he was ostracized by other kids at school. His family was burdened with huge financial problems, which forced his mother into bankruptcy.

He paid a price in other ways that neither you nor I could ever imagine. The last thing he needs is for an ugly episode of a generation ago to be back on page one. None of his friends know anything about that scandal, and I'm positive he wants to keep it that way."

"But Ricki," he said, then stopped because she talked right over him.

"Since it didn't seem relevant to the mess he found himself in today, through no fault of his own, I decided not to mention it, a decision I don't regret. And besides, I can't believe, for one moment, you didn't already know all about this. Why, you're one of the best detectives in the LAPD, maybe the best, yet you also chose not to discuss it during our meeting today. Either you did a thorough background check on Arnie at the very beginning, or he told you about it himself when you spent a couple of hours with him Monday evening."

Ricki stopped to take a breath, but to Lieutenant Hogan, she still appeared calm and collected. Then it dawned on him. Arnie had told her he'd discussed his family history with the lieutenant in great detail right before running into her at the Red Barn on Monday night. She was making a not-so-subtle hint that why should she have mentioned it since she knew he already knew all about it. It was his job to share that information with the team, not hers. After all, he's the one running the investigation.

Hogan made up his mind about Ricki, and it was not a tough call. She would continue in her role, not only because his boss, Captain Coogin would probably insist on it, but because, if there had to be a female working under him, it might as well be her. He wondered how someone that pretty could also be that smart. They would get along just fine as long as she remembered who was boss.

"Okay, Ricki," said Hogan, his tone softer, less combative. "I understand where you're coming from, but, it would have been wise if you had been up front about it from the start. This kind of thing cannot happen again. No more secrets, okay? All five of us working this case must have all the information. Got it?"

"Yes sir, I do," said Ricki. "I made a judgment call that seemed right to me, but you're the boss, and I promise to follow your lead."

"Anyway," said the lieutenant, "as you know, your point is now irrelevant, since the press has gotten wind of Arnie's background. I'll bet it will be in tomorrow's *LA Times*, complete with photographs of Arnie as he appeared at thirteen, and as he looks today."

"Shit," said Ricki, while wiping her forehead with her bare hand. "I feel so badly for Arnie about this. Shit."

"Well, events are now moving faster than Apollo 11 on its way to the moon," said Hogan. "I don't believe I've ever encountered anything like this in all my life."

Ricki took a five-minute timeout to go to the restroom. There was a second point she was going to make to the lieutenant, but now she was glad she had forgotten about it. When the time was right, everyone in the LAPD would know that she had been keeping an eye on Arnold Taylor long before her involvement in this case, and they would know the reason.

When she returned, Ricki observed Lieutenant Hogan looking out his fourth-floor window at the headlights and taillights of vehicles heading north and south on Van Nuys Boulevard. When he turned to face her, he appeared as dark and somber as the night.

"What bothers me," Hogan said, "is that while we've solved the identity of the killer, and know for sure he's dead, this case is far from over. I'm convinced that Crosetti didn't act alone. More people are involved. Maybe I'll have a better handle on this when I talk with our one viable suspect, Sandi Taylor. But I have a problem believing that she had Crosetti kill four of Arnie's clients when, if she wants to be free of him, all she had to do was have her gangster boyfriend kill Arnie."

"Ready for some good news yet, Lieutenant?" asked Ricki.

"Yes. I had momentarily forgotten there was such a thing. Please go ahead."

"After our meeting broke up, Merrill got a hold of Arnie and learned that Carol Lohman is the name of Sandi's redheaded pal. So it's very likely she's the one who was with her when she met Frankie Crosetti.

"Arnie told him that for a while, the two gals were pretty close, but he hadn't seen Carol or heard his wife mention her name for some time, maybe even a year. Since Merrill caught Arnie at home, he gave Merrill Carol's phone number from Sandi's address book."

"So, when are you going to call her?" asked the lieutenant.

"I already have," said Ricki. "We're having breakfast tomorrow morning at Denny's at 8:00, you know, the one in Mission Hills on Sepulveda."

"There's one thing you must remember when the two of you get together, Ricki. Make sure she knows your meeting with her is confidential, and she is not to mention it to anyone. Not a soul. Do you understand why I'm making such a point about this?"

"Of course," said Ricki. "You don't want her to talk to anyone about our interview because my name might get back to Arnie."

"You've got it. Good luck."

Chapter 15

Thursday Morning, March 13, Mission Hills

Always punctual, Ricki Wright arrived at Denny's at 7:50, got a small booth for two, ordered coffee and water, and kept her eye on the front door.

She had no idea what Carol Lohman looked like other than that she had red hair. Ricki assumed there was nothing particularly striking about her, such as weighing three-hundred pounds, or being as tall as Kareem Abdul Jabbar, or resembling Maureen O'Hara. She also had a feeling this was going to be a very important meeting. She didn't know why, but when she had experienced this feeling in the past, it turned out to be true about ninety percent of the time.

She had just asked for a coffee refill when, at 8:15, Carol walked in the door and told the hostess behind the counter she was looking for someone. Ricki stood, walked a good ten paces, extended her hand to introduce herself, then pulled her police badge from her purse.

Ricki, dressed professionally with gray slacks and a dark-blue blouse, took a quick glance at Carol Lohman before proceeding. Outfitted in a knee-length red skirt and white blouse with a low neckline, a generous amount of cleavage was evident that would get any man's attention. She would be a very pretty woman if her skin was not so white, her blue eyes a bit warmer, and her nose a little less pointed.

After being seated, Carol apologized for being late, and ordered coffee. Ricki then pulled a small notebook from her purse and began the interview.

"I know from our brief telephone conversation, Mrs. Lohman, that you're aware I'm visiting with you because you were with Sandi Taylor when she met Dan Turner. We now know Turner was really Frankie Crosetti, a mobster who was shot to death Tuesday morning behind Bob's restaurant in Toluca Lake."

"That's correct, Officer," said Carol. "Back then, Sandi and I'd meet every couple of weeks or so for cocktails somewhere, and on that particular day, it was at the Holiday Inn in Panorama City. It was too long ago for me to remember the day of the week or the date, but I sure remember that afternoon this sleazy looking guy started buying us drinks."

"You say he was 'sleazy looking,'" said Ricki, "but your girlfriend, Sandi, enjoyed the attention?"

"She sure did, and I could never understand why. Not then, not afterword, when we stopped seeing each other, and certainly not now."

"I'm already aware that you eventually left, and the two of them remained there," said Officer Wright. "So, since he was paying for the drinks, and you and Sandi were such close friends, what prompted you to leave?"

"Well, a couple of things. First of all, he was flirting with Sandi, not me. I got the free drinks only because I happened to be with her. Sandi attracts men like Elvis attracts teenage girls, Ms. Wright. She's beautiful, with great legs. She is a bit flat-chested, but then, so are Grace Kelly and Audrey Hepburn.

"But the real point is, I'm not in competition with her or anyone else. I'm divorced, no children, thirty years old, have a good job at Warner Bros. I don't lack for men in my life. I have plenty of dates, and a couple of men who would marry me in a heartbeat. The thing is, I don't go to bars to get picked up by guys, but to visit with girlfriends, like Sandi."

"What do you do at Warner Bros.?"

"Actually, I'm a secretary at Reprieve Records," said Carol.

"I'm a big Sinatra fan myself," said Officer Wright. "And come to think of it, the newer Sinatra albums I have are all on the Reprieve label."

Carol nodded.

Ricki liked this woman. She liked her a lot. In fact, she'd love to go out drinking with Carol Lohman once this inscrutable crime was solved.

"Okay," said Ricki, "you left because you were odd man out, so to speak, but I suspect there were other reasons you said adios. Right?"

Carol looked surprised. "How'd you know that?" she asked.

"Well, the obvious answer to that comment is you don't like being around sleazy looking guys, which is reason enough. But there's more, isn't there?" asked Officer Wright.

"Oh, you're good," said Carol. "Now I know why you're a cop. The real reason I left, and it's the reason why I don't see Sandi anymore, is because I'd grown tired of her cheating on her husband. Her constant affairs with guys who couldn't hold a candle to Arnie. Not that he's perfect by any means. Given what he went through as a kid, it doesn't take Einstein to conclude he probably has major issues. I mean, how could a child raised in an atmosphere of such violence and instability be otherwise, especially with his known-world watching? But he doesn't deserve a wife who cheats on him for no reason other than she finds him boring and she needs the excitement that comes from having sex with a new partner."

The waitress appeared. "Are you two ready to order?" she asked. Neither had looked at the menu, but both knew what they wanted. Carol ordered bacon and eggs, sunny side up, hash browns and sour dough toast. Ricki requested a waffle, two scrambled eggs and a cup of fresh fruit.

"The truth is," said Carol, "Sandi's a nymphomaniac. She told me so herself, and I've never doubted it. She loves sex. Claims she can never get enough. I suppose the only thing that's kept her from becoming a porn star is her strong Lutheran background and the fact that she's so close to her 'holier than thou,' self-righteous, pompous father."

Ricki let that comment rest for the moment. She wanted to get back to something else. She was dumbfounded by something she had just heard. After they ordered breakfast, followed by a few moments of silence, she said, "Did I hear you correctly? You mentioned issues Arnie might have as a result of his childhood. How do you know about his childhood?"

"How do I know? Are you kidding? Sandi's probably told every friend she has about Arnie's family. She refers to his dad as, 'his criminal father.' She might as well put a full-page announcement in the *Los Angeles Times*."

Ricki took a deep breath and thought about how embarrassed Arnie would be if he knew his wife had a mouth bigger than Martha Raye's. But then, she really shouldn't have been all that surprised, given other information she had regarding Sandi's mean streak.

"You say she's had numerous affairs over the years? How do you know that?"

"Because my ex-husband, Al Lohman, worked as an agent for Bear Republic for a couple of years. He didn't make it in the business, and has moved on to other things. But he told me that everyone in the office except Arnie Taylor and Michael Wong knew that Sandi was having a torrid affair with another Bear Republic agent. And it wasn't her first fling. Michael didn't know, of course, because he would have told Arnie."

"Tell me more about this, Ms. Lohman. Like, how long did this go on, why did it end, and most importantly, what was the name of the agent, if you happen to remember?"

"I'd say it lasted for a year or so. According to Al, the relationship ended because Sandi wanted to divorce Arnie and marry the guy, but there was a problem. He was already married, with two small children, and he never had any intention of leaving his wife and marrying Sandi. To him, Sandi was just a good lay, or as the agent once told my ex, 'nothing gives me greater pleasure than screwing Arnie Taylor's wife.'"

"Do you happen to remember his name?" asked Ricki.

"I sure do," said Carol. "Bill Kaiser."

Ricki's eyes widened, her heart pounding like a bass drum. She gulped down her glass of water because her throat had suddenly gone dry.

"You mean the John Bircher, NRA guy who allegedly hates Arnie because of his liberal political views?"

"Yep, that's him," replied Carol Lohman

Chapter 16

Thursday Morning, March 13, Chatsworth

Lieutenant Hogan had scheduled the appointment with Sandi Taylor for 10:00 at her parents' house in Chatsworth. It was Hogan's original intent to have Sandi come into his office at the Van Nuys City Hall, but he changed his mind. She might be more forthcoming in a friendlier, more familiar environment. Anyway, if there was a problem this morning, he would order her to come to his office, where she would be put under oath.

Before leaving for Chatsworth, about a twenty-minute drive, Hogan received a call from Ricki Wright. She gave him a brief account of her visit with Carol Lohman. Information concerning Sandi Taylor's numerous affairs, including her liaison with Bill Kaiser, consumed most of the conversation.

The Lieutenant and Officer George Porter were greeted at the front door by Sandi's father, Hans Schwartz, who ushered them into the living room where his wife, Lenore, and their daughter Sandi, were awaiting them.

Schwartz, wearing brown slacks and a white, long-sleeve shirt, walked with the precision of a 19th Century Prussian Officer. A man with a dignified bearing, he displayed the forced smile of an undertaker while shaking hands.

Lenore, who got up to greet the two officers, was dressed in a simple blue and white full-length dress. Her bearing and tone was a combination of indignation and anxiety. Her blue eyes, though filled with tension, were her best feature. She was as thin as a rake. Lenore looked like a shrunken, used-up, older version of her daughter.

When Hans introduced his daughter, she gave both officers a smile that was almost pathetic in its artificiality. Remaining silent, she held out her hand for the Lieutenant to shake, then Officer Porter.

After the introductions were made, Mr. Schwartz asked the Lieutenant if he and his wife could remain in the room while the two officers interviewed their daughter.

"Yes, you can stay," said Hogan, "as long as you remember that we're asking her the questions, not you. That doesn't mean you can't interject a comment at some point, if you think it would be helpful, but it's Sandi we're here to talk to."

Sandi's mother and father sat on the sofa, their daughter on an oversized, cushy recliner adjacent to them. The two officers sat on straight-backed, comfortable but utilitarian chairs across from the three. A large coffee table with a vase filled with fresh flowers were the only objects between the officers and the family. On the far wall across from the sofa, a nicely framed Van Gogh print hung over the fireplace, the famous artist's use of yellow adding some brightness to the surroundings. The room was nicely furnished, not lavish, but homey and inviting.

Officer Porter removed a notepad and pen from his inside left coat pocket as his boss opened the discussion:

"Mrs. Taylor, we're here to ask you some questions concerning all the trouble your estranged husband is in, and the extent to which you may, or may not, have some information that would be helpful to us.

"While you are not under oath, we expect you to be truthful. If we suspect you're not, and it turns out we were right, there'll be consequences later on that could be very, very damaging for you. Have I made myself clear?"

"Yes, Lieutenant, I understand. I will tell you everything I know, but please call me Sandi. Everyone calls me Sandi."

"I appreciate that, Mrs. Taylor, but since this is an official visit, my partner and I always follow the rules of etiquette appropriate to LAPD investigations."

Hogan pursed his lips and looked at her for a moment or two before asking the first question. There was no doubt about it—this was one pretty woman, slim, about 5' 5", nice legs, and outfitted conservatively in a pale-blue dress with a high neckline. A natural blonde, she had greeted them with a beautiful smile, even though he could tell it was forced. After all, Sandi was in an unenviable position given the fact that, her marriage was on the rocks. Her disdain for her husband was an object of gossip not only among friends, but throughout her husband's office as well. Her pale face and reddened eyes gave the impression she'd been crying a lot.

"Mrs. Taylor, when did you first become aware that someone was killing your husband's clients?" asked Hogan.

"Well, Arnie didn't say squat about it until the second murder. I read the newspaper almost every day, or at least I scan it, but when he told me about the second one, I didn't remember reading about the first one. He tried to pretend it was all a coincidence, but I could tell he was very concerned."

"Was his concern focused on the victims, or was there a broader issue?" asked the lieutenant.

"Mostly, he was concerned about his clients, the victims. Both those who had been killed, and those who might be objects of target practice in the future. That is, if there really was a serial killer going after his clientele. He was also concerned that if this continued, his career would be in jeopardy. His clients would leave him, Bear Republic would give him the boot, and then, what other life insurance company would want him? He would be damaged goods. He was terribly upset about the whole ordeal, that's for sure."

Officer Porter knew that Hogan started out with soft questions, both to get her to relax a bit, and to get her talking. It seemed to be working. While Hogan paused, Officer George Porter entered the conversation.

"Please tell us, Mrs. Taylor, when you first learned of the third and fourth murders."

"All I remember about the third one is, he said there was now a good chance Bear Republic would notify the police. Neither my husband nor the company had been contacted by the police or the press, so it was obvious they were unaware that all three had purchased life insurance from Arnie. This was a fact the police would want to know."

"But that didn't happen until the fourth murder, right?" asked Officer Porter.

"I guess so, Officer, but Arnie and I haven't spoken for three days. All I know is what I read in the papers."

Her tone was contemptuous. A deeper, darker personality surfaced as she resettled herself in her chair, crossing her legs in the process.

"What happened when you heard about murder number four?"

"Well, Arnie and I had a really ugly argument the night before, which was Sunday. When he got home late Monday afternoon, he walked right by me without speaking, called his office, and then ran out of the house and drove away like he was preparing for the Indy 500. I knew it was the office he had called because I heard him say the name,

'Angie,' who is the switchboard operator. I also knew there had been another killing."

"How did you know that?" Porter asked.

"I just knew, that's all. My husband and I have been married a long time, too damn long, and I had never seen him that upset. Not even the night before when we had the worst argument of our marriage, probably the final one. He was totally rattled."

Lieutenant Hogan reflected on the fact that everything she said was consistent with what he already knew, except for one small detail. But now it was time to play hardball, and he took over the questioning again.

"What did you do after Mr. Taylor left the house Monday afternoon, Mrs. Taylor?"

"What do you mean, what did I do?" she said.

"Did you call your parents, watch an "I Love Lucy" rerun, get in your car and drive somewhere? What did you do?"

She glanced at her mother and father, paused a moment, then responded.

"This is really a private matter, Lieutenant, which has nothing to do with the reason you're here, and everything to do with my private life and the end of my marriage."

Lenore Schultz then jumped up from the sofa and asked if anyone wanted coffee, water, or a soft drink. The lieutenant said he and Officer Porter would pass, but thanked her anyway. Hans shot a cold glance at his daughter, who was looking at Lieutenant Hogan.

"You said a little while ago, Mrs. Taylor, that you would tell us everything we wanted to know."

"Yes, I did, but you told me you'd be asking questions concerning the trouble Arnie is in, and the extent to which I may, or may not, have relevant information. You're asking personal questions that have nothing to do with the serial killer. To be blunt, you're now asking questions that are none of your business."

In Hogan's mind, this woman had the delicate sensitivity of a python.

Sandi smiled narrowly, then scratched the side of her face with her right hand.

"Yes, but"—

"God Dammit, Sandi," stormed her father, "answer the Lieutenant's question, or I will, and then you can go with him to the police station to answer the rest of his questions."

Lenore turned as white as a Polar Bear, placed her hand on her mouth and looked at her husband, but remained silent.

"You did go somewhere," said Lieutenant Hogan, "and a little while ago you made a slight misstatement when you said, "everyone calls me 'Sandi.' At the Panorama City Holiday Inn, you're known as 'Sandra,' isn't that right? And you were less than candid when you said that what you did later on Monday afternoon has nothing to do with why we're here. It has everything to do with why we're here.

"Now, tell us about the rest of your evening at the Holiday Inn, including who you were with, and why you were with him."

Eyes focused on her father, Sandi brushed the side of her face with one hand, then coughed nervously. Fighting back tears, she began to speak.

"I went to the Holiday Inn bar to see my boyfriend, Dan Turner. We had been seeing each other for a good six months and I had fallen in love with him. I'm sure you know the rest of the story. It turns out 'Dan Turner' doesn't exist. His real name was Frankie Crosetti, and he was not only a mobster, but the killer of my husband's clients. I'd say the bastard got what he deserved."

She stopped, and cried uncontrollably for several minutes while the other four people in the room remained silent. It struck Hogan as odd that neither parent attempted to comfort her. He figured Lenore had been watching her daughter cry for the past couple of days, and was either immune to these fits of emotion, or was just too exhausted to react. Hans was a different story. He folded his arms against his chest, and had that look of grave disappointment that comes when a father discovers his daughter, his little girl, is no angel.

"Did you ever talk to Crosetti about any of your husband's clients, Mrs. Taylor?" asked Hogan.

"No," Sandi answered, before he could even finish the question. "How could I? I've never had any interest in Arnie's business, and while we've socialized on occasion with a few clients that he especially likes, I really don't give a shit about any of them."

"Did you ever have access to Mr. Taylor's briefcase?" asked the lieutenant.

"Access? Well, yes, I guess I did. He brought it home almost every night, and sometimes would work for an hour or so. You know, put the finishing touches on apps he was going to be handing in the next morning, that sort of thing. He usually kept it in the front guest room which also serves as a kind of home office."

"Did you ever go into the briefcase for any reason?"

"Absolutely not," said Sandi. "As I've already said, I have no interest in my husband's business."

"Are you willing to swear under oath that you never knew this so-called Dan Turner was a mafioso, and that you never gave him information concerning the four victims?"

The Lieutenant wondered why so many pretty girls go for the dangerous ones.

She forced a half smile. "Yes, I am willing to swear to that under oath. Why don't you put me under oath right now? Then, maybe we can put all this behind us.

"Look, I've made some big mistakes, real whoppers, that's for sure. But I would never knowingly get involved with a gangster, and I had absolutely nothing to do with the death of four innocent people. What in the world would I have to gain by being involved in such a shameful act. I want a divorce, that's all, not a bunch of dead bodies and my husband a front page story again."

"Again?" Asked Lieutenant Hogan.

"Yes," said Sandi. "You see, when he was a kid. . ."

"We know all about that, Mrs. Taylor. Since it's irrelevant to this case, I'm surprised you've alluded to it.

"Did you know any of the four who were murdered?" asked the Lieutenant.

"Know them? I never even heard of them."

The lieutenant looked over at Officer Porter, who was jotting something down on his notepad. When he finished, Hogan nodded for him to proceed.

"Just one more question about Monday evening, Mrs. Taylor, then we'll move on to a different topic. How did your evening with Crosetti end?"

"Rather abruptly," she said. "The bartender, Stan, told him he had a phone call, and when Dan returned from behind the bar, he looked really pissed off. He said he had to go. He gave me a quick kiss, and left. I never saw him again."

"He didn't say who called him or where he was going?"

"Not a word," she replied.

Officer Porter removed a photo from his inside right coat pocket. He handed her the picture. "Ever seen this guy before?" he asked.

"Yes, he's an insurance agent with Bear Republic. I don't know his name, but he comes into the Holiday Inn lounge occasionally."

"Did you ever point out to Crosetti that a colleague of your husband was in the room, a fellow agent?"

"No, I was afraid he'd have a temper tantrum, and would insist on meeting somewhere else. I wasn't at all bothered by his being there. Arnie hardly knows the guy, which is why I don't even know his name. And I love the Holiday Inn cocktail lounge. And since I was about to divorce Arnie anyway, why did it matter if this guy knew I had a boyfriend? By then, I was sure Arnie was aware I was seeing someone, but odd as it seems, he never seemed to give a damn one way or the other."

"What's interesting," said Officer Porter. "is that you're apparently unaware that this man, Whit Payne, was murdered Monday night while sitting in his own home having dinner. Crosetti killed him after leaving the Holiday Inn that evening, so we're pretty sure the phone call he received had to do with Payne's murder. Didn't you see this in the *LA Times*? The article identified Crosetti as the killer, and there was even a picture of Whit Payne alongside the story."

For the first time, Hans Schultz came to his daughter's defense. "Officer, we've all been so focused on Crosetti being the killer of four of Arnie's clients, I can understand why Sandi never noticed it. I read it, and so did Lenore, but we saw no reason to mention it to our daughter. She had enough to worry about concerning the four other victims without calling her attention to Whit Payne's murder."

Lieutenant Frank Hogan picked up the questioning of Sandi Taylor again.

"Did you have another lover prior to Crosetti?"

Sandi shot a quick glance at her father, then closed her eyes for a moment. She asked her mother to please get her a glass of water, then looked at the lieutenant.

"Yes, I did," she said.

"And who was that?" asked Hogan.

"Bill Kaiser, another Bear Republic agent."

"Do you want to tell us about it, or would you prefer us to start asking specific questions?

"Since you seem to know everything already, I'll save you the effort and just spill it out," said Sandi.

"Bill and I had an affair that lasted about a year. I was physically attracted to him, but the main thing was, like Dan Turner, I mean Crosetti, he was so different from Arnie. Less reserved, more fun. We had some important things in common. We're both conservative Republicans, which may not seem like such a big deal, but at home it got so bad

Arnie and I couldn't even discuss politics anymore. Bill was a member of the John Birch Society, and so were my parents.

He's also from the Midwest, like my mother and father, and is a big Badger fan. You know, the University of Wisconsin?"

She stopped for a moment to catch her breath. Lenore had returned to the living room and set a glass of water next to a lamp on the table beside her. Hans was silent, looking at his wife, at the fireplace, at the Van Gogh print on the wall, at Officer Porter—everywhere but at his daughter.

"There's something else about Bill Kaiser, something very important, that you haven't mentioned, isn't there?" asked Hogan.

"I don't understand what you mean," said Sandi.

"Something that sets him apart from all the other agents in the building? Something that has to do with your husband?"

"Oh, yeah. He despises Arnie. He can't stand him, and it all has to do with their political differences. And, yes, that attracted me to him as well."

"Two more questions and we're done, Mrs. Taylor. How did you and Mr. Kaiser happen to get together?"

"It started at an awards banquet a couple of years ago. Arnie was at the bar holding court with a small group of friends, and I struck up a conversation with Bill, who was alone that night. One of his kids was sick, so his wife couldn't come."

"With all due respect, Lieutenant Hogan," said Hans, "it's now my turn to ask just what this prior affair has to do with the four victims and Frankie Crosetti?"

"Thanks for intervening, Mr. Schultz. You've given me a perfect segue into my last question.

"I want to know, Sandi, if you're aware of any connection between Kaiser and Crosetti. After all, Kaiser despises Arnie, and Crosetti went to extremes to make his life miserable. There could very well be a connection. Especially since obtaining the information about the four victims appears to have been an inside job."

"I doubt it," said Sandi. "but there is a connection between Bill and one other guy in the agency who hates Arnie as much as he does, maybe even more. In fact, the two of them have formed a very close relationship over their mutual dislike of my husband. No one else in the office knows about this, not even Rolene Ward, who usually knows everything. Or thinks she does.

"His name is Dominic Amalfitano. You know, the agency manager? With him, it's all about Vietnam."

Chapter 17

Thursday noon, March 13, North Hollywood

Gladys Doleshal left a message late Tuesday morning for Mike Slovak, after Arnie left her house in Burbank. Gladys never had any reason to call this number before, but his instructions were clear. In an emergency, she was to dial Mike's number. A woman would answer with the salutation, "Melanie speaking, how may I help you?"

She would then leave the designated message, "have Mike call O.F.," and hang up. Mike would return the call to "Old Friend," as soon as he got the message. When he called around 1:00 that afternoon, they discussed Arnie and the four murders. Without hesitation, Mike agreed to meet Gladys's youngest son for lunch at noon on Thursday at the Villa Sorrento.

Gladys was told to tell Arnie that he might be up to a half hour late, but not to worry, since it was by design. He would explain over lunch.

Arnold Taylor felt his heart racing as he pulled into an empty parking spot in front of the Villa Sorrento in North Hollywood. He hadn't seen Mike Slovak for twenty years, unaware back then that he was a hit-man for Mickey Cohen and the mob prior to moving in with the Taylors. By now, Mike had been a fugitive from justice, and on the 10 most wanted list, going all the way back to 1947 and the slaying of Bugsy Siegal. Twenty-eight years. Arnie was only seven when Slovak joined the Taylor household to be the family's fix-it guy and all-around handyman.

At a couple of minutes before noon, Arnie walked into the restaurant and took a booth at the rear of the dining room. Here, he and Mike would have a modicum of privacy and not be overheard if they kept their voices down. He smelled pizza, heard the theme from "The Godfather" in the background, and ordered a Miller's High Life. When his beer arrived, he told the waitress someone would be joining him in a little while, and the two of them would be having lunch. A little less nervous now that he was inside and seated, he gave the room a quick glance. There was a counter along the left side as you entered, with an open kitchen behind it. An Italian couple were shouting back and forth, an obvious mom-and-pop operation. The one waitress, maybe nineteen or twenty, was a young version of the woman in the kitchen, minus about forty or fifty pounds.

There was no one seated at the small counter, but four of the tables, and one of the other three booths, were occupied. A family of four, including two little boys, both under six or seven; two couples in their late thirties or early forties, and a family of five were seated at the tables. Seated at another booth was a couple that looked old enough to be Arnie's parents, probably in their sixties. They appeared to be deep in quiet conversation while sharing a salad.

By 12:40, the place had pretty much cleared out, except for the older couple in the booth. The two got up to leave, but after walking the woman to the front door and giving her a kiss on the cheek, the man turned around and headed back into the restaurant.

"Hi, Arnie. Long time no see."

Arnie recognized Mike's voice instantly, even though he hadn't heard it for two decades. Speechless, he jumped up and the two threw their arms around each other.

"I've been watching the front door for nearly forty minutes and, holy shit, you've been sitting a dozen feet from me the entire time," said Arnie. "Even after Mother gave me a brief description of the new Mike, I still didn't recognize you."

It occurred to Arnie that his mother had understated how different Mike looked. He must be at least sixty pounds heavier, and, with his shaved head, looked like a cartoon character. A kind of fat version of 'Mr. Clean,' minus the earring. Wearing jeans, a Hawaiian shirt and cowboy boots. The only thing that hadn't changed was Mike's friendly, casual manner.

The two sat down and ordered a large pizza: pepperoni, Italian sausage and Canadian bacon. They chatted a good ten minutes about some of the fun times in the old days when Mike lived with the Taylors. Before everything went to hell. The days he would join them in the front yard, and Arnie and his brother, Danny, and Mike would throw the football around.

"I'll bet I know how you answer when anyone asks if you're a Dodger or an Angel fan," said Arnie, indirectly referring to the fact that LA didn't have any professional major-league sports teams back in those years except the Rams.

"I'll bet you do, too," said Mike. In unison the two then said, "Detroit." That was always Mike's standard answer to any question about team loyalty. He liked Detroit, where he was born and raised. Period.

"You know, Arnie, you remind me a lot of your father," said Mike. "Your self-assurance, the way you talk. You even look something like him, especially the shade of your blue eyes."

"This isn't the first time I've heard that, Mike, but I like to think I'm more like my mother. That I'm my mother's son, so to speak."

Mike laughed. "So to speak? That's your dad, Arnie, but never worry, you are your mother's son. You definitely have her personality. Anyway, everything I've just said I meant as a compliment."

"I know. Thanks."

The pizza arrived. They were the only customers in the restaurant, and after the waitress brought two large mugs of beer, it was time to get serious.

There was silence for a few moments while Arnie wolfed down two slices of pizza while Mike took a bite, and then a sip of his beer. Arnie couldn't help but reflect how odd this scene was—talking and laughing with an old friend who, incidentally, was a gangster. And he was not only a target for the LAPD, but probably for rival gangs as well.

"Why do you use your real first name, and what is your last name these days?" asked Arnie.

"First, the cops would never suspect I'd go around town using my real first name, so I think this might throw them off a bit. Secondly, I still use an Italian last name because, if it worked for so many years, when I was Sam Palumbo, then I must be believable as an Italian. Why risk trying to pose as Polish or Armenian or as a Jew? My Italian last name is Bianchi. Mike Bianchi."

"How long have you been here?" Asked Arnie. "I was told you would walk in maybe half an hour or so after I got here."

"I've been here since 11:35," said Mike, as he glanced at his watch. "About an hour."

Arnie then asked, "Why so early?"

"Because I wanted to see if anyone was following you," said Mike. "If ten people walked in here, one after another, I would be able to spot in an instant, which one was tailing you, if, in fact you were being followed. I'm good at this, Arnie. God knows I've had enough time to become an expert."

"But why would anyone be following me? I haven't done anything."

"More than likely, it would be the police," replied Mike. "And it shows how incompetent they are that no one is watching you every second of the day. Why? Because you'd think they would want to know if you are in contact with me, given the mess you're in. If one of them had come in here, I would have kept on visiting with my girlfriend and would not have left until at least an hour after you did."

"What's your girlfriend's name?" asked Arnie.

Mike smiled. "I don't remember," he said.

They had finished the pizza and Mike motioned for the waitress, Marie, to bring two more beers. The Dean Martin "Volare" recording, which had been playing softly in the background, was now turned up to a louder pitch, which made it easier for them to discuss matters of life and death without being overheard.

"Are you aware that the killer of your four clients, Frankie Crosetti, is dead?" asked Mike.

"Yes," said Arnie. "Lieutenant Hogan, the officer in charge of the investigation, called me early last evening with the news. Of course, I also saw the story in this morning's *Times*. I knew this Crosetti guy had been killed behind Bob's Big Boy Toluca Lake, but I didn't know until last night he was the one we've been looking for. By the way, I was at Bob's with Lieutenant Hogan right before this happened."

Arnie continued. "The Lieutenant also told me what I already had figured out. This case isn't over—we need to know how Crosetti got the information, and why those four particular clients were singled out. In other words, what the hell is this all about?"

"Well, Arnie," said Mike, "I'm going to tell you a couple of things I want you to know, but keep in mind, this information must not go any further. And, at the same time, I'm going to tell you as little as possible, because if the police discover we've had this meeting, the less you know the better. You're going to be in deep shit if they learn you and I have talked. In the war they called it, 'collaborating with the enemy.' Your ass will be put over a hot stove that you'll feel for the rest of your life. Not a word to anyone, not even your mother, your best friend, or God himself. I mean it, Arnie."

"I understand. I'm smarter than I look."

"Okay," said Mike. "Here's the inside story."

"Your mother showed her usual smarts when she asked for my help, but I had already beaten her to the punch. I was pretty sure after the third shooting, and positive after the fourth on Monday, when you were identified as the insurance agent for all four victims, that I knew what's going on.

"I shot and killed Crosetti's brother, Tony, a year or so ago. The Crosettis are part of a small gang that's at war with my people, the old Cohen gang, whose names you don't need to know. The Crosetti gang operates almost entirely here in the San Fernando Valley, dealing in drugs, prostitution, gambling, that sort of thing. More than anything, our dispute with them is over turf. I've known for some time that Frankie Crosetti was trying to smoke me out, to find and kill me, for what I did to his brother. When the news came out after the fourth murder that you were the agent of all four victims, I was positive I was right.

"You see, somehow he learned that I had a connection with your father a long time ago, that I had lived with your family, that we all got along very well, and, somehow, this is the most confusing part, he learned you were a Bear Republic life insurance agent working out of Panorama City."

"How would he find out about my past?" asked Arnie. "I never discuss it with anyone. My best friend doesn't even know about it."

"Well, somebody knows about it," said Mike, "somebody who knows, or knew, Frankie Crosetti. Your mother told me your wife is pretty nasty, that she's moved out of your house, and that she dislikes—maybe even hates—you. She knows about your childhood, right?"

"Yes, of course she does," said Arnie. "but for all her faults, I've never thought of Sandi as a blabber mouth, and besides, how would she even know someone part of an underworld gang? Anyway, I'd think she'd be too embarrassed to admit she married the son of a well-known felon."

Mike shrugged and looked toward the counter.

"Marie, could you bring us a couple of more beers?"

"No thanks, I've had enough," said Arnie. "Make that one more, Marie," said Mike.

"Before Bear Republic hired you, did they do a background check?"

"Yes, but I doubt they were checking that far back," Arnie replied. "But, come to think of it, I gave them three references, two of whom do go back that far. It might have come out then. To tell you the truth, I've always been curious about what's in my personnel file and who has read it."

"Who are the two you listed as references?"

"Ann Swendsen, a family friend, and Harry Sax, my boss at the *Herald-Express.*

"Well, I remember Ann very well. A real classy lady. She might have mentioned it, but I doubt it. I never knew Harry Sax, or even heard his name, so I don't have an opinion about him."

"Well," said Arnie, "Ann's still very much alive, but probably wouldn't remember whether she said anything about it or not. She and Clyde retired in Oxnard. As for my old boss, I heard a couple of years ago that he died."

"Anyway, let's move on," said Mike. "After the fourth murder, I was convinced that Frankie Crosetti was the assassin and that he figured sooner or later you would ask me to step in and he would then take me out."

Mike continued. "So, on Tuesday morning of this week, just two days ago, I followed you from the moment you backed out of your garage. After getting on the 405, I hadn't even reached the Balboa Boulevard turnoff when I realized you were being tailed by someone else. I got close enough to see that it was Crosetti. A little later, he followed you into Bob's, and when he came back out, about fifteen minutes after you left, I shot him as he was getting into his car. Your mother called me an hour or two later."

"My God," shouted Arnie. Mike held up his right hand as a reminder for him to lower his voice. "But why was Whit Payne murdered? What does he have to do with all of this?"

"I haven't given the Whit Payne situation much thought," said Mike, "but I do have one question to ask you about him."

Busy processing everything he'd just learned, Arnie was slow to react. Mike picked up his beer mug and took a long swallow while he waited for Arnie to speak.

"Go ahead, Mike. What's your question?"

"Was Whit privy to any information about your present or your past life that nobody else in the agency knows about?"

"Yes, my present life. He told me my wife was having an affair with some guy she met a couple of afternoons a week at the Holiday Inn. Whit was divorced, and he liked to drop by there and have a beer or two before going home."

"Did he know the man's name or give a description of what he looked like?"

"Yes," said Arnie. "He told me his name was Dan Turner and he was probably Italian, about my height, on the heavy side, but otherwise, a pretty average looking guy."

"And you never mentioned this to anyone?"

"Only my mother and my best friend, Michael Wong."

"And as far as you know, Whit never told anybody?"

"He promised me he wouldn't," said Arnie. "and he was a pretty closed mouth kind of guy. He minded his own business and, frankly, didn't socialize much with anyone."

"Arnie, have you read the description of Frankie Crosseti in the paper or heard it on TV?"

Mike leaned forward over the table, lowered his voice, and looked right into his friend's eyes.

"Arnie . . . Crosetti was your wife's boyfriend."

For Arnold Wayne Taylor, the world changed in a second. He sat there rigid with shock. The woman he had loved and been married to for twelve years was in cahoots with the hoodlum who was killing his clients. He pulled a handkerchief from his pocket to stop the tide of tears flowing down his cheeks, but it didn't do much good.

Arnie decided to have another beer after all. He and Mike then spent a good half hour discussing various ramifications of this information. Mike did almost all the talking while Arnie sat there in frozen silence. The whole situation was beyond comprehension.

Mike glanced at his watch and mentioned it was nearly 3:30, they had been visiting for more than two and a half hours, and he needed to go. That was okay, Arnie was exhausted. Besides, Arnie was anxious to share all this with the Lieutenant. Without, of course, mentioning his source. He would only tell Hogan that the description in the press of Frankie Crosetti matched Witt Payne's description of Dan Turner, close enough to conclude they were one and the same.

"There's one more thing I want to share with you, Arnie, along with the fact we may never see each other again.

"You're aware of the old saying, 'the more things change, the more they stay the same'? Well, that's kinda what's going on right now. There's a third Crosetti out there, another brother, who lives somewhere here in the Valley. I don't know his first name or what he looks like, but, one thing I do know is, he'll be coming after me.

"Whether or not he'll try to get my attention by killing another of your clients remains to be seen. I certainly hope not, but we won't know for a while."

"Why is that?" asked Arnie.

"I'm surprised you ask. Surely you know the murders are taking place every forty-five days, and the last one was just three days ago. That's well thought out on their part, not just a random act. I use the word "they" because I'm sure that even though the Crosettis are our enemy, there are other people involved helping them, including someone in your office, which leads me to one more point.

"These killers are down to a system in more than one way. Not only do they operate on a time schedule, I'm positive their choice of targets are not random. Those poor victims all have something in common. The Crosetti gang's betting I'll solve the puzzle, then show up at the right place in forty-two days, where they will be waiting for me. And I do mean "they." It's going to take more than one of them to gun me down."

"So, my job is to solve the puzzle," said Arnie, "since you don't know anything about my book of business."

"Book of business?"

"That's trade talk, Mike, for 'clientele.'"

"That's right, only you can solve the puzzle." Said Mike. "I already know through informants at the LAPD that there's a woman undercover officer working on this. She thinks they may be loosely linked as drug dealers, or something of that sort."

"She's on the wrong track," said Arnie. "There has to be something else. I'll do some brain work, to the extent I have one, which is questionable at this point. I'll make this my number-one priority, which isn't difficult. I've been suspended by Bear Republic as an agent until further notice, so it's not like I don't have plenty of time on my hands. I'll start removing files from my office and take them home, or to my mother's, and see if I can come up with anything. Since I have around 700 clients, this won't be easy."

"Good luck, Arnie, and don't try to reach me unless it's absolutely necessary. Then, go through your mother. I may drop in on you sometime, when you least expect it. It will never be at your home, though, or at your mother's.

"These are not forgiving people, Arnie, and I have now killed two of the Crosetti brothers. Let's just hope the remaining brother and his cohorts give up on the strategy of getting to me by involving you and your clients.

"But since we don't know what they're next step is going to be, you must always be careful. Stay alert, be aware of your surroundings, wherever you are."

Chapter 18

Monday Morning, March 17, the San Fernando Valley.

At 6:50 am, the 1975 black Cadillac Eldorado turned right off of Ventura Boulevard in Encino, drove to the end of the driveway adjacent to Rossi's Ristorante, and parked behind the building. There was another Eldorado already there. It was a blue '73 model. Parked on the far side of the lot was an early '60s Plymouth Valiant. In need of a wash and minus a couple of hubcaps, the beaten down heap looked out of place.

A robust, dark-haired man about 5' 6", wearing a blue suit, stepped out of his automobile. He walked a good ten feet, gave the backdoor one knock, then opened it and walked in. His lone surviving brother was standing at the counter pouring himself a mug of coffee.

"You're right on time," said Rocky Crosetti, "the coffee's ready." He set his mug on the counter, took several steps, then threw his arms around his brother and gave him a big hug.

"It's great to see you, Rocky," said Vincent Crosetti. "We have some serious shit to talk over, as you know. I've only got about forty-five minutes."

Rossi's Ristorante was a front for the Crosetti brothers, a popular Italian eatery where they often gathered in the back office to plan their Underworld activities. They owned the building, but the restaurant itself was run by Jerry Rossi and his family, longtime friends.

The office was about three-hundred square feet. It was furnished with a round table in one corner with five chairs. As you entered the room from the back, there was a wet bar against the left wall. On the counter next to it was a coffeepot, several mugs, and some cocktail glasses. A dozen or so bottles of hard liquor were stored in a cabinet below, along with some weapons, including a shotgun, a .25 automatic and two .38s. The wall to the right was adorned with photographs from long ago, including one of the four boys taken when they were kids, and one of their mother and father on their wedding day.

A door opposite the one in the back of the room opened into the restaurant, with a mural of Rome on one wall, and the Tuscany landscape on the other. The kitchen was on the right toward the front of the building.

"There's a couple of things on my mind, Vince," said Rocky, "but first you might want to tell me what ya think we should do now. This whole thing's so fucked up, I'm not sure where we go from here. One thing for sure, this mess was your idea to begin with. It's your job to fix it."

"Before you start in on me," said Vince, "let's get one thing straight. It was you and brother, Frankie, who decided we had to find Mike Slovak and kill him for what he did to Tony. What I did was devise a plan, a damn good plan, that would get Mike to come out in the open where we could wipe out the son of a bitch once and for all. The plan I came up with was full-proof."

"Yeah," said Rocky, "full-proof that Slovak would come out, but he was supposed to show up during one of our executions of Arnie's clients, where we 'd be waiting for him. Not in the fuck'n parking lot at Bob's Big Boy. Slovak was the last thing on Frankie's mind when he started to get into his car."

"There's one thing I'm sure we can agree on, Rocky, and it has to do with Frankie. He's our brother, we loved him and all that stuff because he was family. But he was always the loose cannon, the one most likely to bring us all down. His getting involved with Taylor's wife is unforgivable. I mean, how stupid can one man be. His failure to use his goddamn head could be the end of all of us, depending on how much the bitch knows. Sad to say, but we're really better off with him out of the picture."

"Yeah, you're right," said Rocky. "I spent Wednesday and Thursday night in this room all by my lonesome. Got drunk, smoked cigars into the wee hours of the morning. But as I sobered up, I came to the same conclusion. We're better off without him.

"So, Mr. Genius, just where are we at this point? What do we do now?. Or should we do anything at all? Sometimes the best thing to do is nothing. Maybe we should just call it quits. Ya know, call the whole thing off."

Vince Crosett's face reddened and his tone of voice hardened as he looked right into his brother's eyes. "We can't quit now, Asshole, not when we're behind. The time to quit is when we're ahead. Am I the only one who has any brains in this fucking family?"

Vince continued. "First, we've got a plan, remember? The problem is, by the fourth killing, dumb-shit Arnie still hadn't figured it out. If he had, he would have asked Slovak to help him. You would have been killing Slovak while Tony took care of our client-targets. And there's no way the police could figure it out even if they went through every goddamn one of Arnie's files. I even wonder if anyone at this point has noticed that the clients are being knocked off in alphabetical order.

"But we're getting somewhere. We now know that Arnie has brought Slovak into this, just like I said he would. How do we know? Because Slovak knew that Frankie killed all four of the victims. That's why he took him out."

"The question is, how'd Slovak know?" asked Rocky.

Vince got up from the table and stretched, then walked over to the counter for a second mug of coffee.

"If you want a cigar, Vince, they're in the right-hand bottom cabinet. And get me one, too."

Vince returned to the table and sat down. He tossed a cigar across the table to Rocky, lit his 'Cuban,' took a sip of his refill, then stared at his brother before responding to his question. "The answer to your question, Rocky, is obvious. Slovak decided to tail Arnie to see if anyone else was following him. Either the cops or the killer. He saw Frankie following him, so he began following the follower. Arnie went into Bob's to meet with Hogan, the dumb ass in charge of the investigation. Frankie went into Bob's, watched the two of them, and some time after Arnie left, Frankie left. Only he never made it into his car."

Vince raised his right thumb, index and adjacent finger, and pointed his hand like a pistol.

"Boom, Boom. One more Crosetti dead. Mike Slovak, alive and well. The legend lives on."

"That's your best guess?" asked Rocky.

"Not a guess, Rocky. A fact. We have an informant inside Homicide, remember? And not just any informant. This guy's one of us—part of our gang.

"One more thing. Hogan and his crew are very suspicious that Arnie has contacted Mike, since they know Slovak killed Frankie. So they're probably going to be tailing Arnie now, in hopes that they'll at least get Slovak, even if they never discover what our operation and motives are all about. And that would be a bigger coup for them than catching us. Remember, Mike Slovak is a much bigger fish. We're small fry."

"So, what do we do now, Vince?" asked Rocky. "Got any bright ideas?"

"Yes, I do. We need to wrap this up," said Vince. "It all boils down to three big questions.

"First, do we get rid of Arnie? The only reason to do that is a good one. It would really make Mike Slovak shit his pants. That's probably reason enough.

"Next. Do we knock off that dumb blonde, Sandi Taylor? She was seeing Frankie and, who knows what the moron might have told her. He always did have a big mouth. To kill her is to eliminate an important potential witness. If we have to choose between the two Taylors, I vote to kill the wife. She knows a hell of a lot more than he does. In fact, he doesn't know shit."

"What about kill'n both of them?" asked Rocky.

"Of course, that's always an option, but I'm not sure it's the best one," said Vince. It's easier to eliminate just one enemy at a time. The more folks we start killing at this point, the more likely there will be a mistake.

"Finally, do we continue with our plan or scratch it? We've got one guy left on the list to bump off. One client who has something very important in common with the other four. I'm betting that since Arnie is no longer walking around like a fuck'n zombie, suck'n his thumb in denial, he'll solve the puzzle before we kill the last one. Let's see, that's thirty-eight-days from now, April 23d or 24th. We'll have to look at a calendar to get it right.

"Oh, and you can bet your ass that when Arnie comes up with the answer, he won't go to Lieutenant Hogan. He'll go to Mike Slovak, his hero. He'll trust Slovak before he'll trust the cops."

"How do you know that?"

"Because Arnie's smart enough to know that the LAPD's been looking for Slovak since Truman was President. He's outfoxed them for something like thirty years."

Rocky stood, paused, then said, "Okay, Vince, I get what you're saying. You've always been the one with the smarts. Anyway, my opinion is that to eliminate Arnie and his wife would put more pressure on us than we need. The chief of police and the sheriff would have every cop in Southern California looking for me . . . Rocky Crosetti. Not you,

Vince. Me. They may not know what I look like or where I am, but they know I'm around somewhere. They don't even know you exist."

"That's right, Rocky, they don't, which is to our advantage. I am in the thick of things, just as you are, but I'm invisible. But the best part, not only am I the unknown brother, I'm your identical twin. Talk about confusing the enemy.

"Our first order of business, then, is to kill the dame. Like I said, we don't know what she knows, which puts us in a very bad position. She knows something, that's for damn sure. And it's your job to find out where she is, and do what needs to be done. Start by assuming she's staying with her parents. They live in Chatsworth somewhere. Their last name is Schultz.

With that, Vince Crosetti, aka, Dominic Amalfitano, got up from the table, walked out the door, got into his Cadillac and drove to his day job as agency manager at Bear Republic in Panorama City.

Chapter 19

Van Nuys City Hall, Monday, March 17, 9:45 AM

Hogan sat behind his desk in silence as his team entered his office for a brief meeting. After the four officers were seated and ready, he gave them a 'good morning' in a soft voice. He straightened his tie, sat back in his chair, and tossed a quick, sober glance at each of them.

"A little while ago, Captain Coogin dropped by for a brief visit. The moment he came through the door, I had a pretty good idea what was on his mind. Unfortunately, I was right. This was one of those times I'd rather have been wrong."

"He's calling off the investigation," said Officer Merrill, "because we now know the identification of the serial killer, and he's dead."

"Close. Very close. But no cigar. And Gary, please let me continue uninterrupted, at least until I'm able to explain why I've called this meeting."

The lieutenant continued. "As I was saying, the captain wanted to discuss the status of our case from the viewpoint of his boss, Inspector Lewis, and Deputy Chief Fleming.

"The consensus of the three of them is that there will not be a fifth murder. That being the case, they feel we can continue our investigation with a much smaller staff."

Officer Grant raised his hand. "Go ahead, Jim," said Lieutenant Hogan.

"Are they assuming Crosetti got the client information by himself? There is no accomplice?"

"Apparently," said Hogan, "but Coogin didn't actually say that.

"Which brings us to the real issue at hand, the bad news. I need to reduce our team by half, which means that two of you are staying, and two of you will be moving on to other assignments."

"Well," said Officer Merrill. "I think it's obvious how this will play out. George. . ."

"That's enough, Gary. The situation being what it is, we don't need accusations and sour grapes entering the discussion. And for your information, the choice of who gets to stay was left entirely to me. And it wasn't an easy decision. You're all doing a terrific job, but George Porter and I have worked well together for years. So yes, he's staying."

Officer Porter did not react, but remained as stoic as always. Hogan guessed Porter wasn't at all surprised that he'd be one of the two to remain with the shrinking team. The group sat in silence while, after fumbling with some papers on his desk, Hogan looked directly at the only female on the team.

"Ricki, you'll continue as a member of this smaller team, working with Porter and me."

Officer Wright flashed a quick smile, but remained silent. Less than thrilled, Officers Goodwin and Merrill shot cold stares at their female colleague, then looked back at the Lieutenant.

Hogan's tone of voice hit a new high for the morning.

"I know what you're thinking, Jim and Gary, but you need to get something straight. You need to get a couple of things straight. First, as I've indicated, this decision was not forced on me by higher ups. It was my decision and mine alone. It has nothing to do with her being female. Nothing to do with affirmative action.

"Everyone here, including Ricki, knows that I was not happy when she was assigned to this unit. That said, she's done a first-rate job. She's as good at obtaining information as anyone in this room. And her approach with those she's interviewing has been creative and productive. She's also quick with sensible suggestions during our team meetings. Ricki's staying because I want her to stay. Period."

Hogan stood and walked around to the back of his desk, shook hands with Officers Merrill and Grant, wished them well, then advised them to return to their private offices, where they would be hearing from Captain Coogin regarding their new assignments. He also instructed them to leave all of their notes from this case with his secretary, Rosa Lee.

After escorting the two disgruntled officers to the door and closing it behind them, Hogan approached Ricki Wright and George Porter and offered his congratulations on their being selected to remain on the team.

Leaning against the back of his desk, Hogan then confirmed what they already knew.

"I'll be meeting alone with Arnie Taylor in a couple of minutes. Ricki, you'll be having lunch at noon today with Rolene Ward, Amalfitano's secretary, and I'll be interviewing her boss at 2:00 this afternoon. That is, if he's finally back in the office. George will be with me during the Amalfitano meeting, and our 4:00 p.m. appointment with Bill Kaiser at some Republican bar on Sepulveda. I can't remember the name of the place, but I have it written down in my notebook."

"Sonny's," said Officer Porter.

Ricki raised her hand. "What if Arnie's waiting outside when I leave your office?"

"I want you to remain in here with me. When he comes in, we'll tell him what's going on. Why you had to lie to him about your career in law enforcement when you met at the Red Barn, and that you had no involvement with this case at that time."

"With all due respect, Lieutenant, I think that would be a big mistake," said Ricki. "There's a very sensitive side to Arnie that you're not aware of. In fact, very few people are. Remember, I've known him for twenty-five years, and I guarantee you, if he walks in here to see you and finds me here as well, he's going to be mortified. He's going to feel betrayed. He's going to be so devastated that I didn't tell him the truth about my job, it will more than likely be the end of our friendship. And, by the way, the end of my participation in this case."

"So, what do you suggest we do?" asked Hogan.

"I suggest I get the hell out of here pronto and arrange to see him alone as soon as possible. Like tonight, or this afternoon if I can get a hold of him. I will then be in a position to explain the whole situation without him feeling blindsided. I can do this in such a manner that not only will his feelings be assuaged, but our likelihood of breaking this case wide open will be greatly enhanced. Trust me."

"With all due respect, Ricki," said Lieutenant Hogan with a smile, "why should I trust you on that last point?"

"Because, even though we've seen little of each other over the past couple of decades, Arnie trusts me. I'm convinced he'll share information that you'd never be able to get out of him. There's a mutual understanding and respect between the two of us that I've never had with any other male, including the two bozos I married. I'm certain he would say the same about me. Of course, that's not saying much, given that witch of a wife he has."

"The answer for now is no," said Hogan. "It just doesn't feel right. I'm open to reconsidering it in the future, however, depending on how events unfold."

Chapter 20

Panorama City, Monday, March 17, 8:30 AM

Arnie Taylor decided to take the long way in to the office. Rather than getting on the south-bound San Diego Freeway, he drove to Van Nuys Boulevard and headed south.

He had an appointment with Lieutenant Hogan at 10:00 at the Van Nuys City Hall, but first he wanted to stop at the office. He hadn't been there since last Wednesday, and he didn't want anyone to think he was hiding because of all the uproar. Arnie wanted to reassure his friends in the office that he was going to be all right.

Sandi's affair with Frankie Crosetti had been leaked to the *LA Times* by an anonymous source. This juicy piece of information, which received a "no comment" from the LAPD, came just two days after Arnie's childhood trauma had been publicized.

Everett Ward Taylor, dead for twenty years, was long-forgotten by most Angelenos old enough to remember the corrupt and violent lawyer. But now he was back, and millions throughout Southern California remembered him. On Friday the *Times* had a lengthy article recounting the yearlong scandalous episode of the mid '50s, accompanied by photographs from their archives featuring Gladys, Everett, and the thirteen-year-old Arnold. There was also a current photo taken of Arnie leaving the Panorama Towers Wednesday afternoon after he learned of Whit Payne's death. His expression suggested a combination of anger and sadness.

Overall, the press was kind to Arnie. One reporter wrote that as a youngster he had been forced to bear the sins of his father in the public arena. And now as an adult, he was back in the same arena. Only this time he was faced with the tragedy of a faithless, possibly criminal wife. Some people were just plain unlucky, seemingly able to attract misfortune like garbage attracts flies. The *Times* writer, who had covered the Taylor saga twenty years earlier, concluded that Arnold Wayne Taylor was like a patient who had survived brain cancer only to suffer a massive heart attack.

To get himself into a better frame of mind, Arnie spent the weekend at home alone. Silence, loneliness, the absence of dialogue, were nice for a change. He wanted to be certain that, not only could he handle the crises of the preceding week, but that he could manage any additional firestorm. He knew there was a limit to what the human mind could endure, but he wanted to be dead certain that his anger did not dissipate into self-pity. He had proven in the past that he was a survivor. He was determined to prove it again.

On Saturday, Arnie listened to Bach and Brahms, Rachmaninov's Concerto Number Two and the Chopin Waltzes, followed by a two-hour nap. Sad melodious music and books provided insulation against the disasters of his not-so private world, helping him put his problems in perspective. On Saturday and Sunday, he also immersed himself in "The Powers That Be," a newly released book by David Halbertstam, which he liked so well that he got through nearly 300 pages. He read the LA Times on both days, but never turned on the radio or TV.

Sunday night, he searched through the writings of Montaigne, Voltaire, Benjamin Franklin, and others for the source of the aphorism, "Industry is the enemy of melancholy." He couldn't find it, but he had seen or heard it somewhere, and was determined to apply it to his current situation. He would follow this sagacious advice to keep his sanity, to plod on day after day by mobilizing all the mental and physical energy at his disposal until this fiasco was history. Then—and only then—could he make thoughtful decisions which would determine the future course of his life. And he knew he could do it. He had done it once before. This time, he was older, more mature, more experienced in handling tragedy.

As Arnie entered the Panorama City area, he slowed down to get a close look at people walking along the sidewalks, entering and exiting retail establishments, standing at crosswalks waiting for traffic lights to change.

It was a different scene from when he first arrived in this neighborhood in 1964. There were now more Hispanics and blacks, some of whom wore the trappings of success. Lots of males of all complexions with long hair, some dressed in jumpsuits and tracksuits. The hippie look had all but disappeared. He saw a couple of guys wearing leisure suits. Some women wore pastel colors. Many were wearing low cut dresses, very low cut. Some of the younger ones were even braless.

Taking in the sights while pondering the scene along Van Nuys gave Arnie the comforting illusion of normality. Everyone needed an occasional escape from their private hell, and for a good ten minutes, it was his turn.

Arnie chuckled to himself. His hair had covered his ears for several years now, and a month or so ago, he had purchased his first leisure suit. He planned to wear it on weekends and for social events. He would be sufficiently formal and suitably casual at the same time. While working, however, the only acceptable form of attire was still a suit and tie. This would always be the case, which was fine with him.

After turning right from Van Nuys onto Titus, he passed the north side of the Towers and swung an immediate left to enter the large parking lot.

When Arnie entered the Bear Republic office on the sixth floor, Rolene smiled, got up and gave him a hug. Aware that everyone within view was watching, he could feel his light complexion turning red, but he didn't care. He was making a quick stop at the office to say hello to his friends, and if anyone wanted to demonstrate how they felt about him, that was okay. In fact, it was wonderful.

He proceeded to walk the thirty feet to his office, but was stopped twice as small groups of agents and staff members greeted him with handshakes and hugs. Maria was so excited, she threw her arms around him and gave him an innocent kiss on his cheek.

After ten minutes of chit-chat with friends alongside Maria's work area, Arnie walked into his office and sat down. There were maybe two dozen or so phone messages spread around his desk, all on the personal side. Maria had been instructed by Rolene, in Mr. Amalfitano's absence, to refer all business questions to Judy Isenberg, the manager of the GSO. There was also a pile of mail, note cards from clients who preferred not to express their sympathy and concern via telephone messages.

Arnie had been looking over the messages and mail for about ten minutes when Maria walked through the door, all the way up to his chair behind the desk. She leaned over and spoke in a voice so low he could barely hear her. "Mr. Kaiser would like to visit with you."

"Where is he?" asked Arnie.

"Right outside, next to my desk. He says to tell you he comes as a friend." Maria grimaced as she spoke the last sentence.

"Tell him to come in."

Bill Kaiser, eccentric, extroverted, and by far the most successful and assertive agent in the office, walked up to the front of Arnie's desk, extended his arm, shook hands, and sat down.

"Do you mind if we close the door, Arnie? There are some matters we need to discuss that are private."

Arnie called out for Maria to close the door, then looked straight at Kaiser and realized he had never seen the man look so serious.

"Well, Bill," said Arnie, "I must say I'm surprised to see you. You're probably the last guy in the office I would expect to be in here right now, but please go ahead. I'm all ears."

"First, Arnie, I want you to know how truly sorry I am that all this shit is happening. Whatever differences we have over politics, and just about everything else . . . no one deserves the hand you've been dealt. No one. And I feel awful that your life has become such a nightmare.

"It's kind of you to come and tell me that, Bill. I appreciate it very much. I really do."

"That was the easy part, Arnie. Now for the hard part." Kaiser paused for a moment.

"I wasn't at all surprised to read that Sandi was involved in an affair. Not one bit." Arnie looked straight at Bill. Unsmiling. Expressionless.

"Well, whatever it is you feel you need to tell me can't be all that bad, Bill," said Arnie. "I mean, it's not as though you're in here to tell me you had an affair with my wife a year or so ago that had gone on for about a year. Is it?"

Still looking across the desk, but now grinning from ear to ear, Arnie saw a Bill Kaiser he had never known before. He saw a humble side of a man he was convinced didn't have a humble bone in his body. A man scratching the side of his nose, his face down, nervously clearing his throat.

"I didn't think you knew, Arnie, which is really stupid of me. I blabbed it to a couple of guys who, I guess, couldn't keep quiet. Anyway, I really feel bad about the whole thing. The affair itself, and the fact I couldn't keep my damn mouth shut. By the way, how did you find out?"

"I have my vays," said Arnie. He spoke with an exaggerated German accent.

Kaiser's eyes widened as an uneasy, forced smile came upon him.

"Oh, I get it," he said. 'Hogan's Heroes.' Right."

"Anyway, I've known for a long time, Bill. While it hurt when I first heard about it, the fact that probably everyone in the building knew is what really caused the pain. But I got over it. Real fast. Let's say, about five minutes after I learned about it. My real regret is that she didn't leave me and marry you. Oh, how that would have changed my life. For the better. Forever."

"I'm sure it doesn't matter now, Arnie, but for whatever it's worth, she came on to me. I was having big-time problems at home at the time and, well, Sandi's a beautiful woman."

"You don't have to explain, Bill. I understand, I really do. And I'm sure you're wondering why I didn't care that much at the time. Well, for one thing, you weren't the first. Or the second. Or third. Only God knows how many men she's been with the last four or five years. She's had more lovers than Mickey Rooney's had wives.

"How could I let such a pathetic situation go on so long ? First I was in denial, then I just didn't care. Plus, I suppose I was just too busy building a business, which is a pretty lousy excuse. So I kept putting it off, letting it hang over me like a black cloud, which is ridiculous. That black cloud is now a category five hurricane.

"The fact is, given all the chaos and embarrassing publicity surrounding my family when I was a kid, all I ever wanted was a normal, quiet life. You know, a nice loving wife who would give me children. Someone who would always be there for me, provide a healthy atmosphere for all of us. I was determined there would never be any unfavorable attention focused on me, or my family, by the world outside."

Kaiser held up his right hand to stop Arnie. "You don't need to explain anything to me," he said. "I just feel really rotten about the whole thing. The hurt I caused you, your four dead clients, all the fuck'n publicity. Everything."

Arnie resumed talking. "Anyway, I was about to acknowledge the fact that I've been a failure. A complete failure. I'm now the center of a story, a national story, that's more sinister, despicable and highly publicized than the one my father starred in a generation ago."

He paused for a moment, fearful he was choking up, that his emotions were getting the best of him. His eyes swelled with tears. He needed to stop. Now.

He glanced at Kaiser, who looked as sorrowful as Arnie felt. The number-one producer in the agency had his handkerchief out and was wiping the sweat off his forehead, then dabbed at a couple of tears running down his cheeks. He held up his right palm to silence Arnie, then began to speak.

"My personal problems are minuscule compared to yours, Arnie, but they're monumental to me. I've suffered through my own living hell, what with an unloving wife who has told our therapist she would prefer that the two of us live as brother and sister. She thinks that now that we've had our family, we shouldn't sleep together anymore. So I'm now the current resident of our guest room. Denise seldom speaks to me because she thinks I'm abrasive. Me, the Casper Milquetoast of the Amalfitano Agency. She says she should have married a cultured Frenchman rather than an overbearing, opinionated, gun-toting Kraut. Anyway, you get the point."

"The two of you are in therapy?" asked Arnie

"We were, but I don't go anymore. She goes by herself. I told her I've had enough of that pompous, know-it-all, dumb-shit Jew. Hitler may have gone too far, but he had a point about God's chosen people."

Arnie made no comment. After all, Bill was in his office for all the right reasons. There was no reason to spoil it by taking issue with a stupid, offhand remark.

"Another thing I want you to know, Arnie. For the first time in my life, I'm going to church."

"Really," said Arnie, more as a comment than a question. "Where are you going?"

"Van Nuys First Baptist," said Bill. "I'm going by myself. Denise doesn't have any interest in going anywhere with me, and that includes church. I'm telling you this because I know you've been active in your church for some time. Hey, please don't mention this to anybody around here. It might ruin my image as a tough guy."

Kaiser laughed so loud anyone within thirty feet of Arnie's office would think there was a party going on in there.

"I just have one question," Arnie said. "What happened that caused you and Sandi to call it quits?"

"What happened? I finally decided she had to go. But I couldn't figure out a way to do it. That is, without inflicting considerable damage on her psyche that would come back to bite me on the ass."

"So, how did you finally manage it?"

"It was easy. She basically said, 'Marry me or else,' meaning for her, this was no fling. She said she wanted each of us to get divorced, then get married. And get this, she was adamant that Denise have the children one-hundred percent of the time.

"Whoa. This ain't gonna happen, I told her. No fuck'n way. No offense, Arnie, but I would never marry someone like her. I have two children, a boy, seven, and a girl, four, and—"

"Can you hold that thought for a moment, Bill?"

Arnie called for Maria to come in for a moment, then asked her to call Lieutenant Hogan and tell him he was running ten or fifteen minutes behind.

"Sorry for the interruption."

"No problem," said Bill. "In fact, I'm meeting with the lieutenant at four o' clock this afternoon."

"Really?"

"Yeah," said Bill. "At Sonny's. You know, the bar over on Sepulveda south of Nordhoff."

Arnie knew the place, all right. It was pretty unforgettable. The walls were decorated with photographs of Barry Goldwater, William F. Buckley, Ronald Reagan, and other prominent conservative Republicans. The owner, a veteran of both Korea and Vietnam, had various decorations and awards in frames on the wall, including two Distinguished Flying Crosses. Looking at the wall, one might well conclude this guy had more decorations than Audie Murphy. The music was strictly country western. Not exactly Arnie's style, though he did like Willie Nelson and Johnny Cash.

"Anyway," said Kaiser, "I know you've got things to do, so I'll wrap up my story real fast. Even if I wanted a divorce from Denise, I would never have married Sandi. She's made it very clear she doesn't like kids, and having a pretty good idea how mean she can be, I'd never trust her around Greg and Melissa.

"In fact, I'd never have had anything to do with her in the first place if I'd known she had aborted a child right after the two of you got married. I didn't learn about that until we had our last argument. I fuck'n couldn't believe it."

Arnie glanced at his watch, folded the cards and phone messages on his desk into a neat pile, and pushed his chair back.

"Thanks, Bill, for coming in for a friendly visit. And for expressing your concern for my well-being. Also, for sharing something private about your life. It won't go any farther."

"It would serve me right if you put out a press release, Arnie. Hey, we should get together once in a while over a brewsky or three. You know, shoot the shit. But no politics."

Arnie agreed, under one condition.

"You stop calling me a communist, Bill, and I'll stop calling you a fascist." They both laughed, shook hands, and Bill Kaiser walked out.

Arnie was on his way out the front door of the agency when he noticed Amalfitano's office door was open and the light on. He stood outside the doorway and saw the boss reading from a stack of papers about a foot high on his desk. He maneuvered his position until the boss could see him, then said, "Welcome back, Dom, we've missed you. I'm sorry about your sister. My oldest brother, Robbie, died of cancer two years ago, so I kinda know what you're going through."

Dom tossed Arnie a cold stare.

"Thanks. I appreciate your condolences."

He then resumed reading the paper on the top of the stack.

Arnie pulled out of the parking lot, got back on Van Nuys Boulevard, and headed toward City Hall to meet with Hogan. He took a deep breath, exhaled, and concluded that his weekend of solitude was reaping dividends. He had gotten through two potentially tough moments without becoming rattled.

First, there was Kaiser's comment about Sandi's abortion in the spring of '63. He had long suspected it, but never questioned her. He knew she would deny it. Now It had been confirmed. His marriage to Sandi Schultz was based on a lie. In the overall scheme of things, the murder of five innocent people was far more serious than taking the life of a fetus, as awful as it was. Anyway, at this point, he would let it go. It was the least of his problems. His wife had always been rotten to the core. That it took him so long to realize this was his fault. And his problem.

Then there was Dominic Amalfitano's ice-cold response to Arnie's greeting this morning. Why, he didn't even express concern about Whit Payne. What a supercilious asshole. This incident would be reported to Hogan at their meeting.

He knew the LAPD was furious that the killings had not been reported until the fourth one, which Arnie felt was the responsibility of the agency manager, not him. Anyway, he was far more amused by Amalfitano's pissy attitude this morning than he was aggravated.

Having recently installed a tape deck in his Gran Torino, Arnie decided he wanted music, but nothing classical. Not now, on a nice, sunny morning. After fumbling through a couple of Neil Diamond and Bob Segar tapes, he decided on Elton John. He fast-forwarded past *Yellow Brick Road* and *Crocodile Rock*, then settled on his current favorite, *Don't Let the Sun Shine Down on Me*. By the time he reached his destination, he had played it twice, singing along as he drove.

While he had retained his composure through a tough morning, now he had to deal with Lieutenant Hogan. An entirely different matter. During their two previous visits, and at least a half-dozen phone conversations, the Lieutenant had never had one positive word to say regarding unfolding events. Hogan had called him at home last night and told him to come in to his office at 10:00. His tone was serious, so Arnie assumed something new had come up. Probably bad news.

Arnie didn't see an open parking place as he circled City Hall. He finally found a spot on a side street a couple of blocks away, on the other side of Van Nuys Boulevard. He pulled into an open space behind a beautiful, brand-new, yellow '75 Corvette. Never especially interested in cars except as a means of transportation, this one got his attention. After getting out of his Gran Torino, he spent a minute or so admiring this beauty, then walked on to his destination.

Chapter 21

Van Nuys City Hall, Monday, March 17, 10:22 AM

Lieutenant Hogan was a bit miffed at Arnie for being late, even if he had called ahead to let the Lieutenant know he was running behind. He decided, however, not to say anything about it. After all, the poor guy was carrying around an awful load of weight these days, what with a broken marriage, public humiliation, and a business in jeopardy, perhaps its continued existence at stake.

After being ushered into Hogan's office by Rosa Lee, Arnie apologized for his tardiness, commented on what a beautiful day it was, and sat down.

"I'm happy to hear that," said the lieutenant. "It was still dark when I got here. I haven't even looked out a window. I'll be out on a couple of appointments this afternoon, though, both of them pertaining to your case."

"Yeah, so I hear," said Arnie. "That is, I know you're seeing Bill Kaiser at 4:00 at Sonny's. Oh, you'll really love that place, I guarantee you."

"How do you know I'm meeting him? And how do you know when and where?" asked Hogan.

"He told me. He told me a whole lot of other stuff, too. I stopped at my office this morning to visit with friends and look over my messages, and before I knew it, Kaiser was at my door. He said he wanted to talk."

"Really," said the lieutenant as he leaned back in his chair. This morning was turning out to be full of surprises. He had a number of items he wanted to go over with Taylor, but they could wait.

"Tell me about it. I thought he avoided you like poison ivy." The Lieutenant smiled, but Arnie's face wore a serious expression.

"It's hard to know where to start," said Arnie, "he had so much to say."

Hogan reached into his left-hand drawer and pulled out a note-book, picked up a pencil from his desk, then gestured with a nod for Arnie to begin.

"Bill came in to tell me that he and Sandi had an affair that lasted for a year and ended about a year ago. He was unaware that I'd known about it almost from the start. He apologized profusely, even becoming emotional about it. He also told me how sorry he is about the mess I'm in, saying, in so many words, that nobody deserves to go through the hell that I'm now living. He said he wanted us to lay our political differences aside, that he regrets the way he's treated me, and that he wants us to be friends from here on out."

Arnie pushed his chair away from the front of Hogan's desk and stretched his legs as far as they could reach. Lieutenant Hogan sat impassively, his right hand rubbing his lower lip, and waited for him to continue.

"I guess you might say the two of us smoked a peace pipe." said Arnie.

"Do you believe he's sincere?" asked Hogan.

"Yes. His body language certainly indicated it, and in my business, being able to read body language is important. He teared up a couple of times, Lieutenant. He also shared some personal stuff about his marriage, which really surprised me. He says he's now going to church. Who knows, maybe some spiritual nourishment will give him a broader perspective on the vagaries of life that, sooner or later, confront all of us."

"Has it not occurred to you that this might very well be nothing more than an act to take the heat off him as a serious suspect?" asked the lieutenant.

"Of course it has, Lieutenant. I'm no fool."

Lieutenant Hogan was surprised by Arnie's tone, and his reddened face. Ricki had said he was sensitive—now he was seeing evidence of it.

Despite Arnie's positive attitude, Hogan was dubious about Kaiser's sincerity. It all seemed too convenient, too contrived. But the fact was, he had never met Bill Kaiser. He'd gotten an earful about him from Sandi Taylor, and from Arnie himself, but had never seen him in the flesh. That was about to change. He decided he would not reach any conclusions about the matter of Kaiser's motives or honesty until he interviewed him later today. And it might take a good deal longer than that.

Lieutenant Hogan continued. "Anyway, Arnie, I hope you're right about Kaiser. If nothing else, the annoying harassment you've taken from him over the years will stop, and that's certainly a positive. We'll take whatever positives we can get at this point, right?"

Arnie didn't comment.

"Now, I'd like to move on to four more items," said Hogan, "the first being Mike Slovak."

He stopped briefly to watch Arnie's reaction, but didn't notice anything other than that he remained calm and quiet.

"The fact that your old friend, Mr. Slovak, murdered the serial killer who had taken out four of your clients is quite a coincidence, don't you think?"

"Yes, I'd say it's a coincidence," said Arnie. "But from what I read in the newspapers, there's a war going on in the underworld between two factions, and Slovak killed Crosetti because he knew Crosetti was out to get him. You know, for killing his brother. I'm happy Mike killed Crosetti rather than the other way around. I'm happy that the asshole who killed four of my clients is now dead. I'm happy that there's more than a remote possibility that there will be no more killings, but, of course, that remains to be seen."

"Do you think that—"

"Wait just a minute, Lieutenant, you need to know what I'm unhappy about," said Arnie.

Hogan raised his eyebrows, folded his arms against his chest, and stared straight into Arnie's eyes.

"I'm unhappy about the leaks coming out of your department concerning my wife's previous affairs. That she's been a serial adulterer for years. I'm unhappy that the LAPD didn't get the killer, that it took somebody else to finish him off. And I'm really unhappy—make that, pissed off—that you refer to Slovak as my 'old friend.' And if you're wondering if I've seen him or been in touch with him recently, you can forget it. The answer is no. I repeat, no.

"That's NO."

Frank Hogan felt his heart rate accelerating, his temper rising. After a brief moment of silence, he asked, "Is that all?"

"No. There's an accomplice out there somewhere that we need to find. I'm not aware of any progress toward that goal, but it's certainly not Mike Slovak. We're wasting precious time talking about him. I was hopeful when I walked in here that I would learn something important. Instead, you want to talk about a guy who's evaded capture by your department for nearly thirty years, and rub my nose in the fact that

I know him. I haven't seen him since I was thirteen years old, so, I'm sorry, I can't help you find him.

"By the way, did you say you had other matters to discuss?"

After taking a deep breath and a few moments to reflect, Hogan decided he didn't have anything more to say about Slovak. Arnie had a point. The lieutenant's approach to the subject was not tactful. He failed to consider what a sensitive subject this was for Arnie twenty years ago, and perhaps even more so now. And for the second time during this interview, he failed to remember how sensitive Officer Wright had said he was. Normally, he didn't give a damn about someone being sensitive when he was doing his job as an investigator, but Arnie was a victim, not a suspect. And he, Hogan, needed to have him on his side if he was going to get anywhere with this case. He needed to have his confidence and his full cooperation. And the last thing he needed was for Arnie to get even more upset and go tell the press the LAPD was so obsessed with catching Mike Slovak they were all but abandoning the search for Frankie Crosetti's acomplice. That Arnie might go that far seemed like a bit of a stretch, given how little Hogan had said about Slovak, but anything was possible given the stress Arnold Taylor was under.

Arnie was also right about the leaks to the press. It was obviously a humiliating experience to have his marital problems exposed in the public arena. It must have made him feel like a total jackass.

"No harm intended, Arnie, with respect to Mr. Slovak. As for the leaks to the press, it's been a serious problem in our department for some time, but I do believe we're about to solve it. And I mean solve it real soon, like within the next day or so."

Hogan decided not to share the news with Arnie about leaks also going to the Mafia. That would only make the LA Police Department appear to be more inept than Arnie already thought it was. More inept than Keystone Cops running around with fire hoses.

"There are a couple of other items I'd like to discuss, Arnie. First, is it your impression that Mr. Amalfitano and Bill Kaiser are very close friends outside the office? Like, do they hang out together, do their families get together, that sort of thing?"

"No," said Arnie, "that's not my impression at all. In fact, you're dead wrong if you believe that's the case."

"I don't have an impression, or an opinion, about the matter, Arnie. That's why I'm asking you." Lieutenant Frank Hogan was getting annoyed again, just as he was beginning to calm down after all the fuss over Mike Slovak.

"I'm sorry, Lieutenant, I didn't mean to be so brusque. It's just that, well, they're the most unlikely pair imaginable. Kaiser's loud, outgoing, overbearing, the life of the party. Dom is the exact opposite, an introvert. In fact, when he speaks, it's sometimes hard to hear him because his voice is so soft. In addition, Dom does not believe in mixing with us peons. I think that comes from his military background. You know, that line between officers and enlisted. He was an enlisted man in the Marines, a sergeant. But now that he's a big-shot agency manager, he walks around his domain like he's Napoleon."

That's interesting," said Hogan. "A kind of self-important guy who enjoys having power?"

"Exactly," said Arnie. "He's all business. That's all he thinks about."

"Anyway, as far as socializing with the agents, Dom gets all of us together for the awards banquet, in February, and sometimes, he throws a Christmas party at his house. That doesn't mean he never takes agents to lunch, because, from time to time, he does. But it's always been my impression it's strictly for business reasons and not because he especially enjoys our company. For example, he might want to get us jazzed up for a sales campaign, or, if I write a big case, he might feel he should reward me in some way."

"So, are you saying he doesn't give Kaiser any more special attention than he gives the rest of you?" asked Hogan.

"No, that's not what I'm saying. He does give special attention to Kaiser, but only because he's the number-one producer in the agency, and has been for several years. So, I'm certain Dom spends more time with him than anyone else. Which is as it should be. But I'm equally certain he doesn't spend any more time with him than he thinks he has to."

Lieutenant Hogan was puzzled. This was a direct contradiction from what Sandi Taylor told him and Officer Porter. He got up to stretch for a moment, then sat down again, and folded his hands together on his lap.

"I'm surprised to hear this, Arnie. My associates and I have heard otherwise."

"Well, Lieutenant, I have no idea with whom you've spoken, but they're mistaken. Why, you ought to hear some of the things Kaiser says about the boss. He says he's never seen anyone make so much money who works so little. He says Amalfitano doesn't deserve all the override he makes off of Kaiser's sales, that he's worthless when it comes to giving him technical help. He complains that he always has to call home office when he has questions regarding complicated estate planning cases, since he knows Dom never has the answers.

"Oh, and get this. Kaiser's said more than once that he wouldn't be surprised if Dominic Amalfitano is part of the Mafia. When he brings this up, he always pronounces the boss's full name very slowly to emphasize the fact that he's Italian. I've even heard him say in a soft voice, 'You know, it's those quiet ones you have to watch out for. I wouldn't want the son of a bitch on my blind side, that's for damn sure.'"

"Does Kaiser give any reason for bringing this up other than the fact that the boss is Italian and speaks softly?"

"Yes," said Arnie. "He wonders where the hell Dom is when he's spending so much time away from the office. Everyone's noticed he's away a lot. You might want to ask Rolene Ward about that. And please understand, I don't mean to be presumptuous by that remark. I'm more than aware it's not my business to tell you how to do your job."

Lieutenant Hogan had a couple of more questions, but they didn't seem that important anymore.

"Thanks for your input, Arnie. You've been very helpful. I'll get back to you in a day or so."

After his visitor was out the door, the lieutenant took a couple of minutes to reflect about Arnie's little temper fit regarding whether or not he was in contact with Mike Slovak. Hogan did not believe a word of it. With twenty years as a police officer behind him, nearly all of it in the homicide division, he was pretty good at detecting what was real from what was made-up. Arnie was undoubtedly a very good insurance agent, and there was no question he was well-rounded intellectually, but as an actor, he left something to be desired. Marlon Brando he was not. Hogan was certain Arnie was in touch with Slovak, and that his denial was a lie.

The Lieutenant phoned Officer Wright to let her know it was now safe for her to leave her office. Also he had some information to share.

"Arnie says there's no way Bill Kaiser and Dominic Amalfitano are friends. He says Kaiser goes around ridiculing the boss behind his back all the time. As you know, this contradicts what Sandi Taylor told George Porter and me. Keep in mind, though, that Sandi also said even Rolene doesn't know there's a relationship between the two. Anyway, find out what Ms. Ward has to say on this subject, if anything. It could be of value. Oh, I also learned Dominic is away from the office a lot, and the agents have no idea where he is or what he's doing. Ask her about that, too. Good luck."

Ricki smiled as she hung up the phone. After saying "hello," she never got another word in. She'd get the information he wanted, but she had another question for Ms. Ward. A question, to her knowledge, nobody had thought to ask. Maybe someday Frank Hogan would have enough confidence to allow her to interview a male of interest. But then again, maybe that was too much to hope for.

As Arnie walked to his car, he thought hard about the conversation about Mike Slovak. He knew Hogan was going to bring up the fact that Mike had done him a huge favor by taking out Frankie Crosetti. After all, there was a good possibility there would not be any more murders, thanks to his friend. But he also knew it wouldn't be easy to lie his way through an interrogation regarding his relationship with the fugitive assassin. While he could tell a 'little white lie' as well as the next guy, he had no experience in being deliberately untruthful regarding serious matters. And to tell an outright lie to the police would be unthinkable, given normal circumstances. But these were not normal circumstances. He had to lie. There was no way he would betray Mike. He just hoped he'd pulled it off. He knew honest people made poor liars.

Chapter 22

Panorama City, Monday, March 17, 12:05 p.m.

As Officer Ricki Wright headed into Rothbard's Delicatessen a couple of blocks from the Panorama Towers on Van Nuys, she held the door for the woman behind her. Before they reached the female cashier near the entrance, Ricki turned to the stranger and said, "Are you by any chance Rolene Ward?"

She was, the appropriate introductions were made, and the two ladies were ushered to a booth against the right wall about halfway through the crowded restaurant. The room was filled with smoke, the smell of pastrami and corned beef, the roar of conversation.

"Wow, this place is really busy," said Ricki, as she held up her badge for Rolene. "And I've never even heard of it before."

"It's mostly locals who come here," said Rolene. "You know, people like me who work in the area, along with those who live nearby. I've never been to a Jewish deli I liked any better than this one, including Katz in New York."

"Well, I sure love the smell," said Ricki. "I got a good whiff of deli sandwiches as soon as I walked through the door. I could do without all the noise and the smoke, but that's part of the price you pay to eat in a great place.

"I assume you have to be back at the office by one, is that right?"

"Normally I get an hour for lunch," said Rolene, "but since Mr. Amalfitano was away most of last week, he said I could take longer today if I needed to run errands. He's always been thoughtful about stuff like that. Anyway, I can give you all the time you need. I'm not sure I can tell you anything meaningful, but I will certainly try my best to be helpful."

"By the way, I love your green dress. It's really beautiful," said Ricki.

"Thanks, my Saint Patrick's Day outfit."

Ricki found Rolene friendly. She also thought she was pretty. A brunette with long, straight hair parted in the center, Ricki thought of Ali MacGraw in *Love Story*. Dressed conservatively, she could have passed for a high school teacher, an accountant, perhaps even a lawyer.

A waitress named Maggie approached with two glasses of water and asked if they were ready to order.

"I know what I want," said Rolene, "but my friend has never been here before, so she might need a menu."

"No, I know what I'd like," said Ricki. "I'll have pastrami on rye with potato salad and a Coke, please."

"I'll have my usual," said Rolene. "A reuben sandwich, also on rye, potato salad, and just water, please."

"Please understand, Ms. Ward, that our conversation is strictly confidential and that nothing you say will ever get back to anyone connected with the agency, nor will your name appear in the newspapers. I work undercover. Which means you are not to discuss our meeting, nor are you to share my name, with anyone. The only exception to this confidentiality is if, in the event of a trial, you are called on to testify about the information you give me this afternoon."

Rolene said she understood, and was open to any questions Officer Wright might have, with one proviso. That her name was Rolene, and she preferred to be addressed that way. Ricki agreed.

"For starters, is there anyone in the agency whom you might suspect somehow got into Arnold Taylor's files and gave the information to Frankie Crosetti?"

"Wow, you get right to the heart of the matter, don't you, Officer Wright?" said Rolene, as she smiled. "Nobody will ever accuse you of beating around the bush, that's for sure.

"Anyway, the answer is no. Anyone could have obtained a key to Arnie's office. It wouldn't have been difficult at all, especially if they got hold of a master key."

"Who would have access to a master?"

"I have one, Mr. Amalfitano and Judy Isenberg, the manager of the GSO.

"Oh, and so does the night janitor. It's a possibility that someone picked up one of the three, if we it left sitting out. Anyone could have gotten a hold of one and had a copy made. There's a little shop that makes keys less than a block from the office."

"The culprit, then, wouldn't have had to take a key from Mr. Taylor's office, or from the desk of his secretary, Maria, but could have gained entry from stealing a master key. Is that what you're saying?"

"Yes, that's correct," said Rolene. "And my own personal opinion is that one of our three master keys was taken rather than the key to Arnie's office."

"Why do you think that's the case?"

"Easy," said Rolene. "There are only two keys to Arnie's office, other than the masters. One of them is on Arnie's personal keychain, along with his car keys and house keys, etc. Those keys go wherever Arnie goes. And Maria has a key, which is also on her keychain, which goes wherever she goes. I've never seen Maria's keys on her desk. She's very meticulous about everything."

Ricki coughed, raised her right hand, and waved it back and forth directly in front of her face. A man in the booth behind her was smoking, and it was blowing her way each time he turned sideways to look at his companion.

"Okay," said Ricki, after regaining her composure. "I have a question. Do you have your master key with you right now?"

"No," said Rolene. "It's locked in my desk. But more than once I've been careless and left it on my desk after opening an office for someone to get into for one reason or another. And I've noticed Mr. Amalfitano's key on his desk from time to time, but he doesn't make a habit of it. Anyway, it wouldn't make a lot of sense for someone to sneak into his office and walk off with his master key. He might be back when the dummy reappears to return it."

"I agree," said Ricki.

Rolene continued. "Which leaves us with Judy in GSO. I'm not sure just how she handles her master key, but she's a good manager, a smart woman with lots of commonsense.

"I doubt she'd be sloppy and leave her key laying around on her desk or on the counter where the agents leave their apps. But it's a possibility that its happened. You know, people are human. We all lose our concentration and do stupid things once in a while."

They stopped talking while the waitress set their plates on the table. Ricki felt she understood the situation surrounding the mystery of the keys sufficiently. It was time to change the subject and move on.

"This is a leading question, Rolene, but I'm going to ask it. In your mind, is Bill Kaiser maybe just a little more likely to be a suspect than others, given his well-known dislike for Arnie?"

"No, absolutely not, Officer," said Rolene. "I've heard office gossip about him being involved in this tragedy, but I don't buy it. For one thing, it would be too obvious. Everyone knows he dislikes Arnie because of his politics. It seems to me more likely that the culprit is someone who hates Bill and set him up. Of course, that same someone would have to hate Arnie as well. I have no idea who that might be."

Ricki looked around the room for a moment, then took a bite of her sandwich as Rolene continued.

"There's another reason I don't buy into the theory that Kaiser's the bad guy. I'm convinced that, in spite of his big talk and overbearing personality, he's got a big heart. I don't think he'd hurt a flea."

"So you think maybe he was setup? That's interesting."

"There are a hundred theories out there," said Rolene. "The switchboard operator, Angie, is quick to blame Bill, so she doesn't accept my setup theory. But that's because she's so protective of Arnie, and she knows Kaiser's always bad-mouthing him."

It was obvious to Ricki there had been a lot of talk around the office about the four murders and the killing of Whit Payne the previous week. "I have more questions, Rolene, but there's light at the end of the tunnel," said Ricki. "I've heard that Amalfitano and Kaiser are as close as Siamese twins."

Rolene laughed, then washed down a bite of her sandwich with a drink of water. "Who in the world told you that?"

"It doesn't matter," replied Ricki, "but based on your reaction, there's obviously no truth to it."

"Let's put it this way. The boss tolerates Kaiser because he has to. Bill, on the other hand, feels he doesn't have to tolerate Amalfitano. Agency managers come and go, and in Bill's mind, he's far more likely to outlast Amalfitano than the other way around. By the way, he's right. If Kaiser left, there would be a significant drop in overall agency production. When the boss leaves, it really won't matter much.

"In response to your question, the only thing Amalfitano and Kaiser share is mutual animosity."

"What do you think of Arnie?"

Rolene cast Ricki a serious glance. Her face reddening, she was silent for a moment, appearing to be choosing her words carefully,

"As the agency manager's secretary, I'm neutral concerning all our agents. But as a human being, just like everyone else, I have my favorites. Let's just say, I like Arnie a whole lot, and leave it at that. Okay, he's by far my favorite agent, but if you quote me on that, I'll deny it. Even under oath."

Rolene laughed nervously at her last comment and looked away for a moment. Ricki recognized deep feelings in her voice. Rolene had just implied —practically expressed—that she was in love with Arnold Taylor. She could tell by her coloring, her body language, her tone. There was no doubt in Ricki's mind that if Rolene went after Arnie when this whole mess was over, she might very well succeed. But then, she had no idea how Arnie felt about Rolene, at least in terms of a romantic relationship.

The two ladies discussed Dominic Amalfitano for a while. Rolene said he was easy to work for as long as you did your job. She'd never seen him lose his temper in the outer office, but she sure had witnessed it behind closed doors in his private office, usually over a home office underwriting matter.

"Is he a real hands-on, every day in the office kind of manager?" asked Ricki.

"I know where you're going with this one, Officer. Somebody's been talking. He's gone a lot. A lot more than he should be, at least in my opinion. I'd say he's gone about thirty-five to forty percent of the time. But he's able to get away with it."

"How's that?" asked Ricki.

"Because he has one of the top five producers in the whole company in Bill Kaiser. In addition, he has a hard-core group of about a dozen above-average producers, of which Arnie Taylor is one. They all work hard, do their job, bring in a lot of business, and seldom require the boss's attention. The fact is, they prefer he stay away. He's not popular with anyone in the office. Anyway, this agency has so much talent it could run itself if it had to."

Maggie returned to their booth, picked up the empty plates and asked if they wanted pie or ice cream for dessert. They both declined, but Ricki asked for a refill of Coke, then thanked Rolene for recommending Rothbard's. She added that she would be having lunch there again, some time.

"It seems like quite a coincidence that Mr. Amalfitano left for the rest of the week just as the office scandal was accelerating. What the with news of the fourth murder, and Whit Payne's violent death," said Ricki. "Do you know for certain that his sister passed away and that he really was in New York for the rest of last week?"

"The answer to both of your questions is yes. Sarah died early Tuesday morning. I know that because I had a couple of conversations with another sister, Delia, last week. I'm the one who arranged the flight for the boss, as I do for all of his airline travels. I also ordered flowers for the funeral and called the mortuary to make sure they had arrived. Sister Sarah did die, and Mr. Amalfitano did fly to New York for the funeral."

Ricki glanced at her watch, then asked what she believed to be the most important question of the day. But she was determined to ask the question in such a casual way it would appear to be an afterthought. A Columbo kind of thing. "Something just occurred to me about Whit Payne. Do you have any idea who the last person in the agency was to see him alive?"

"Yes, in fact, I know for certain who saw him last." Rolene took a moment to finish off her glass of water. "It was Mr. Amalfitano."

"How do you know that?" asked Ricki.

Rolene leaned forward, looked straight into Ricki's eyes, and lowered her voice.

"I know that because I worked late last Monday. Mr. Amalfitano had a lengthy letter to the home office that he wanted to dictate for me to type, and then give it back to him to look over for any last minute changes before I left for the day."

"What time was that?" asked Ricki.

"Oh, I finished about twenty minutes to six, told him good-bye after he approved the letter, and walked out the front door. At that moment, he was the only person left in the agency. On my way to the elevator, I stopped to visit the ladies' room. and was in there five minutes, maybe more. As I was getting on the elevator, Whit was getting off. He asked if Mr. Amalfitano was still there and I told him he was.

"Whit then said to me, 'That's great. There's something I think he needs to know.'"

Ricki smacked her lips together, took a deep breath, exhaled, then asked, "How do you know Amalfitano hadn't left when you were in the restroom?"

"I didn't," said Rolene. "I just assumed it. But when I got off on the ground floor, I walked right past his Cadillac on the way to my car. He was there all right."

"Have you shared this information with anyone?"

"No," said Rolene, "you're the only one who asked. To tell you the truth, with everything else going on, it slipped my mind until you brought it up.

"Anyway, it's obvious you think it's important."

Ricki gave Rolene a serious stare. "When we're talking about murder, everything is important."

Chapter 23

Monday, March 17, 1:20 p.m.

As soon as Ricki got back in her car, she called Lieutenant Hogan.

"I'm glad I caught you, Lieutenant. I was afraid you might be out having lunch somewhere on your way to see Amalfitano at two o' clock."

"You barely caught me in time. I'm going to be out of here in five minutes, with a quick stop at McDonald's. What's up?"

"Plenty," said Ricki. "For starters, Rolene Ward confirmed two pieces of information Arnie gave you. First, there's no way Bill Kaiser and Amalfitano are friends, and secondly, the boss is away from the office a whole lot more than anyone thinks he should be. As much as 35-40 percent of the time, she says."

"That's interesting. Anything else?"

"Well, she doesn't believe for one moment Kaiser's the bad guy, insofar as getting into Arnie's files. She says he's all macho, but inside, he's got a heart the size of Rhode Island. My notes say that Arnie pretty much told you the same thing."

"That's correct," said the lieutenant. "Anything else?"

"Yes. I think we've finally got our first real break in this case.

"Dominic Amalfitano was the last person in the agency to talk with Whit Payne. When Rolene was getting on the elevator Monday evening with the boss the only one left in the office, she ran into Whit, who asked if Amalfitano was still there. When Rolene told him he was, Whit responded by saying, 'That's great, there's something I need to tell him.' Rolene then walked by the boss's car when she reached the parking lot."

"What time was it when this took place?" asked Hogan.

"Around quarter to six, maybe five minutes later at the most."

"Good work, Ricki. Thanks."

****

On their way to Bear Republic, Lieutenant Hogan briefed George Porter on Ricki's interview with Rolene Ward. As they approached their destination, the lieutenant summarized the situation.

"Anyway, George, while Ms. Ward's information appears to shed some new light on our situation, there's no way we can prove that Amalfitano talked with Payne some time before six o' clock last Monday, but it certainly appears that he did," said Hogan. "Nor does it prove he made the phone call to Crosetti at the Holiday Inn, even if he did talk to Whit."

"I'd say the evidence is pretty conclusive," said Officer Porter, "but it's possible the big boss was on his way down one elevator while Payne was coming up on the other one."

"The problem with that theory is, it contradicts what Ms. Ward told Ricki. She saw Whit on the sixth floor, and when she exited the elevator and walked out into the parking lot, Amalfitano's Cadillac was still there."

Porter picked up the conversation again. "Or, Amalfitano might have been in the Men's Room when Payne got off the elevator. Seeing that the manager was not there, the door to his office locked, he went to his own office. Meanwhile, the boss walks out of the bathroom and takes the elevator to the ground floor."

"Yeah, that could've happened," said Hogan, "But if Amalfitano did talk to Payne, and called the Holiday Inn, we'd have a whole new situation, wouldn't we?"

"You bet your ass we would. But I doubt we can prove it. And it would still leave a question unanswered. Why would a successful businessman like him be involved with the Mob, and, if he is, what motive would he have to arrange for Arnold Taylor's clients, or Whit Payne, to be murdered. It doesn't make any sense."

"No. It makes no sense at all," said Lieutenant Hogan.

At exactly two o' clock, the detectives entered Amalfitano's large, airy office as Rolene closed the door behind them. On the wall opposite the door a giant studio window, a not so picturesque parking lot six floors below. Dominic Amalfitano sat behind his desk smoking a cigar. He wore a white shirt, red tie, and charcoal suit. His eyes looked foggy, which Hogan hadn't noticed when they first met a week ago.

They exchanged the usual pleasantries, the lieutenant introduced

Officer Porter and the police officers each took a seat.

"First, Mr. Amalfitano, on behalf of the two of us, I want to express our deep sorrow over the loss of your sister. As one who's experienced a couple of deaths to cancer in my own family, including my father, I have some idea of what you've been going through. We're both truly sorry."

"Thanks, Lieutenant, I really appreciate it. By the way, would either of you care for a cigar?"

"No thanks, but we appreciate the offer."

"Now, just what is it that brings you in here today?" asked Amalfitano. He fidgeted for a moment, moving a couple of pencils around on his desk. Opening a desk drawer and then closing it, for no apparent reason.

Porter had his pen and notebook ready. Hogan, baffled by what he'd just heard, sat stiff in his chair, his hands folded on his lap, his eyes focused on the agency manager.

"Everybody in the world knows the killer is now dead. It's safe to say his killing days are over, it's done. I'm surprised you're here, my first day in the office in nearly a week, for Christ's sake."

His tone matched his language.

"I'm surprised you feel that way, Mr. Amalfitano," said Hogan. "Especially since you told me barely a week ago you were anxious to assist us in this investigation no matter where it led. The truth is, we know the *who,* but we don't know the *why*. And we don't know the *how,* either.

"In other words, we know Frankie Crosetti killed all five individuals, but we don't know *why* they were killed, nor do we know *how* he got the information from Taylor's files. Perhaps most puzzling of all is what Whit Payne's death has to do with the four client killings. Certainly there's a relationship. And certainly five murders is reason enough for us to be here, even if it is your first day back."

Amalfitano took a puff of his cigar, glanced up toward the ceiling and exhaled enough smoke to inhabit the kitchen of a cheap hamburger joint.

"You'll have to excuse me, gentlemen, if I appear gruff or rude. But all these killings involving our clients, along with Whit Payne's brutal murder, have my head reeling. And the fact that my favorite sister, Sarah, also died last week, only adds to my grief."

Hogan and Porter waited for him to continue.

"My boss in San Francisco is threatening to close down this entire operation and assign all our agents to other Bear Republic offices, including Glendale, and the new one in Thousand Oaks. Oh, and, in the process, give me a one-way ticket to Topeka." His attempt to smile failed.

"So I'm as anxious as you are to wind this up. ASAP. It's just that, well, you're wasting precious time asking me a bunch of questions, which is why you're here. Nobody has a more vested interest in getting to the bottom of this than I do. That's for damn sure. But I haven't even been here for a week, and whatever answers you're looking for are more than likely out there where the agents work, not in my office. Or out there in the streets somewhere."

Officer George Porter spoke for the first time. "We understand the position you're in, and you have our sympathy, but if we're going to clean this up, we're going to have to take some time to ask you a number of questions. Is that okay?"

Hogan stared at Porter. They were here to ask the boss questions, and it didn't matter one damn bit whether it was okay with him or not. Amalfitano was also looking at Porter, his bold eyes bulging as he gave him a once-over.

Porter continued:

"We know you have something like forty agents here, but there must be at least one—possibly even more—that you might consider more likely to be involved in this hideous undertaking than others."

"That's a stupid question, if, in fact, it's even a question. Bill Kaiser detests Arnie Taylor, Charlie Anderson is quick tempered, Richard Crowe once took a swing at some guy across the street at the Classic Cat, Dale Trudeau can't hold his liquor. Probably half the agents out there cheat on their wives. Does that mean one of them might be a likely suspect in four murders of policyholders, not to mention Whit Payne? I don't think so."

There was something about Amalfitano's eyes Hogan hadn't noticed when they met the first time. Something he didn't like. They had the stigma of passion, ruthless passion. They were wide and dark, almost black. A dark impenetrable forest.

"Bill Kaiser's name keeps coming up during our interviews. Do you think . . ."

"Bill Kaiser's not guilty of anything other than being one of the best life insurance agents in the country," said Amalfitano. "He's also a blowhard and a bit of a playboy. And yes, I'm sure you've heard he keeps an arsenal in his house sufficient to invade North Korea. But that's because of his far-out political beliefs.

He's the last guy I'd suspect of going out and murdering innocent people. If I were you, I'd leave him alone. You'll only be wasting your time. And his."

Hogan couldn't help but think that this last statement had more to do with Kaiser's value to the agency than anything else. He didn't want his star player distracted by this mess. It might hurt his production. And Amalfitano's pocketbook.

"The one you need to be questioning is Arnold Taylor," said Amalfitano, "you know, Mike Slovak's good friend. Slovak obviously knew that Crosetti was the killer of Arnie's clients, so he probably knows how Crosetti got the information. In fact, if you guys would leave us alone— all of us but Arnie— and go out and find Slovak, a buck will get you ten that you'll have this whole case settled."

Lieutenant Hogan twisted in his chair, pulled out a pack of Salems from his inside breast pocket, along with his lighter, and lit up. With a slight shake of his head, he nodded to Porter to remain silent. He was playing one of his favorite games—the first guy who talks, loses.

Only the guy behind the desk wasn't playing. Amalfitano took a couple of puffs of his cigar and sat there wearing more than a hint of a smirk on his face. Hogan noticed that suddenly the boss looked a bit more calm, and a whole lot more cocky, if that was possible. The man had a predatory air about him. Hogan knew that Amalfitano had just delivered him a not so subtle message:

This is your problem, not mine, so don't waste my time. You and your stupid ass colleagues have been looking for a real killer, Mike Slovak, for decades and have come up with nothing. So get the hell out of my office and go do your job, so I can do mine.

While sitting there waiting for Amalfitano to say something, Hogan noticed pictures on the wall to his right that had escaped his attention during his initial visit to the office. It was a collage of photographs of the agency manager's family, including two young girls and a boy at various stages of their lives. There were also pictures of him and his wife on their wedding day, and a more recent photo of his wife with the three children, two of whom appeared to be in their early teenage years. Amalfitano was either a genuine family man, or he wanted people to think he was.

It was time for somebody to say something.

"You have a very attractive family," said the lieutenant, as he gestured toward the wall."

"Thanks. They mean everything to me. They're the reason I come to work every day and bust my ass."

"As far as Arnie's concerned," said the lieutenant, "we've been working with him all along, and will continue to do so. But we really have no reason to believe he's guilty of anything other than being a victim of a vicious plot perpetrated by one very sick puppy. Like you, he's a victim who has everything to lose, and nothing to gain."

Hogan's comment that Arnie was no more culpable in this matter than Amalfitano was made for no other reason than to mislead the boss into thinking he was not a suspect. In fact, in Hogan's eyes, he was now more of a suspect than Kaiser. Something didn't smell right, all of a sudden. The Lieutenant was determined to get to the bottom of it.

"Tell me about your relationship with Kaiser? Are the two of you close friends, or is it strictly a business relationship?"

"Strictly business, Lieutenant. He's by far the biggest pain in the ass in the agency, but he's worth it because of all the business he brings in the door. Let's just say he's a hell of a producer, but other than that, I have no use for him."

"Why is that?" asked Hogan.

Amalfitano's tone raised a decibel or two. "He thinks I should be at his beck and call every hour of the day, including weekends. And when I'm doing something else important and he has to get in line, he really gets pissed off. He's even called Home Office to complain about me, telling them, in so many words, that I'm a worthless, piece of shit. So, no, I don't like him. Not one goddamn bit."

Hogan was beginning to wonder if Amalfitano liked anybody. In any case, the boss had just confirmed what Lieutenant Hogan and his staff had learned from everyone else, except Sandi Taylor, who had a totally different story of their relationship. He made a note to have Sandi come into his office and take a lie detector test. Since a suspect had to agree, that might not be easy. Then he remembered—she had offered to take one during their interview the previous Wednesday. In fact, she's the one who brought it up.

At this point, Hogan concluded that Amalfitano was right about one thing—meeting with him was a big waste of time. The lieutenant would ask one more question, then get the hell out of there. And the only way to ask that question was to get right to the point. Maybe catch the arrogant bastard off guard.

"When was the last time you saw Whit Payne, Mr. Amalfitano?"

For the first time, the boss looked surprised, even stunned. Like he'd just learned his wife had been caught in bed screwing her brains out with the next-door neighbor. He took another puff on his cigar, which looked to Hogan like an obvious tactic to stall for a little time.

"Well, let's see. I didn't see him Tuesday morning, but I was only in here for a couple of hours that day, and then I was off to New York."

"He was dead by then, Mr. Amalfitano. He was murdered while eating dinner at home Monday evening. If you don't know that, then you really do need us here to bring you up to date."

Hogan had lost his patience. He was now ready to play the role of the 'bad cop.'

"That's right, he was. But you have to remember that, since I was three thousand miles away the rest of last week, my memory might not be as quick as yours.

"Anyway," he continued, "I didn't see him Monday, so I guess the last time I saw him was the week before last. And I have no recollection at all as to when that might have been. He was never in my office much, so when I did see him, it was usually wandering around visiting with other agents, or in the GSO."

"You're sure you didn't see him Monday, say, right before you went home that night?"

"Of course I'm sure. What's all this shit about? I was in my office until a little before six that evening, and the only other person here was Rolene. She was typing a letter for me that had to get out that night. She will confirm that we were the last two people in the office. I dropped off the letter at the post office on my way home."

"So, did you and Rolene leave together?"

"My recollection is, she left a minute or two before I did. I remember locking the front door, which must have been right after she got on the elevator and headed down."

Dominic Amalfitano's face flushed with anger as he pushed back his chair and stood glaring at Lieutenant Hogan.

"What is this, a fuck'n interrogation? And what difference does it make anyway?" The agency manager's tone even more contemptuous and accusatory than earlier.

Hogan stood and glared for a brief moment.

"Thanks for your time, Mr. Amalfitano. We'll be on our way now."

Officer Porter got to the door first, opened it, and, as the two of them walked out, the lieutenant turned around and took one last glance at the irate Dominic Amalfitano. They parted on mutually suspicious terms.

****

Amalfitano told Rolene to close his office door, that he didn't want to be disturbed for a while. He then dialed a phone number, which was picked up on the third ring.

"Rocky, it's me, Vincent. That asshole, Lieutenant Hogan, has somehow learned that Whit Payne was in my office Monday night after Rolene left."

"How'd he find out?" asked Amalfitano's brother.

"Beats hell out of me. Maybe she saw him drive into the parking lot when she was driving out. That's all I can figure.

"Anyway, if he has hard evidence Payne and I talked, then I'll be linked to the phone call to the Holiday Inn. Remember, our informant in Homicide told us the cops know from two sources that someone called Frankie."

"I know the dame told the cops about the phone call. Who else did?" asked Rocky.

"The bartender, you dumb ass. Who do you think?"

"So here's the deal," said Amalfitano. "You need to arrange for our guy to take out Taylor's wife. Don't **you** do it. It has to be someone outside the family. Someone that leaves us totally out of it. Pay him ten grand. Tell him this is a very important job, which is why he's getting so much dough. And why he can't fuck this up.

"And Rocky, I don't want this job done tomorrow. It's too soon after today's meeting. It might look like I ordered the hit to take the heat off me over the Whit Payne visit. A little later in the week will be fine.

"One more thing. Since she's staying with her parents, our friend will have to kill all three of them. Unless Mommy and Daddy get lucky and are out somewhere when he shows up."

"Consider it done," said Rocky.

Amalfitano hung up.

Chapter 24

Following Monday afternoon's explosive meeting with Dominic Amalfitano, Lieutenant Frank Hogan got a phone call from Police Headquarters downtown. His wife had been rushed to the Glendale Adventist Hospital Emergency Room at 12:50 after a suicide attempt. This was her third effort to end her life.

A neighbor, convinced her friend was home because her car was in the driveway, rang the doorbell several times, then peeked through the window. She saw Gail Hogan lying on the floor motionless. She ran home, called for an ambulance, then waited in the front yard until police and medics arrived twelve minutes later.

When Hogan arrived at the hospital a little after three thirty, he learned she was conscious and would recover. Medics on the scene had found an empty container of Valium and a fifth of Johnnie Walker Red on a table in front of the sofa. The bottle of Scotch was about two-thirds empty. The prescription, dated only three days earlier, March 14th, for fifty pills, was empty. Her stomach had been pumped shortly after her arrival at the hospital.

While it was unclear when she would be released, Hogan was advised the family should plan on her not coming home for at least a week.

He called their daughter, Michelle, in San Diego, and asked her to come home to spend time with her mother at Glendale Adventist, at least through the end of the week. By then, Hogan would be available full-time for the weekend.

"The reason I moved down here in the first place was to get away from Mother, and all her booze and pills. And now you're asking me to stop everything I'm doing and rush back home?"

"Yes, Honey, that's exactly what I'm asking you to do. She's your mother, you're our only child. She can't help it. She's sick. Alcoholism is a disease."

"I know, Daddy, I know. I've been hearing that all my life. She made my childhood so miserable, it's a miracle I'm not an alcoholic myself. Fortunately, I'm afraid to go near the stuff. The truth is, she stole my childhood, and since I'm no longer under her control, I'm determined to stay away from her. She's toxic, Daddy."

Hogan's heart skipped a beat. Arnie Taylor had uttered that same expression– "he stole my childhood" when referring to his father during their initial interview.

"Listen to me, Michelle. you're nineteen, you've got your whole life ahead of you. I'm involved in a high-profile investigation, which means I can't just disappear like a bear hibernating in the woods. I've got an important job to do, lives are at stake."

"You just don't get it, do you, Daddy? You've always been a big part of the problem. Since I was twelve, you've been on some important case. I've been left to deal with my drunken mother alone. No more, Daddy. No more."

They argued for another ten minutes. She finally told him she had exams to take on Tuesday and Wednesday, but would drive up there Wednesday night, and return to San Diego on Saturday.

He was about to thank her when she said, "After this, before you leave her alone, how about filling an empty Johnnie Walker bottle with gasoline. Then, she'll be out of her misery, and our problem will be over."

Hogan hung up on her.

By Wednesday, matters had gottten worse. When Michelle arrived, her boyfriend Tad, was with her. Her father swallowed hard, then said that it was okay, they had a spare bedroom. Michelle said, "no." They would be sleeping in her bedroom. She was a big girl now, she was on 'the pill,' and she was making her own decisions. She was getting on with her life, and she didn't need, or want, any advice from her father or anyone else.

Later that night, Hogan sat in his favorite chair and drank most of what was left of the scotch Gail had not downed. Musing over his current problems, both at home and at work, he decided he wanted to see Father O'Reilly sometime Sunday morning, either before or after mass. He wanted to know how to begin proceedings leading to an annulment.

Frank Hogan spent the rest of the night sleeping in the chair.

Chapter 25

North Hollywood, Monday, March 17, 5:40 p.m.

Rolene Ward was home about ten minutes when she kicked her shoes off, and took her first sip of wine. She liked Chablis, and usually had a glass or two after work. She also liked to watch the nightly news on NBC with John Chancellor and David Brinkley, but tonight, she didn't turn it on. She was preoccupied mulling something over. Something very important. The last thing Rolene needed was the distraction of bad news blaring from the television set. There was enough bad news at work—she didn't need an earful while trying to relax after a busy day at the office.

She purchased her first house three years earlier, combining her modicum of savings with a small inheritance from her father to make a 40% down payment. The house was on Califa Street in North Holly-wood, between Laurel Canyon and Whitsett Avenue. The twenty-eight-year-old dwelling was not large, 1,300 square feet, but with a bath and a half, two bedrooms, and a sizable living room with a fireplace, there was more than enough room for her. It only had a one-car garage, but then, Rolene only had one car, so that wasn't a problem. The fact was, she loved her house, and was thrilled to be a homeowner.

When she read The *Times* account of the shootings outside Arnie's apartment when he was a boy, it struck her that the Taylor's family address on Magnolia was almost directly south of where she now lived. No more than a mile or two away. Small world.

Rolene's dilemma concerned Arnie. She wanted to invite him over for dinner next Saturday night, but was agonizing over whether or not that was a good idea. She weighed the positives and the negatives of extending such an invitation. The more she considered it, the more complicated it seemed, and the more frustrated she became.

On the positive side, she could provide a home-cooked meal. Not that he wasn't getting that from his mother at least a couple of times a week, but it wasn't the same. At her house, he would also be getting an innocent form of female companionship with someone his age, something his mother could not provide. Something he might find appealing, given all the ramifications of the violence overwhelming his world. It would also give the two of them an opportunity to visit in a casual environment. A chance for them to discover if there was anything there that might lead to a more meaningful relationship. When she had been to his house the previous summer, there had been a half-dozen others in attendance. This time it would be just the two of them.

On the negative side, she didn't want to appear too aggressive. After all, two of the five murders had been committed in the past week. Was it too soon? Maybe he needed some breathing room, some time away from friends, especially friends from the office. Then there was the issue of his divorce. Maybe she should at least wait until he hired an attorney and filed papers.

Finally, given her responsibilities at work, was it appropriate for her to take the lead in asking a coworker to come to her house for a meal? She decided, with all the scandals revolving around the agency, issuing such an invitation was a trivial matter. On a scale from one to ten, it would register a zero, compared to the other problems currently confronting her workplace. In any case, she didn't care. She knew what she was going to do. She was going to call him.

Rolene stretched her legs out on the coffee table. She picked up the bottle of Chablis, refilled her glass and took a healthy swallow, just for good measure. She turned sideways to reach for the phone, located on a small table adjacent to the sofa. Even though she seldom had any reason to call him at home, she had memorized his number. Before she could pick up the handset, the phone rang.

****

March 17, Monday Afternoon

Arnie spent the afternoon with his mother. First, she treated him to a couple of gin and tonics at the Yankee Peddler Inn in Toluca Lake, followed by a hearty lunch consisting of a Roquefort salad, open-face steak sandwich, and baked potato. For desert, a slice of cherry pie, his favorite. His mother ordered a dish of vanilla ice cream.

Gladys Doleshal treated him to a movie at the Alex Theater in Glendale. She thought a nice, unhurried lunch, followed by a light comedy, would do him some good. She suggested *Shampoo*, with Warren Beatty, Julie Christie and Goldie Hawn. She knew it involved political satire, which her son enjoyed. She had been a big Goldie Hawn fan since the early days of *Rowan & Martin's Laugh-In*. Her strategy paid off. They both enjoyed the film. Arnie even let loose and relaxed enough to laugh for the first time in a week.

On the drive home, after dropping his Mother off, Arnie thought how nice it would be to get away once or twice a week. Just for a few hours and have some fun. Not with Mother, fun with a nice, unattached, female. One who could laugh, but had a serious side. One who could hold her own intellectually, who actually read books and had her own opinions on serious subjects. One who could make him feel good about himself, who could like him for who he is, rather than despise him for who he is not.

He didn't have to give much thought to the one he had in mind. He knew plenty of single women. Some were divorced, some had never been married. Some had children, some didn't. One worked for Bear Republic. She was three or four years older than him. She was divorced, no children. Her name was Rolene Ward. She was the one.

Arnie wondered if it might be too soon. Rolene might think he was jumping the gun, given the fact he was still married. Well, he wasn't going to let that stop him. He wasn't going to waste precious time. Life was too short.

The truth was, he'd been living alone since he was ten, and it was getting old, just as he was. When his father began neglecting the family, spending almost every evening out of the house, his mother had little time for Arnie. She was too preoccupied with his father's bizarre behavior, which accelerated for another three years, until it all stopped in a surge of violence. After that, during his high school and college years, he had no close friends, by design. He was reluctant to let anyone get too close. After a couple of years of marital bliss, he was alone again. Living with a stranger who posed as a wife.

He had another concern. As a boy, he had a front row seat to indescribable domestic violence. After a twenty-year hiatus, news of those events involving the family had resurfaced. Now that he was again surrounded by tragedy, was it possible single women might consider him damaged goods? Likely to suffer from depression or anxiety? This was more than a remote possibility. Well, he was about to find out.

The worst thing that could happen would be a polite "thanks, but no thanks" from Rolene. As a life insurance agent, he faced rejection on a daily basis. He was certain he could handle it. Well, almost certain. It would be a different kind of rejection. It would be personal.

Arnie walked into his house a few minutes before six and walked to his desk in the office at the end of the hall. The list of agency personnel phone numbers was in the top right-hand drawer. He headed toward the kitchen, taking a wineglass from the cupboard, he filled it to the brim from an open bottle of Chablis from the refrigerator,. He sat down at the kitchen table took a healthy swallow of wine, just for good measure. Finding her number near the end of the alphabetical list, he dialed and waited for her to answer. He had not made a call like this for fourteen years. His heart skipped a beat as she answered the phone.

"Hi, Rolene, it's Arnie Taylor."

Chapter 26

March 17, Monday, 5: 50 p.m., The San Fernando Valley

Rolene was astounded to hear Arnie's voice on the other end of the line.

"I can't believe it, Arnie," she said. "I was just about to call you. That's why I picked up the phone so fast. This really is a coincidence."

She was sorry as soon as she said it. Since he had called her first, she would have preferred that he not know she was about to call him. But it was too late. She had been caught by surprise, and had just blurted it out.

"You were going to call me? Is there more bad news at the office?"

"No, no, nothing like that. I was going to ask if you'd like to come over Saturday evening for a good, old fashioned home cooked meal."

"That sounds great. How many people are you expecting? Is there something special you're celebrating?"

"Yes, it's something special, but not a party. It will be just the two of us."

"Why, that's really nice of you," said Arnie, "but I'd like to make a counteroffer."

"A counteroffer?" she asked, her voice projecting a hint of nervousness.

"Yes. I was wondering if you'd like to join me for dinner tomorrow evening. That is, if you don't have other plans. It's rather late notice, to say the least."

Rolene laughed. "Well, I'd love to tell you that I'm booked every night for the next three months, but it's simply not true. I seldom do anything after work on weeknights other than watch a little television, then cuddle up with a good book. Anyway, 'yes,' I'd love to go to dinner with you tomorrow night."

"That's great. I'd like to take you to the Odyssey, you know, the restaurant up on the hill near my house."

"Okay," said Rolene, "but I'd feel better if you'd let me meet you somewhere closer to the Odyssey rather than have you drive from Granada Hills all the way to North Hollywood, and then back again. And you'll also be doing that when you take me home."

"That's very considerate of you, Rolene. But I don't mind the drive at all. And I promise to get you home at a decent hour."

****

Tuesday, March 18

Arnie told Rolene he would pick her up at 6:30 the next evening, which would give her enough time to get home from work, cleanup, and get dressed. They had reservations for 7:30, which allowed her the opportunity to show him her house. The two of them could relax for a little while over a glass of wine before heading for the Odyssey. The restaurant was about a 25 minute drive, nearly all of it freeway.

It was a little before six thirty when Arnie rang the doorbell.

"Wow, you really look terrific," he said.

"Well thank you. You look pretty terrific yourself."

Wearing a pale-blue, knee-length dress which showed off her legs, Rolene also wore dangling sapphire earrings and matching necklace, which brought out a sparkle in her blue eyes he had never noticed before.

Arnie handed her a bottle of wine. She thanked him, then invited him in. He walked through a small entry way which led to a good-size living room, or den, he wasn't sure. He was about to comment on her house and furniture when she said, "Arnie, do you realize we match? Your light-blue leisure suit is about as close a match with my dress as possible. How did you know what I was going to wear tonight? Do you have some sixth sense you never told me about?"

She gave him a playful smile, as though he had been keeping something important from her for the ten years they had known each other.

"Darn," he said. "My secret's out. I have extrasensory qualities no one ever imagined."

She led him down the hallway, pointing out a bathroom on the right, a guest bedroom at the end of the hall on the left, and her bedroom at the end of the hall on the right.

As she was leading him back through the house to the kitchen, he stopped in the living room to admire the beautiful brick fireplace with a raised hearth.

"I just love your house, Rolene. Everything about it. Your fireplace is a real attention-getter, for sure. But I'm especially struck by how new and clean everything looks. You've really made this house a home."

"Thanks, Arnie, it's very thoughtful of you to say that."

They walked into the kitchen, where she removed a chilled bottle of Chablis from the refrigerator and put the bottle he brought in its place.

"Let's sit in the living room and visit for a while before we go," she said.

"Sounds good to me. We have at least a half an hour. I'll open the bottle."

Arnie seated himself at one end of a full-length sofa. Rolene sat about ten feet across from him in a recliner. After he offered a toast to a nice evening together, they each took a first sip.

Rolene had something to say.

"I want you to understand, Arnie. I have no intention of talking business tonight, or referring in any way to all the negative stuff going on in our lives, with one exception. If you feel like you want, or need, to vent to someone who understands your environment at work, and knows all the players, then please don't hesitate to unload. I don't mind at all, and I think you'd find me to be a good listener. And, of course, you can feel secure that anything you say will not go any further."

Arnie took another sip of wine, set his glass on the coffee table, and smiled. "I appreciate that, I really do. Let's just see how the evening unfolds. If the situation at work comes up, then at least I'll know how you feel about going there."

She asked him what he'd been up to the past couple of days. He told her about his visit with his mother the day before, the nice lunch followed by going to the movies in Glendale. He started to tell her about "Shampoo," but she had seen it, so they each recalled a couple of scenes and shared a few laughs. Like Arnie's mother, Rolene loved Goldie Hawn.

After nearly thirty minutes of chit-chat, they headed out the door and began the drive to the Odyssey.

They arrived on time, and were immediately escorted to a larger room by a pretty, buxom brunette who could have passed for sixteen. She seated them at a table for two in a far corner with a window view. A nice breeze that afternoon had blown the smog away, which made for a picturesque setting. With twelve stories, and the only tall building in the area, the Panorama Towers was easy to spot. It was easily the tallest building in the north central Valley.

"You know," said Rolene, it's possible we might run into someone we know from the office. I'm sure you've thought about that."

"Yes, I have. I doubt it, though, on a Tuesday night. But anything's possible. Hey, it's a free country, and if we want have dinner together, so be it. As my mother would say, 'I really don't give a rat's behind.'"

"I don't care either," she said, "but if anyone sees us, no matter who it is, I'd bet you a hundred dollars that by nine o' clock tomorrow morning, everyone in the office will know about it."

"Gosh, I never thought of that," he said. "But being seen with you would certainly help my image, that's for sure."

Before she could reply, the waitress appeared, greeted them, and asked if they wanted to start with something from the bar. Arnie looked at Rolene and said, "Please order whatever you'd like. I'm going to have a gin and tonic with a twist of lime, Bombay Sapphire."

"I'll have a vodka martini," she said. "Very dry. Smirnoff."

'Sandi likes vodka, too," he said, as the waitress headed toward the bar.

"Oh my God. The last thing I want to do is talk about her. And here we are, barely seated, and I mention her name. Damn."

"Don't think a thing about it, Arnie. It's only natural. You've been with her a long time. It will take a while before you realize, internally, that you're not with her anymore. Believe me, I know what I'm talking about. I've been there. You'll eventually put her behind you and life will go on. I promise."

Her eyes filled with kindness, her tone soft and caring, Arnie perceived an innocent, natural prettiness. Rolene was the girl next door, a brown haired Doris Day who could charm the fox out of the henhouse. Her whole being invoked substance, a brain behind that pleasant face, a heart inside her chest.

His first date was going well. Very well. He tossed her a shy smile.

"We were talking earlier about *Shampoo*," he said. "Do you go the movies often?"

"Oh, I guess two or three times a month. Sometimes with a date. Sometimes with a girlfriend. Sometimes, I even go alone."

"Really? I haven't gone to a movie alone since I was seventeen. It was a Sunday afternoon and I saw *The Bridge on the River Kwai*. A girl I had a mad crush on told me she was now going steady with somebody else. Knowing for sure it was the end of the world, I buried my teenage sorrow in a dark movie theater in Burbank. It turned out the film was so engrossing, I quickly forgot about good old Sally whats-her-name."

The waitress appeared with their drinks. "Would you care to order dinner now, or would you like to wait a while?"

"Thanks, but I think we'll nurse our drinks for a while," said Arnie. "Besides, we haven't even looked at the menu yet.

"We better decide now," he said to Rolene, as the waitress walked away, "or she'll be back before we know it, and we'll have to go through the drill all over again."

After they each made up their mind, Rolene picked up the conversation.

"Anyway, going to a movie by yourself isn't so bad. Especially if you live alone and have some time on your hands. You want to get out of the house. For me, that day is usually a Sunday."

"That makes sense," said Arnie, "you work all week and probably spend Saturdays cleaning house, grocery shopping and running errands."

"Exactly. As for 'River Kwai', I enjoyed the movie, but I think it's more of a man's film. There are no women in it, except for maybe twenty or thirty minutes. And the movie runs nearly three hours."

"It's my all-time favorite," said Arnie. "But to tell you the truth, I've never thought about the lack of women. I guess you're right about that, but for me, it's the perfect movie."

"I do like David Lean films, though," said Rolene. "Especially *Dr. Zhivago*, though Pasternak's book was better. And I enjoyed *Ryan's Daughter*, even if it was panned by the critics."

Arnie couldn't believe what he was hearing. An attractive female who not only knew who David Lean was, but could discuss his films in detail. And she even read books. Sandi wouldn't have a clue who David Lean was, where he was from, or what he did for a living. Nor would she care. She either liked a movie or she didn't. That was it. There was never any discussion regarding plot, character, theme, the quality of acting, or anything else.

"So, Rolene, what's your favorite—?"

Arnie stopped in midsentence. Through his left side peripheral vision, he noticed a party of three following the young-looking hostess. They proceeded toward the table about six feet away from where he and Rolene were seated. His breathing accelerating, his heart vibrating at a furious pace, Arnie jerked his head to the left to verify what he thought he saw from an angle.

He glanced at Rolene, nodded his head in the direction of the approaching customers, then pushed back his chair and stood.

Sandi and her parents were within conversational distance when they stopped cold and stared, first at him, then at Rolene.

"And to think I've always believed we live in a large city," said Arnie. He made no effort to smile.

Arnie thought Sandi looked pale, even ill. She also seemed somewhat detached from her surroundings. Hans Schultz's demeanor was combative, Lenore's, convivial. She walked right up to her son-in-law, gave him a hug, and whispered, "I'm so, so sorry about everything, Arnie. I really am."

"Me, too," he replied.

Arnie withdrew from Lenore's embrace, nodded toward his dinner guest, and said, "This is Rolene Ward, Mr. Amalfitano's secretary. Sandi, of course, has known her for years."

Hans turned to the hostess and said, "Please find us another booth in a different section. We'll meet you back in the front entry area."

The three started heading back toward the entrance when Sandi stopped and turned around. She looked at Arnie, gestured toward Rolene, then said. "It didn't take you long, did it?"

Chapter 27

March 18, Tuesday, North Hollywood

"Let's get the hell out of here," said Arnie, after Sandi walked away.

"Are you sure?" asked Rolene, "Hey, we got here first, and we have as much right to be here as they do. But the important thing is that **you** be comfortable. So, wherever you want to go is fine with me. I'll have a great time wherever we are."

They drove out of the parking lot in silence. Arnie was trying hard to mask his mental state, but Rolene wasn't buying it. She had never seen him so discomfited. He was now solemn, silent. His hand shook when he unlocked and opened the car door for her. It was clear he needed some time to contain his anger, to get himself back together.

"I have an idea. Let's stop somewhere, pick up a pizza and a salad, and go back to my place," she said. "That way, it will be easier for us to visit, and I assure you, nobody will crash the party at **my** house. We can turn on some soft music, get out another bottle of wine, and just lay back and relax. We'll get through this together."

"Are you sure?" he asked, followed by a half-smile. "You know, I would have bet a million bucks the Schultz's would not have gone out anywhere these days, yet alone the one restaurant I selected for the two of us. It shows how smart I am.

"I want to say 'no', it would be unfair for you to end up entertaining me in your home when my purpose tonight was to take you out for a good time at a classy place. Not that your house isn't classy," he added.

They drove in silence for a few minutes before he asked her what her favorite pizza was. Twenty-five minutes later, they were back inside her North Hollywood home.

While Arnie opened the bottle of wine he'd brought, Rolene set up TV trays in the living room. She thought they would be more comfortable in there than sitting at the kitchen table. She also turned on her stereo and put on a small stack of records, including Barry Manilow, Linda Ronstadt, The Eagles, and The Carpenters. While he got himself seated, she removed two more bottles of wine from a cupboard in the kitchen and placed them in the refrigerator. She was thinking—and hoping—that this would be a long night, notwithstanding her need to be at the office by eight the next morning.

After they'd finished eating to the accompaniment of Barry Manilow, Rolene could tell Arnie was beginning to perk up.

He smiled and said, "As I was saying before we were so rudely interrupted, what's your favorite movie, Rolene?"

"I don't really have a favorite," she said. "But if we break it down by category, you'll have a pretty good idea which ones I've especially enjoyed."

"Okay," said Arnie. "We'll compare."

"Favorite Hitchcock film?"

"*Rear Window*," she answered.

"Mine is *North by Northwest*."

"Favorite western?"

"*The Magnificent Seven*."

"Great choice, but I prefer *High Noon*."

"Greatest mystery?"

Rolene thought about this for a few moments. "I like Agatha Christie's stories, so I'm going to say, *Witness for the Prosecution*."

"Bingo. That's my favorite, too."

"Favorite romantic drama?"

"That's a tough one." She paused. "*An Affair to Remember*."

"I'm going to name an old black-and-white film that came out during World War ll," said Arnie. "And, no, I don't mean *Casablanca*. The movie is *Random Harvest*."

"Wow, I wasn't thinking that far back. The truth is, I've never seen it. I've read the book, though, by James Hilton. It was one of a couple of hundred volumes I inherited from my father when he passed on. The book, by the way, is a real tearjerker, so I have a pretty good idea why it's on your movie favorites list." "One more," he said. "Favorite romantic comedy?"

"*Pillow Talk*," she said.

"Mine is *What's Up, Doc*."

Arnie said it was obvious she was quite a reader. She said she was.

"I completed two years at Valley Junior College, majoring in English Lit. I was planning to go on to UCLA and eventually teach high school English. But after Bob left, I was hired by Mr. Rupert at Bear Republic for more than double what I was making at Larue and Palmer, and with better benefits. Since I was alone in the world, and wouldn't be getting financial help from anyone, I decided to delay my education for a while. You were already at the agency when I arrived, so you pretty much know the rest of the story. I've been there ten years and enjoy my job, especially, the money. Oh, and I've met some great people."

Rolene threw a beautiful smile his way, then gestured with both hands extended, so that he would know she meant him.

Arnie's face lit up as he shook his head sideways. "You're amazing. I haven't had this much fun in years," he said.

"How have you remained single all these years? It doesn't make sense."

"There's an easy explanation for that. There are no good "available" men out there . They're all married. Unless you happen to catch one at exactly the right time, say, following a divorce or, unfortunately, the death of a mate, they're taken. There can be problems when they are available, too. Like children. There might be too many, or they might be bratty, which can be a deal-breaker. Don't get me wrong. I love kids, and always hoped to have some. But that's not the same thing as raising someone else's and making it work."

"Of course, a man's at risk, too, when it comes to finding a divorced woman with kids," said Arnie.

Rolene nodded, and continued:

"I don't think I would have a problem getting picked up in some bar, but . . . sorry, that's not for me. I've been set up a few times, and while I've known that to work out for some friends, it's never worked for me. So here I am, single at thirty-seven. No real complaints. Overall, life's been good."

Arnie knew she was a little older than he was, and he had it about right. Four years. No big deal. Except when he was eleven and she was fifteen.

The next couple of hours consisted of trivial banter back and forth while they made their way through the stack of LPs on the stereo. Rolene shared funny stories about certain agents. She told him that James had been trying to convert her to Christianity for several years. She kept telling him she was a Christian, and had attended a Methodist Church, but he said she needed to be 'born again,' or she'd never get to heaven.

"Have you told Amalfitano about this?" asked Arnie.

"No, I'd never do that. He'd fire him in a heartbeat. James means well. He just doesn't use good judgment. He should keep his religious beliefs to himself when he's in the office."

"Personally, I don't believe in trying to convert others to my point of view," said Arnie, "whether it has to do with religion, politics or anything else."

Rolene's face reflected a sly grin. "I'm surprised to hear that. You're certainly not one to keep your political views a secret. Everyone knows you're a Democrat."

"That's true, but it's because I love to engage in spirited discussions involving a healthy exchange of views. It's never my intent to change someone's mind, but to help them to understand where I'm coming from.

"I must admit, though, my willingness to give my opinion has gotten me in trouble more times than I can remember. But that's never going to change. I guess you could say, it's who I am. I love politics, I'm well informed, and if someone objects to my opinions, that's just too damn bad."

The subject of Bill Kaiser's political extremism came up. When Arnie mentioned he thought Kaiser lived in Cloud-Cuckoo-Land, she laughed so hard she started coughing.

After several hours of music, conversation and wine, Annie looked up at the clock on the wall separating the living room from the kitchen. "My God, Rolene, it's nearly 12:30. It's tomorrow, already. I've got to get the hell out of here. You have to be at the office by eight."

"Relax, Arnie, I've been keeping my eye on the time, there's nothing for you to worry about. For one thing, I've decided not to go in tomorrow, or today, as it turns out. I've piled up a lot of sick leave and I'm going to call Angie as soon as the office opens and have her tell Mr. Amalfitano, I'm not feeling well.

"And you don't need to worry about going home, you're not going anywhere. We've consumed two and a half bottles of Chablis, so there's no way I'm going to risk your getting into an accident or getting a DUI while driving home."

"But Rolene, you know I can't stay here tonight."

"Of course you can. I have a guest bedroom down the hall, as you know. You can sleep there. I'll cook you a first-class breakfast in the morning, before you get on your way."

"You're right, Rolene, I've had too much to drink. But, I'd feel better sleeping on the couch. That way, you'd have more privacy."

"Nonsense," she said. "You're not sleeping on the couch, the guest bedroom will be fine. End of conversation. And by the way, I always have an extra tooth brush available for visitors like my mother or brother, or, in this case, you."

Rolene Ward got up from her chair, walked over to Arnie, and motioned for him to stand up.

"I'm going to bed," she said, "but first, I need a good night kiss."

Arnie got up, put his arms around her, held her tight for a moment, then gave her a prolonged, but innocent kiss on the lips. She responded in kind, and turned around and walked down the hallway to her bedroom, closing the door behind her.

Chapter 28

March 20, Thursday, Van Nuys City Hall

When Lieutenant Hogan arrived at the office in Van Nuys, Thursday morning, he had been absent for two long days. With the approval of his boss, Captain Coogin, he would be leaving for the hospital by 11:00 and would be out for the rest of the week. He didn't trust his daughter to stay at the hospital with her mother. He felt someone needed to be there for Gail, and since she had almost no friends, he would be there.

At 9:00 he met with Wright and Porter. They had already been informed that he would only be in for an hour or two.

Since Ricki had been briefed by George Porter on Tuesday regarding the tempestuous meeting with Domonic Amalfitano, Monday afternoon, Hogan decided not to mention it. He was more interested in hearing about Porter's meeting with Bill Kaiser. Porter had already left his report of the interview for Hogan to go over prior to their meeting this morning, but the lieutenant had not looked at it.

"So George, tell me about Kaiser. This loud-mouth, self-important, top producer. Not to mention, adulterer. What's your take on him?"

"Well, of course, I don't know what he's usually like, but he sure turned on the charm. He couldn't have been more pleasant. He's an interesting guy. I watched him down three beers while I had my usual Coke."

"How long did your meeting go?"

"Almost exactly thirty-five minutes."

"That's not very long."

"It was long enough for me two learn that he had nothing to say we don't already know. Except for one thing."

Hogan and Ricki Wright sat quietly, their eyes focused on Porter while he paused for a moment. It occurred to the lieutenant that the silence was intended for effect. Like he had something important to reveal, and he wanted to do it with some sort of dramatic flair. General MacArthur resurrected as Officer Porter.

"To say Bill Kaiser dislikes Arnold Taylor would be an understatement. He despises him. He was reluctant to talk about Arnie initially, but, eventually, he let loose with some foul language that was so gross, I'd rather not repeat it in front of Ricki. It's in my notes, though. It's all here."

Hogan sat in silence, not for dramatic effect, but because he was confused.

"Did he indicate the reason for such animosity? Is it strictly a matter of their political differences?"

"I think that's part of it, but I'm convinced there's more. The subject of his affair with Sandi Taylor came up, and though he didn't say so outright, I think he probably heard some pretty bad stuff about Arnie from her."

"Anything else?

"Yes, one more thing," said Porter. "Whenever I shifted the conversation to Amalfitano, he kept bringing up Arnie again. He thinks Arnie is behind all the killings."

Hogan shook his head. "That makes no sense, George. Why would he think that?"

"He says there are rumors around the office that Arnie has gotten tired of the life insurance business. He's talked about becoming a journalist, writing a book. If that's true, his future in the business is not an issue, since he won't be around anyway. But Amalfitano's future is a different story. Arnie wants the big boss out, preferably by sending him off to prison or the gas chamber.

"Oh, and get this. Kaiser says to me, 'Can you imagine Arnold Taylor as an Edward R. Murrow or a Drew Pearson? He'd be right in lockstep with those two leftist assholes.'"

Lieutenant Hogan rubbed his lower lip a couple of times. With a tone indicating incredulity, he asked Porter, "You do realize this contradicts the information from Rolene Ward, as well as from Arnie himself?"

"Hey, don't shoot the messenger. I'm just telling you what I saw and what I heard, and the conclusions I've drawn as a result. And don't forget, it matches what we learned from Sandi Taylor. Kaiser detests Arnie."

"Yeah," said the lieutenant, "if anyone can believe her. By the way, I wanted to have her come into the office this week for a second interview. With a lie detector, if she will agree to it. In any case, I want her questioned again, but since I'll be away until next week, it will have to wait."

Hogan continued: "Did Kaiser indicate that he and Amalfitano are close?"

"No, that never came up," said Officer Porter.

"You didn't ask him?" Hogan shook his head, then expelled a deep sigh.

"That's interesting," said the lieutenant. "After hearing Sandi Taylor on the subject, you'd think they were as close as Woodward and Bernstein. Of course, Amalfitano told us otherwise."

Ricki jumped into the conversation for the first time. "Well, somebody's lying, that's for sure. If we knew **why**, then we'd know **who**."

"That's all. We're done," said Hogan. "I've got a couple of other matters to tend to before I get out of here."

"Lieutenant, may I make a suggestion before we go?" asked Officer Wright. He nodded for her to proceed.

"I think there's a possibility Kaiser's messing with us. That he's jerking our chain."

"Why would he do that?"

"Well, he's got a big ego, right? He was expecting the man in charge of the investigation to be there, not just an underling. No offense intended, Porter."

"All I can say is, he damn well better not be messing with us," said Hogan. "Not when there are five dead bodies out there. If he doesn't realize he could be next, then we've been overestimating the hotshot."

The Lieutenant got up, motioned for the two of them to leave.

Officer Wright's phone rang just as she opened her office door. It was Lieutenant Hogan.

"Ricki, would you please come back? I want to talk to you alone."

***

When she returned to his office, she noticed something different about her boss. He was no longer upbeat, or wearing that mask of command that those with rank often display when there's work to be done.

He looked tired and worried, even despondent. After staring at the clean top of his desk for a minute or two, he began to speak in hushed tones.

151

"We need to talk. I need to speak with you in a manner more confidential than either of us could have imagined a week ago. Between the bizarre twists of this strange case, and my domestic problems with an alcoholic wife and wayward daughter, I'm not certain where to turn. You can't do anything about my problems at home, that's for sure. But maybe, between the two of us, we can get this case moving in the right direction."

"You have my word, Lieutenant, I'll do what I can."

Hogan placed his hands on the desk, folded them together, and leaned forward a little bit.

"In the larger picture of our investigation, Ricki, I think we're off script—way off script."

Ricki smiled, set her notebook and pencil on the back of the lieutenant's desk, and pushed her chair closer to the desk. Her body language suggested to Lieutenant Hogan that she was in total agreement that something was wrong, that their focus needed to be redirected. She was all ears.

"Feel free to throw out any suggestions, Ricki. You've demonstrated more than once that your creative, no-nonsense, modus operandi gets results."

"Thanks, Lieutenant, I appreciate that very much."

"For starters, I think we're wasting way too much time worrying about what Arnie thinks about Kaiser or Amalfitano, or what Kaiser thinks about Arnie. It's all a bunch of bullshit. Kaiser's not the killer any more than Arnie is.

"But Kaiser did say that Amalfitano is away from the office a lot more than he should be, confirmed by Rolene Ward. And Arnie did say that the boss had turned on him since the fourth murder. Amalfitano made it clear that Arnie's the one we should be investigating—Arnie and, as he put it, "his friend, Mike Slovak.""

"It appears he is trying to put the blame on Arnie," said Ricki. "That seems strange, to say the least. It is also obvious Amalfitano has an obsession with Mike Slovak."

"Exactly," said Hogan. "Very strange. There can't be any reason in the world why Arnie would be part of a plot to execute his own clients."

"You're right, of course," said Ricki. "But we could say the same thing about Amalfitano, couldn't we?"

"Yes," said Hogan, "and while this might be a bit of a stretch, what if Amalfitano is somehow involved with the mob? What if he's very close to the Crosetti brothers. What if Arnie is their means of getting Slovak into the picture so that they can take him out?"

Ricki stared straight at Hogan, immobile, attentive to his every word, then responded.

"That's possible," she said. "As a big shot, successful agency manager, he may think he's somehow immune from suspicion, whereas Arnie might be expendable. But, we'd have to ask ourselves how the Crosetti's knew about Arnie, his long-ago relationship with Slovak, and that he now works for Bear Republic, unless they learned it from Amalfitano."

The two police officers looked at each other in silence for a moment, then both of them smiled.

"Ricki, you and I are definitely on the same page, and . . ."

"I'm sorry to interrupt you, Lieutenant, but something just occurred to me. I need to get back to Rolene and find out what's in Arnie's personnel file."

"Exactly," said Hogan. "How long it's been in there, and just what it consists of. Keep in mind, in addition to obtaining the information in Arnie's file, you need to ask Rolene to keep you apprised when the boss will be out of the office, and for how long."

Ricki would be pursuing other leads also, including an interview with Arnie's secretary, Maria Tavarez.

As she got up to go, Lieutenant Hogan gave her his home phone number, and the Glendale Adventist Hospital main number. He told her to ask for Gail Hogan's room, number 436.

****

When she got back to her office, Ricki phoned Rolene Ward at work.

"Ms. Ward, it's Officer Wright."

"Well, hello Officer, what's up with you these days?"

"I have a favor to ask of you. One that could help us break this case wide open," said Ricki.

"Go ahead. As you know, I'll do anything I can to help."

"I want you to pull Arnie's personnel file, make notes of what's in there, and then get back to me. Better yet, if you could xerox a copy, that would be even better."

There was a brief silence on Rolene's end.

"I know this is way beyond the rules, insofar as Bear Republic is concerned, but my boss and I think this is very, very important," said Ricki.

"Okay," said Rolene. "It's really none of my business what's in our personnel files, so I've made it a practice to bring them to Mr. Amalfitano when he asks for them, and put them back when he's finished. I never look at them.

"So, you've never looked inside Arnie's file?"

Again, a brief silence. "Well, I did look at his maybe four or five years ago because, well, just because."

Ricki laughed, "I understand, Ms. Ward, believe me, I understand. Anyway, you haven't looked at it since then?"

"No, I haven't. But when the time is right, I'll xerox the entire file, then call you so that you can tell me how you want me to get it to you."

Chapter 29

March 20, Thursday, 5:00 p.m., Granada Hills

It had been a good day. Arnie spent the morning at home reading the *LA Times,* doing some light housework, including getting his barbecue out of the garage and cleaned up. He met his brother, Dan, for lunch at a Mexican restaurant on Balboa in Granada Hills. The two hadn't spent a lot of time together in recent years, because their wives didn't get along, but the brothers remained close. They were bonded not only genetically, but by the shared experience when their father was at war with the entire family. This was their first time together since Arnie's problems had gone public after the fourth murder.

In the afternoon, he drove to Zuma beach. He brought along two books, *Stilwell and the American Experience in China,* by Barbara Tuchman, and Joseph Wambaugh's *The Onion Field,* the latest thriller by the former Los Angeles police officer, but never opened them. A little solitude and the sound of the waves, allowed him to think of the future.

Arnie decided he would call Rolene when he got home. They hadn't spoken since their all-night date Tuesday. He didn't call her Wednesday because it might make him seem too anxious. He was trying to be cool about the whole thing, but in his heart, he knew he wasn't succeeding. She knew he liked her a lot, and he knew she felt the same way. Life was too short. They were too old to be playing games. He would call her as soon as he walked in the door.

As he turned onto Havenhurst, a short block away from his house, he noticed a car parked on the street in front, a vehicle he didn't immediately recognize. He identified the blue '72 Oldsmobile Cutlass, though, when he turned left onto his driveway. It belonged to his mother-in-law, Lenore Schultz.

"Damn," he muttered to himself. "What's that old bitch doing here?"

Arnie stopped his car in the driveway and hit the remote for the garage door. What he saw next was a scene out of a horror movie—a lifeless body hung suspended by a rope tied to a rafter. The other end, around the neck of a body, a step stool on its side on the floor a short distance away.

Arnie knew the corpse had been there a while, since there was no motion at all. The body, a female, still as a desert night. He sat in his car paralyzed by a combination of shock and fear. He felt a freeze in his stomach, and felt his heart beating like a speeding train.

He wondered why Lenore Schultz would choose to end her life in his garage.

Then it dawned on him. The woman hanging in his garage was not Lenore. She was much younger. She was wearing the shortest mini skirt imaginable, one which made the lifeless form appear to be not much more than a pair of legs.

It was Sandi.

Arnie sat in his car and stared straight ahead like a Buddha for the longest minute of his life. He hit the remote to close the garage door, got out of his car, and walked to the back to open the trunk. He picked up a cloth normally used as a dust rag, and walked to his front door. He was positive his wife had committed suicide, but he'd seen enough movies and read enough detective novels to know the police would be checking for fingerprints throughout the house. There was the possibility, however remote, that someone staged this to look like a suicide.

He walked into his kitchen determined not to set foot in the garage until his wife's body was removed. Even then, it would be difficult. He was certain he would never be able to open the garage door without seeing Sandi's body hanging there. At least, not this garage. He wanted to cry, but couldn't. The tears just wouldn't come.

Dark anger began to well up inside him. But the anger soon turned to grief. Not only grief for her, but for himself. Why did she always insist on having the last word? Sandi's suicide was her way of saying, "Now that I've fucked up your life as much as I possibly can, I'm outta here. Deal with it."

Trembling, he picked up his phone to call Lieutenant Hogan, and noticed an envelope on the table. It was sealed with his name on it. It was Sandi's handwriting.

He continued to dial, then heard the voice of Hogan's secretary, Rosa Lee.

"It's Arnie Taylor. Will you please put me through to the lieutenant right away?"

"I'm sorry, Mr. Taylor, but Lieutenant Hogan's out for the rest of the week."

"The rest of the week?"

"Yes. His wife's in the hospital. Is there anything I can do for you__?"

Arnie hung up.

He called Hogan at home, only to learn from his daughter, Michelle, that he was with her mother at the hospital. She gave him the phone number and her mother's room number. Arnie dialed, and got right through to Hogan.

"Lieutenant Hogan, this is Arnie Taylor. I just got home and found my wife hanging in the garage. She killed herself, Lieutenant, she"—-

"Calm down, Mr. Taylor. Please. Try to get a hold of yourself. Have you called the police?"

"Who do you think I'm talking to now, you idiot? You ARE the police."

"Okay, Arnie. I'll contact the authorities immediately. A team of officers will be there within ten minutes or so. I'll also come out, but it will take me thirty to forty minutes to get to Granada Hills from here. Please give me your address—all I remember is that it's on Hayvenhurst."

Arnie gave him the address.

"Oh, and please don't touch anything. Our people will be checking for fingerprints . . . "

Arnie hung up.

He glanced at the kitchen clock. It was 5:07. He picked up the envelope, then set it down again. His mind was on overdrive:

Why did Sandi drive her mother's car rather than her Mustang?

Why did she choose to wear such a sexy skirt? No one cares about looking at a dead woman's legs.

Someone needs to contact Hans and Lenore and give them the news about their precious daughter. Someone else. Maybe the lieutenant can visit them a little later this evening. No way I'm going to tell them.

Why did she become involved with gangsters? All she had to do was leave me, file for divorce, then screw around all she wanted. She could have become a porn star for all I care.

Why am I so depressed and heartbroken about this, but not shedding a single tear? Because she's my wife, we had some great times early on, and there's not a reason in the world her life should have ended this way. I'm not crying because I can't. And I'm not sure I ever will. Not over Sandi. Not after all she's done, all the people who've died because of her.

As Arnie realized her suicide marked the sixth death since the beginning of the client murders, he heard noises coming from the front of the house. The police had arrived. Car doors slammed, the doorbell rang. He looked at the clock. It was 5:15 p.m. on the nose. Exactly eight minutes after he hung up on Lieutenant Hogan. Not bad.

When he opened the front door, Sergeant Mike Smith introduced himself, then did a one eighty and pointed to three more officers, all standing on the front lawn. Sergeant Smith told him the names of each of them, but Arnie couldn't remember a single name when he stopped. Sergeant Smith, Mike Smith, that's the only name he knew or cared about.

Arnie told the sergeant that Lieutenant Hogan would join them shortly. "Yes, I know," replied Sergeant Smith. "We spoke for several minutes on the radios while on our way here."

Arnie told the police officers they couldn't get into the garage from the house. He then walked to his car, grabbed the remote, opened the garage door, and headed back toward the lawn. He didn't want to look into the garage.

"There's a light switch in the far corner, left side," he hollered. "After you guys take a quick look, can we close the garage door so the neighbors won't be able to see what's going on?"

Just as he asked the question, a third police car drove up. It was accompanied by a mobile laboratory. Within a couple of minutes, the garage was filled with three of the six cops, a deputy coroner, a fingerprint man, and a photographer. The lab contained additional lighting, which was needed in the garage. After it was in place, the garage door was closed.

Sergeant Smith followed Arnie into the house. "I need to get a statement, Mr. Taylor."

"There's really not much to say, Sergeant. I arrived home sometime around five, maybe a few minutes after. I opened the garage door with my remote, and there she was, my wife hanging in the middle of the area on the left side where I always park my car. I could tell she was dead, so I closed the garage door and went into the house and called Lieutenant Hogan. I saw that she left me a note, which I haven't read. I was careful not to touch anything, using a dust rag instead. Then, eight minutes later, you showed up. That's it."

"Where were you this afternoon, Mr. Taylor, prior to coming home?"

"I spent the afternoon at the beach. If you're asking if I was with anyone, or saw anyone, the answer is no. I was alone all afternoon."

"You're convinced that your wife killed herself? It does look that way, but it's possible someone killed her and made it look like a suicide. That's why I'm asking you questions about your activities earlier today, and why we brought a fingerprint man along. We really don't know for sure how she died, and probably won't know for another day or so."

"And I'm a suspect?" asked Arnie, his tone one of exasperation.

"Let's just say the entire matter of her death will be investigated. Until we've concluded our research and know for sure how she died, we cannot reach any definite conclusions."

Arnie, disgusted at Sergeant Smith's question since it was obvious to him Sandi committed suicide, turned his back on Smith and started to walk to the back of the house. But he turned and walked toward the front window. There was more commotion outside. He moved the curtain slightly and took a peek. The press had arrived. It looked like three or four of them, including a woman photographer. A van with the letters KTTV turned the corner. It slowed and pulled in behind one of the vehicles the press had come in. Neighbors were now congregating on the sidewalk across the street.

Sergeant Smith stood in the open doorway watching the show, then stepped back into the house, and looked at Arnie.

"You don't have to worry about any news footage of the body, Mr. Taylor. No one but the police will be admitted to the garage and, when they remove her remains, she will be on a stretcher, fully covered."

Arnie was grateful for that. It took some of the sting out of the sergeant's questions concerning his whereabouts that afternoon.

He excused himself, saying that he was going to his bedroom at the end of the hallway to make a phone call. He dialed his mother's number.

When she answered, his first words were, "Are you having a drink?"

Gladys laughed. "Of course, it's past five o'clock. Ray and I are sipping our Vodka."

"Mother," he said, "you need to have a cocktail in your hand, and you need to be sitting down."

"Oh, God. What's happened now?"

He spent five minutes giving her the complete picture, from the moment he noticed Lenore Schultz's car to the present.

"In a way, I'm not surprised, at least not that she's dead," she said. "I've felt all along she would either be spending the rest of her life in prison, or someone would kill her to keep her quiet. I guess she decided to take the easy way out."

"You've disliked her for years, so I shouldn't be surprised you don't seem especially sorry. Nor do I blame you."

"Well, I'm not sorry at all. She's treated you like shit since your wedding day. And she's never been very nice to me, or anyone else in our family. Everything was about **her** family. How long has it been since I've been to your house? Three years? Four? Well, now I can come and visit you and feel welcome."

"Mother, I have a favor to ask of you. Would you please call someone for me and tell her what's happened? Tell her I can't talk with her for a day or two, but that I will be back in touch."

"Of course I will. You want me to call Rolene, that gal from the office you took to the Odyssey the other night."

"Yeah, she's the one. I want her to know about this before she sees it on the news, or reads about it in the newspaper, if it's not already too late. Do you have a pencil?"

After he gave her the phone number, his mother told him that some good would come out of this. Now he would have closure, at least as far as Sandi was concerned. She could never hurt him again. He could now get on with life, hopefully, a new, much better life.

Arnie agreed. In fact, he'd already figured that out himself. After he hung up the phone, he lay on his back on his bed and stared at the ceiling for about twenty minutes. He then got up, removed the receiver from the phone, and threw it on the bed. He didn't want to talk to anyone.

When he returned to the living room, Lieutenant Hogan was there. The detective greeted him with a warm handshake and a friendly pat on the back. This, in spite of the fact Arnie had been so rude to him over the phone and hung up on him. Looking into Hogan's eyes tonight, Arnie gained a new perspective on the man he had come to denigrate. Those sad, brown eyes reflected someone who had known suffering for a long time. He was sure it was personal suffering, not the kind that comes with a cop's job. A job that entails putting your life on the line every day, dealing with the worst, the lowest dregs of our so-called civilized society on a daily basis. People like Frankie Crosetti.

The lieutenant was clearly in charge of the investigation at the house. He told Arnie the fingerprint guy had finished in the kitchen and garage, and saw no point in going over the rest of the house. The deputy coroner stated that Sandi Taylor's death appeared to be a suicide, but he couldn't say for sure until additional tests were run at the lab.

Hogan told Arnie he wanted to know what was in the note Sandi left on the kitchen table. It might shed some light on the killings. Arnie promised he would read it after everyone was gone, except the lieutenant. He wasn't sure how he was going to react. He didn't want a bunch of strangers around, especially when they were there on official business and had no real interest in him as a human being with feelings.

Arnie was anxious that the police wrap up as soon as possible, and remove Sandi's body. He was advised that the lieutenant would tell the press that, while the cause of Sandi Taylor's death appeared to be suicide by hanging, the matter was under investigation and would not be determined for a couple of days. He would also tell them that, "despite deep divisions" Arnie was greatly saddened and in a state of shock."

After the police and lab technicians departed, Arnie was ready to read the note from Sandi. Her beautiful handwriting unmistakable, there was no question she had written it herself. He read it twice, then handed it to Lieutenant Hogan without comment. Hogan looked it over, then told Arnie he would return it in a day or two after making copies.

When he left the house, Hogan escorted him to his car to help keep the press at bay. There were now at least a dozen newsmen milling about on the driveway and the lawn. including a young woman, bright lights on her face, giving updates. "Live, from outside Arnold Taylor's home in Granada Hills . . . "

Arnie had grabbed several books to take with him, some clothes and toilet articles, his checkbook, other miscellaneous items. He needed to call the guy across the street, Bart Morrison, and ask him to keep an eye on his place. He might be gone as long as a week, hopefully somewhere along the coast. Perhaps Santa Barbara, or Monterey.

He would be spending tonight at a hotel somewhere; he wasn't sure where. He was certain it would not be at the Panorama City Holiday Inn. He needed to be alone, away from everybody, including his mother. He didn't want to talk to anyone he knew.

Arnie

There are some matters I would like to clear up before I check out. First, of course I knew Frankie Crosetti was a gangster and that Dan Turner was not his real name. I knew he was a mafioso the first minute I laid eyes on him at the bar. But I got sexually involved with him because we made a deal. He wanted my body, and I wanted him to kill someone. The problem was, he said it would be at least six months before he was ready to do his part because he was on another job that was more important. He said the deal was off unless we had sex at least three times a week. I must confess, I enjoyed it. A lot. I'm not by nature monogamous. I like variety. But by now you've probably figured that out. Anyway, it wasn't until the third murder that I realized he was the one killing your clients. I made a tough decision. I decided that four or five dead clients of yours were worth the one man I wanted dead. So I went along. He said it was nothing personal about you. It all had to do with some guy named Mike. He said you knew Mike and they were using you to get to him because they were sure he would show up to help you out. He was right. Mike did show up, but now Frankie is dead and Mike is alive. I obviously hired the wrong man. The man I wanted dead is the biggest dumb-shit scumbag I've ever known. That lying, two-timing, pompous asshole, Bill Kaiser. If I had been screwing Mike instead of Frankie, Big Shit Kaiser would be dead by now and I would have a reason to stay alive. Anyway, that's my story. And by the way, Fuck You.

Sandi

Chapter 30

March 20, Thursday, 8:20 p.m., Granada Hills

Lieutenant Hogan was on his way back to the hospital when he remembered he needed to call George Porter. While on his way to Granada Hills he had called Officer Porter at his office in Van Nuys. He told George about Sandi, and asked if he would go over to the Schultzes and give Hans and Lenore the bad news. Porter was a good choice because they knew him—he had been there when Sandi was interviewed. He hated to ask him to do it, but felt that it was more important that he be at Arnie's home in Granada Hills, where he might learn something, especially if the troublesome bitch left a note.

Before he picked up his receiver, however, Porter called him.

"Lieutenant Hogan, it's George."

"Yes, George, I'm sure you didn't exactly have a pleasant visit but—

"Listen Lieutenant. Mr. and Mrs. Schultz are dead. They've been shot."

Frank Hogan jerked his head backward, as if he'd just been rear-ended. He was silent for a moment, then cleared his throat. Officer Porter was shouting into the phone.

"Did you hear me, Lieutenant?"

"Yes, I heard you. I was on my way back to the hospital, but now I'll turn around and head out there. It might take twenty minutes or so to get there. While I'm driving, tell me what the scene was when you arrived."

"Okay," Porter said, "but first you should know that there are five squad cars here, a mobile lab, and the press, including several TV stations."

"Why didn't you call me earlier, George. I would have rushed right over."

"I tried, but all I got was a busy signal every time I dialed Arnie's number."

"That's strange," said the lieutenant. "Anyway, what did you find when you arrived?"

"It was maybe ten minutes after seven, the house was totally dark, Sandi's car was parked on the street and the garage door was wide open. There was a Cadillac parked on the right side, the other side empty."

"So you went to the front door, knocked, rang the doorbell, then what?"

"Yeah, I did all that and then I went and sat in my car for twenty minutes thinking that maybe they had run to the store or something. You know, with the garage door open, it appeared they had left in a hurry and would be right back."

"So, how did you finally get into the house?"

"I went to the houses on both sides, but no one was home at either place, both houses dark. Then I walked across the street and a Mrs. Barrett came to the door. I asked if she knew the Schultzes. She said she knew them very well. After I showed her my ID, and asked if she had a key to their house, she said she did and went and got it for me. I then asked her to accompany me across the street to go inside with me. She did, and after we turned on the entry way and living room lights, we walked through the living room and dining room, and there were two bodies on the floor lying in a pool of blood in the kitchen. It appears he was shot in the back while walking into the kitchen. She was shot while standing in front of the sink. She was shot in the back of the head and above her right ear. He was shot in the back and in the back of the head."

"Any forcible entry noted?

"Negative."

"Has the rest of the house been checked?"

"Yes. It appears the culprit was looking for something, or someone, probably Sandi. The closet doors in every room in the house were wide open."

"That's interesting," said the lieutenant. "I'm sure you're right, the gunman was looking for Sandi. I'll be there as soon as I can."

"That's interesting. Very interesting."

Lieutenant Hogan was now talking to himself.

Chapter 31

March 20, Encino, 8:55 p.m.

Arnie Taylor walked into the Hilton Hotel on Ventura Boulevard near Sepulveda, a short distance from the Hollywood Hills. The lobby was empty except for a red-haired, twenty-something receptionist behind the check-in counter, watching television. Her head was turned away, her eyes and ears focused on a late-breaking news story on KTLA.

Arnie glanced up at the TV. A well-known newsman from Channel 5 stood in someone's front yard giving an update.

"This makes three deaths reported in the past three and a half hours, all of them related to the Bear Republic murders. Sandi Taylor, an apparent suicide, discovered by her estranged husband hanging in the garage late this afternoon. And now, Mrs. Taylor's parents, Hans and Lenore Schultz, whose bodies were discovered by police around 7:30 tonight. They had been murdered in what appears to be a gangland execution. Both were shot in their kitchen in an upper-middle class neighborhood in Chatsworth.

"When you add the dead policyholders and Bear Republic agent Whit Payne, the body count is up to eight. This is, without doubt, the most bizarre series of murders I've ever heard of, let alone reported.

"This is Bill Ellis reporting live from Chatsworth. Back to you, Stan."

"Wow, can you believe that?" said the redhead as she handed a registration form to Arnie. "Sorry you had to wait. It's just that, well I can't believe what's going on out there in Granada Hills, and now Chatsworth."

Arnie did not reply. After filling in the form, he handed it back to her.

"I'd like a room for tonight, maybe tomorrow night, too, I'm not sure yet. Preferably on one of the upper floors, a corner room, if one's available."

"We're pretty full tonight, but I think we still have something left."

She looked at the completed form, paused for a moment, then looked up at him, her light-blue eyes wide open, along with her mouth, in disbelief.

"Yes," he said. "It's me. The same Arnold Taylor. I needed to get out of my house tonight."

"I am so sorry, Mr. Taylor. "I've been following this story from the very beginning, and, well, I just can't tell you how badly I feel."

He waited for her to give him directions and his room key, but she stood there, staring at him.

"My room key?" he said.

"Oh, I'm sorry. Room 646, sixth floor, turn left when you get off the elevator, and go to the end of the hall. The room is on the right."

"Thanks," he said.

"Is there anything I can do for you, Mr. Taylor? You know, like send something to eat or drink up to your room? I'll see if I can make it complimentary. My father's the general manager."

"Thanks," said Arnie, "but that won't be necessary."

He turned and walked away, stopped midway to the elevator, and turned around.

"There is something you can do for me. In fact, two things. You can direct me to the bar, and, you can promise me you won't tell anybody I'm here. Please . . . before you know it, there'll be enough reporters in this lobby to fill Dodger Stadium."

"You can take my word for it. I won't tell a soul. You have enough problems without anyone bothering you here. The bar is around the corner to your right."

Fifteen minutes later, after throwing his suitcase on the bed, and rinsing his face with cold water, Arnie returned to the ground floor and walked through the lobby into the cocktail lounge.

The bar itself was full, with most of the tables occupied. He finally spotted an open table in the back corner. Alone in a dark corner is exactly where he wanted to be. With a couple of stiff drinks to help tranquilize the evening's events.

Sandi's suicide had all but drained every ounce of energy he possessed, so he didn't have much left for his in-laws. The truth was, he felt worse about their deaths than he did Sandi's. Much worse. Sandi brought all her problems on herself. Her mother and father were nothing more than innocent bystanders.

Arnie had never been close to Hans or Lenore, nor had he liked them much. There were some real issues between them that could never be fixed. But that was not the point. They were good people—at times, even kind and generous. They just didn't see the world through the same lens he did. Sandi's parents came from a different culture, a different set of prejudices, one that placed more emphasis on the material side of life, less on the cerebral. Arnie believed they were anti-intellectual to a fault. But they had lived good, honorable lives and did their best to raise a respectable daughter. Given the reality that the Donna Reid they loved and nurtured metamorphosed into Lucretia Borgia, their life ended in a tragedy Shakespearean in scope.

It was clear now that when he discovered Sandi in the garage, his night had only begun. He thought about that long night twenty years ago when his father shot his mother four times on the street below the second-story bedroom. Until now, that had been the longest night of his life, a grisly episode that still recurred in nightmares from time to time.

The cocktail waitress appeared, stood in front of him and stared, her eyebrows tilted upward, waiting for him to order. One of his pet peeves was food or drink servers who greeted him with sign language rather than a few friendly words. So he just stared back. Finally, she forced a smile and spoke. "Are you going to have a drink, Mister?" Her tone was impatient, her voice louder than necessary even given the noise all around them. Arnie replied with a question of his own.

"Well, hello there. Are you having a nice evening? I'll bet you're making a fortune tonight. Who are all these people anyway?"

She smiled. "I'm sorry, we're short of help tonight, and some of the men in here seem to think it's cool to behave like Jack Nicholson. That guy over there in the gray suit—she nodded her head in his direction—just called me a dumb-ass broad because I got his drink mixed up with someone else's. Earlier this evening some turd-head grabbed my left boob when I leaned over to set his drink down. I'm sure he was disappointed. Anyway, I'm the only waitress working tonight, and there are more than thirty people in this room, half of them drunk. The other half, crazy.

"Now what's your other question? Oh yeah, who are all these people. EDS has been holding a regional meeting in our hotel since Monday. Tomorrow, they adjourn at noon, thank God. I thought computer nerds were like engineers and accountants. Ya know, quiet, serious types. Well, not these guys. They act like a bunch of horny assholes who got out of the Big House this morning. Let's face it, any guy who makes a pass at me is one sorry, hard-up dude, ain't he?"

She burst out laughing, the kind of laugh that would make anyone smile. Her whole body shook, and the noise of her laughter would have boomeranged from one end of the room to the other were it not for all the noise.

"I'm sorry to hear that," said Arnie. "Now I understand why you seem so hassled. By the way, what's your name?"

"Celeste. I tell everyone 'I'm the Best, call me Celeste', but I'm sure everyone else thinks, 'Poor Celeste, if only she were Blessed.'"

The laugh was back.

"I'll have two gin and tonics, each with a twist of lime. Bombay Sapphire. Both of them doubles."

She frowned. "I hope you're staying at our hotel tonight?"

"Yes, I am, thanks for being thoughtful."

As Celeste walked away, Arnie decided she was probably in her midfifties, more than likely self-supporting. He noticed she was not wearing a wedding ring. She was not young and pretty, like so many cocktail waitresses, but she had a personality that rivaled Joan Rivers. He'd come in here anytime for a drink, just to hear her laugh.

Arnie was determined to do some serious thinking over the next hour or two, along with some serious drinking. His encounter with the waitress had already been a wake-up call. The 'serious thinking' part of his plan had begun.

The poor woman was having a bad night. So was he. Everything in life is relevant—her problems were as real to her as his problems were to him. There was never a good reason to be rude to anyone, since we can never know what the other person's life has been like, or what they're having to endure at the moment.

Life was a bitch and then you die. Arnie knew that by the time he was twelve, but he'd just proved to himself he hadn't yet learned to stop judging others. What was that verse at the beginning of the seventh chapter of Matthew that he liked so much? *Judge not, that ye be not judged*. Well, it was time he started living it.

Celeste was back in five minutes, set his two doubles on the table, and told him the noise level in the lounge was a whole lot different ten or fifteen minutes before he came in tonight.

"See that bald-headed fat guy over there who looks like a wrestler?"

She pointed at one of the tables about halfway across the room. "Well, he stood up and shouted for everyone to shut up, the bartender was turning up the sound level on the television for a special news report. It seems there've been two more murders in that crazy insurance company scandal."

"Really?" asked Arnie.

'Yeah, really," said Celeste. "I suppose you already know the insurance agent—I can't think of his name—came home this afternoon and found his slutty wife hanging inside the garage. Couldn't have happened to a nicer gal. Anyway, now they've discovered that the whore's mother and father were murdered. I guess about the same time the daughter did herself in."

Arnie did his best to fake a look of surprise, as though this was all news to him. "I'd like to ask you a question about this case," he said.

"Go right ahead," said Celeste. "I'm something of an expert by now."

"How's that?" he asked.

"Well, for more than a week now, every couple, every party who comes in here, that's all they're talking about. Frankly, I'm getting sick of hearing about it, but I guess that's better than being one of the eight dead people.

"God, I'm glad I don't do business with those nuts at Bear Republic."

"Here's my question," said Arnie. "Why would someone order the assassination of innocent people just to get at the agent? There might be a larger purpose in mind, like getting this underworld character Slovak to come out of hiding, but why would they kill four innocent people?"

"You're missing the point, Honey" she said. "You see, those folks you describe as innocent are really not innocent at all in the minds of the gangsters."

"But they ARE innocent," he said. "The police have done a thorough search. None of them were drug dealers, pimps, racketeers, or anything like that. And they didn't even know each other. Their only common link was the agent."

"You're still not seeing the big picture, Sweetheart" she said. "Each one of those four victims pissed someone off real bad, so, as a means of getting to Slovak, and probably the agent, too, they were the ones chosen to be executed. Someone in high places didn't like them, for whatever reason. In fact, I'm convinced the big cheese who ordered the killings hated all four of those poor victims. That's why they're dead. Remember, the police say these were not random murders of people who happened to be at the wrong place at the wrong time. They were carefully singled out. Anyway, that's my take on this horrible mess. And don't forget, Sweetheart, I'm an expert."

"Is that what others are saying about the reasons for the murders?"

"Hey, I draw my own conclusions. I've heard everything from piss-ant bullshit, like the agent is the mastermind of all this—Arnold Taylor, that's his name — to Mike Slovak, to morons in the LAPD."

"Some people think Arnold Taylor is behind all the killings?"

"You betcha. See that guy over there?" She pointed to a bearded man in a red checkered shirt several tables away.

"That guy—I call him numb-nuts—says Taylor got the shooting gene from his father, only the old man at least had the guts to do his own shooting. His son, a coward and a real loser, has others do his shooting for him."

Arnie managed a half-smile. "Your take on all this makes a lot of sense. Thanks. I think I understand what's going on much better now."

Celeste left to take some more drink orders. Arnie had an idea a waitress in a noisy bar might have just made more sense about the reason behind the killings than he'd heard since this ugly episode started. He would give a lot of thought, over the next couple of days, to what she had said. But first, he needed to down a couple of gin and tonics and reflect on the sad ending of the lives of Hans and Lenore Schultz. And his wife.

At 10:35, Celeste dropped by his table and asked if he wanted another gin and tonic. He said no. It was time to ride the elevator upstairs to his room. He was exhausted.

Chapter 32

March 21, Friday, 9:30 am, Van Nuys City Hall

Never much of a reader of fiction, Lieutenant Frank Hogan did enjoy Dickens *A Tale Of Two Cities*. He sat in his office on his comfortable high-back chair and ruminated over the lines at the beginning, "It was the best of times, it was the worst of times." For him, these were the worst of times.

First, there was the crisis at home. Daughter Michelle had skipped town sometime Thursday afternoon, no doubt to return to San Diego with that boyfriend of hers who had birdseed for brains. Hogan's wife would not be released from Glendale Adventist until Monday, so he was alone again, with no help from anyone when it came to babysitting Gail.

Then, there was the fact that the murders surrounding the late Frankie Crosetti were not over. Crosetti's life was over, but the killings continued. Sandi Taylor took her own life, but Hogan was positive she would have been murdered, along with her parents, had she not left their Chatsworth home Thursday afternoon. That odd twist put Sandi's fate in her own hands, saving someone the trouble. He wondered if she knew someone was coming after her, and that's why she got the hell out of her parents' house.

In one way, however, it was 'the best of times.' The lieutenant was sure he knew the identity of the man who had shot Hans and Lenore Schultz. He just needed to tidy up a couple of details before taking action.

There was a knock on the door. Officer Ricki Wright opened it and entered the office. She sat down, and looked at the boss with sorrowful eyes.

"Thanks, Ricki, for being prompt. We're about to have a conversation during which I will reveal to you the identity of yesterday's killer. And a big surprise comes with the naming of that person."

Ricki frowned. "You're serious, aren't you?" she said.

"Yes," he said. "dead serious. No pun intended."

"By the way, I apologize for not contacting you last night after Arnie called to tell me his wife had killed herself. So much was going on, between the scene in Granada Hill, and my wife sobering up for an early release date, I—"

"No need to explain, Lieutenant. You knew full well I couldn't go out there anyway. Not with Arnie inside, and TV cameras in front of the house. My mother told me to turn on the TV. I was propped up in bed eating potato chips and nursing a Coors."

"Anyway," he continued, "I was preoccupied with calling Detective Porter to have him go to the Schultz home to give Sandi's parents the bad news about their daughter. As you know, his trip was eventful. They were dead, too."

Hogan's secretary, Rosa Lee, opened the door to his office and peeked her head in.

"Mr. Taylor's on the phone. Do you want to take the call?"

"Sure, I'll talk to him."

Hogan raised his eyebrows at Ricki and picked up the telephone receiver. "Mr. Taylor, how are you doing this morning?"

"I'm okay, all things considered. I'm calling to let you know I'm staying at the Encino Hilton until tomorrow around noon. Then I'll be staying with my mother, probably until Monday, after which, I'm going up the coast for five or six days."

"Really? I figured you went straight to your mother's last night when you left your house."

Arnie cleared his throat. "No, I needed to be alone for a while. The reason I'm calling is, first, I want you to know how to reach me if you feel it's necessary. You already have my mother's number. When I decide where I'm going Monday morning, I'll let you know."

"That's very thoughtful of you."

"There's one more thing, Lieutenant. I don't want anybody else to know where I am during the next several days. Only you, my mother, and one other person will know how to reach me."

"I get it. Michael Wong being the third person."

There was a brief moment of silence.

"No, it's not Michael. It's a female. Let's just leave it at that."

Hogan's face lit up. He tossed Ricki a broad smile, then mouthed, "a woman".

"One more thing," said Arnie. "Is there any way I can be of assistance to you in your investigation before I leave town on Monday?"

"Only if you know someone who drives a '75 yellow Corvette," said the lieutenant. He was half-kidding, half-serious.

"I don't know anyone personally," said Arnie. "Why do you ask?"

"Because two different individuals spotted one around the corner from your in-laws' house last night. It was parked there for fifteen or twenty minutes, about the same time we think Hans and Lenore were shot to death. On the street which runs parallel to the Schultz residence."

"I've only seen one yellow '75 Corvette," said Arnie. "A real beauty. I couldn't stop staring at it. It was parked a couple of blocks from your office at the city hall on"—he hesitated a minute—"Sylvan. Yeah, Sylvan."

Lieutenant Hogan sat up straight in his chair.

"Really? Arnie, this is very important. Precisely when and where did you see this vehicle?"

"The last time I was in your office, Lieutenant, Monday morning. It was parked two, maybe two and a half blocks from the office. On Sylvan, just west of Van Nuys Boulevard. It was parked there when I arrived for our appointment Monday morning, and it was still there when I left about an hour later. The parking lot was full, evidently because something big was going on either in the city hall, or somewhere nearby. So I had to drive that far from your office to find a parking space."

"Thanks, Arnie. You have no idea how helpful you've been. I'll be back in touch later today."

Lieutenant Hogan hung up the phone.

"Ricki, will you please give me an hour or so? Then, I'll explain what's going on around here this morning. By then, I'll have some updated information."

"Of course. By the way, I have some interesting news myself."

"Can you give me a Reader Digest version?" asked the lieutenant.

Ricki got up, walked to the edge of Lieutenant Hogan's desk and dropped a brown eight by eleven envelope stuffed with material.

"For your perusal. Xerox copies of Arnie's personnel file. I picked it up from Rolene at her house last night. Old *LA Times* photos of a young Arnie, his mother, father and brother. And four photos of Mike Slovak, along with details of his relationship with the Taylors."

"Well, I'll be a son of a bitch," said Hogan.

"Oh," added Ricki, "and the last time Rolene had looked through this file, several years ago, none of this information was there."

As she was leaving, Officer Wright stopped at the door and turned to look back at Hogan. She tossed him a knowing smile.

"Rolene Ward," she said.

"Excuse me?" said the lieutenant as he looked up.

"Rolene Ward. She's the woman who knows where Arnie is. Betcha a hundred dollars."

Chapter 33

Friday, 11:25 am, Van Nuys City Hall

Almost two hours later, Ricki was back in Lieutenant Hogan's office. She noticed something smug about him. An air of confidence, even cockiness, she had never seen before.

He stretched his neck upward, then from one side to the other, took a puff on a cigar so big it would make Groucho Marx envious, and began to speak.

"If I were to tell you we now know the identity of the mafioso in our midst, and he was one of the original three men assigned to the Arnold Taylor insurance case, which one would be your first guess?"

"Actually, Lieutenant, that's not a tough question when narrowed down to those three officers. It's Officer Gary Merrill."

"How did you arrive at that conclusion?"

"That's easy. During our first meeting, you told us to be careful and not say a word to anyone about this case because there was a mafia informer in the department, in homicide. You'd hardly finished when Gary Merrill said, 'How do you know that?' Remember? He seemed kinda edgy about it. More than the others."

"Anything else?"

"Yes," she said, "but nothing that specific. Merrill's a little bit too slick for my taste. That guy's as smooth as goose grease. I wouldn't want him on my blind side, that's for damn sure."

Hogan smiled, took another puff of his cigar, exhaled, and stared for a moment at the clock on the wall behind Ricki.

"Well, I hate to disappointment you, but you're dead wrong. The informer in our midst is none other than Officer George Porter. The man I know the best, of any of you. The man I've known the longest. The man I've trusted the most."

Ricki Wright barely managed to restrain from laughing.

"And the man the other two, Officers Merrill and Bryant, are jealous of because they think you favor Porter. He's the fair-haired boy in their eyes. They're probably jealous that he has his own harem, too."

Hogan ignored the comment.

"My discovery of George Porter's subterfuge started a little more than twenty-four hours ago, when he reported to the two of us on his interview with Bill Kaiser."

"Yes," said Ricki. "I remember. His report contradicted everything we had heard previously."

"Exactly. And as I said at the time, it made no sense at all."

Hogan was now standing, walking around the room, puffing on his cigar, glancing at the clock from time to time while sharing his thoughts with Ricki.

"And another thing," he said. "When we were interviewing Amalfitano in his office Monday afternoon, Porter actually asked that stuffy, overbearing son of a bitch if it was okay for us to ask him some questions. Like we need his permission?"

Hogan then mumbled, "He must think I'm a fuck'n moron. Sorry, Ricki."

"Hey, don't be sorry. I've actually heard the word before. Besides, if you ask me, Porter's the fuck'n moron."

"But the shit really hit the fan, Ricki, when Porter phoned me in my car to tell me about the murders of Hans and Lenore Schultz.

"The first thing that struck me was his voice. It was much louder than usual. He seemed overly excited. We've worked a lot of cases together, over the years, some of them brutal, like the Schultz murders. In the past his manner was more detached, more professional. Last night, he was unusually talkative, but he wasn't saying anything. His report made about as much sense as his account of his meeting with Kaiser."

"Of course, none of this proves that Porter is the killer," said Ricki.

"Certainly not enough to convict him in a court of law."

In a reversal of roles, Officer Wright was now walking while talking, gazing out the window, then looking back at Lieutenant Hogan.

"You're right, Ricki," he said. "None of this proves Porter's our man. But the loopholes, the dangling participles, as I prefer to call them, have now been closed.

"For starters, I obtained Mrs. Barrett's phone number before I left the scene around midnight. She's the old lady across the street who unlocked the door so the two of them could enter the house. Her version of what happened when she and Porter entered the Schultz residence was a direct contradiction of what he told me."

Ricki stood still, her arms folded at chest level, shaking her head in disbelief.

The lieutenant continued. "I called Rolene Ward early this morning, about 5:30, and asked her for Bill Kaiser's phone number. I got her number from the phone directory, but Kaiser wasn't listed. I told her it was extremely important. She understood. She said she'd stayed up half the night watching the news. You're right about her. She's very nice."

Ricki sat down and nodded. "I have a sneaky feeling her interest in this case goes beyond everyone else in the Bear Republic office. I think she and Arnie are going to end up together."

The lieutenant gave her a quick smile, then continued.

"Anyway, I called Kaiser and arranged to meet him for breakfast at International House of Pancakes on Ventura Boulevard. He told me what he'd told Porter, but it's a totally different story. He told Porter he thinks Amalfitano is a gangster, and that he and the boss can't stand one another. He's also very nice, in spite of his eccentricities."

Ricki threw up her hands. "Okay, I'm convinced. Porter's the informer, also the killer. So what do we do now?"

"Oh, but you haven't heard the best part of all. Like dessert, I've saved it for last," said Hogan.

"Two on-lookers last night, noticed a 1975 yellow Corvette, parked on the street in front of a house that backs up behind the Schultzes. It remained there for about twenty minutes or so, sometime between three and four o' clock. One of them, a twenty-something female, saw a man get out of the car and walk around the corner. 'A tall, very handsome man,' according to this witness."

"You were talking about a Corvette with Arnie when he called here earlier this morning," said Ricki.

"Yes, I was. Arnie told me he'd seen one parked a couple of blocks away on Sylvan when he was in here Monday. It's the only yellow '75 Corvette he's seen this year. It's not like we're talking about a Ford Maverick or a Chevy Nova, or any vehicle normal folks drive. They're everywhere."

"Why would anyone committing a capital crime drive around in a show-piece like that, one that people would notice and remember?" asked Ricki.

"Arrogance, I suppose," said the Lieutenant.

"Anyway, later this morning after you left my office, I spoke with

Deputy Chief Flemming, who happens to be here in the building today, and he supervised a search for an automobile fitting that description within a five-block radius in every direction."

"And they found it?" shouted Ricki,

"Your goddamn cow-fart'n betcha, they did. But this time it was on Erwin, a couple of blocks east of our building. Different street, different direction. Deputy Chief Fleming had them break in to the automobile. It's registered to a Timothy Mills, of Hacienda Heights, but on the back floor they found a couple of gun magazines with George Porter address labels, and an *Escapade* magazine, also addressed to Porter."

"My God," said Ricki. "It's almost like he's daring us to discover his identity as the mole by leaving a trail of hints everywhere he goes. What an idiot." She shook her head in disbelief.

"I'm waiting for word that Porter's left the building and is on his way to his car to go to lunch. There are at least a dozen cops in civies between our office and the yellow Corvette. All of them here from downtown for a meeting with Fleming. Porter won't recognize a single one of them."

"While we wait," said Ricki, "I have a question about Sandi driving her mother's car instead of her own car, the Mustang. Do you suppose she saw Porter walk up to the front door, and took advantage of her parents' preoccupation with the visitor to get the hell out of the house before they realized it?"

"That's possible, but I doubt it. I think Sandi believed someone was watching the house, and if she drove out of the garage in her mother's car, he would assume Mrs. Schultz was driving it. A normal assumption. I'm convinced Porter's the murderer, and he thought Sandi was there because her car was parked in front, she was the one he was really after. She's the one who had to be silenced. She knew too much. Her parents were collateral damage.

"We'll probably never know the answers to some of these questions, will we?" asked Ricki.

The phone rang. It was the Deputy Chief of Police for the city of Los Angeles. Officer Porter had just left the building. He was heading in the direction of the Corvette on Erwin.

Chapter 34

Friday, 11:55 am, Van Nuys

Deputy Chief Fleming talked so fast, Lieutenant Hogan had trouble catching every word.

"As far as we know, Lieutenant, Porter is unarmed. He left his .38 in his desk drawer. If it turns out he is armed, our men are under strict orders not to shoot unless absolutely necessary. It's imperative we take him alive. He has enough information, I suspect, to wrap up this whole case."

"How are your men going to approach him?" asked Hogan.

"As soon as he unlocks the car door, gets in, and turns on the engine, two police officers are suddenly going to appear on both sides of the Corvette, two on each side by the front door windows, and two behind the vehicle. Total of six. They will appear out of nowhere. There are also officers— "Gotta go, Frank. Sit tight," said the deputy chief.

George Porter, a happy man, walked east on Erwin to his car. A beautiful spring day in the Valley, probably 75 degrees, maybe warmer. Only a short drive from here to the back of Rossi's Ristorante, he would be picking up a paper bag with ten grand in it for the job he carried out late Thursday afternoon in Chatsworth. The two brothers, Rocky and Vince Crosetti, were there waiting for him. There would be slaps on the back, toasts over the three dead potential witnesses—Chivas Regal, no doubt—and pizza right out of the oven from the restaurant facing Ventura Boulevard which served as a front for the gang.

And tonight, he had date with Angela Rapolla, a beauty with twin peaks more scenic than those Sophia Loren ever dreamed of, or, for that matter, cleavage that would make Carol Doda blush. He got turned on just thinking about it. He had two tickets for tonight to see Neil Diamond at the Coconut Grove.

Porter approached his prized vehicle singing in a soft baritone voice a classic from years long gone by—*You are my sunshine, my only sunshine, . . .*

He got into his favorite toy, a brand-new yellow Corvette purchased with funds from another job he'd done for the Crosetti's, put the key in the ignition, and started to pull out of his parking place. Suddenly, there was a knocking noise accompanied by two plainclothes police officers flashing their badges through his left front window, and two more doing the same thing on the far side front window.

Porter didn't hesitate for a millisecond. He pulled out of the parking place, floored the gas pedal, and headed east on Erwin as fast as the sports car could accelerate. Then he noticed a blockade on the corner of Kester and Erwin. Two police cars, a narrow opening between them of maybe four or five feet, designed to stop any pass-through traffic, He drove through the blockade at the center point. The impact of the speeding Corvette making way through a narrow opening between two late-model Fords left an opening large enough to drive a Sherman tank through. While negotiating his way through the blockade, Porter heard dozens of gunshots, but he held his head down and kept going at close to eighty miles an hour until the noise of the shots disappeared, along with the cops trying to follow him.

About an hour and a half later, the Corvette turned off of Ventura Boulevard onto a driveway that led to the back of Rossi's Ristorante. The driver wiped the sweat from his face with a handkerchief, straightened his tie and got out of the car.

While he stood there for a moment glancing at his shiny new Corvette, now ridden with bullet holes, Vincent Crosetti watched him through the open back door.

"Your fancy car is no more. It looks like it's been through a war zone," said Crosetti.

"It has," said Porter, as he walked into the back room.

"You don't have to tell us about it," said Crosetti. "We already know. 'Underworld figure who'd infiltrated the LAPD, and alleged killer of Sandi Taylor's parents, escapes from police,' so says the TV and radio and every news outlet in the world."

"I'd like to explain what happened. . ."

"Wait just a minute, George," said Vincent. "Rocky, why don't you go into the restaurant and bring in the pizza we've been keeping warm. I'm hungry."

After Rocky closed the door behind him, Vincent Crosetti said, "Well, George, it looks like you won't be needing the ten grand after all. Truth is, I'd be a hell of a lot happier if you did need it."

George Porter turned as white as Banquo's ghost while Crosetti removed a handgun, complete with silencer, from his inside coat pocket. At point blank range, he fired two shots into George Porter's head.

Chapter 35

Los Angeles Times

Saturday, March 22, 1975

Editorial Page

*Just when we were certain the Los Angeles Police Depart-
ment had reached the height of ineptitude in their handling of the murders of the Bear Republic policyholders,
we discover they are still climbing the seemingly endless
ladder of complete lunacy.*

*Yesterday, they had in their custody, a police detective
they were positive was not only an informant for the
Mafia, but the man who killed Hans and Lenore Schultz,
the unlucky parents of Sandi Taylor. Mrs. Taylor was not
only the wife of Bear Republic agent, Arnold Taylor, but
also an adulteress carrying-on a torrid affair with Frankie
Crosetti while the goon was killing four of her husband's
clients and a colleague at work. Mrs. Taylor's body was
discovered by her husband hanging in the garage of their
home in Granada Hills, late Thursday afternoon. Her
death has now officially been declared a suicide. While
the LAPD already had more than enough evidence to
arrest and book Officer George Porter for the murder of
Mrs. Taylor's parents, the tip of the iceberg was catching
him with the key to the 1975 Corvette which was parked*

around the corner from the Schultz home while the murders were being committed. Sometime between three and four o' clock Thursday afternoon. Not content with merely proving the corrupt officer had the keys to the car, police on the scene, received orders from high-ranking superiors to wait until Porter turned on the engine before making the arrest.

By now, most readers are aware of the rest of the story. Officer George Porter got away in his racy Corvette, and is still at large. There were twenty-three police officers in the area of Irwin and Van Nuys boulevard, all of whom were under orders to apprehend the suspect alive, if possible, dead, if necessary.

This is only the latest incidence of malfeasance on the part of our police department, which, under the late Chief William H. Parker, was widely considered to be one of the finest law-enforcement agencies in the nation.

The problem started when four murders had already been committed before the LAPD learned that all of the victims had the same insurance agent. This crucial information eventually came to their attention not as a result of careful police work, but because of a phone call from an anonymous tipster.

Then, there was the killing of Frankie Crosetti in the parking lot behind a Bob's Big Boy restaurant the morning after the fourth murder of a Bear Republic policyholder. While Crosetti's death was a good thing, he was not killed by the police, but by a rival mobster, Mike Slovak. Slovak has been on the Ten Most Wanted List for twenty-eight years. The lead investigator was having breakfast with Arnold Taylor, the agent of the four victims, while Crosetti sat twenty feet away, and Slovak was in the parking lot waiting for the rival gangster to come out. It's amazing how often events transpire in the presence of our local police without them having a clue what is going on around them.

Finally, there's the suicide of Sandi Taylor and the murder of her mother and father at about the same time late Thursday afternoon at different locations.

Why wasn't Mrs. Taylor already under arrest and in custody? Surely the police had enough evidence to book her. They knew she had information about the murders. The likelihood of her being silenced was real, and that her parents might very well be targets, too, since she probably shared information with them. At the very least, the house in Chatsworth, where Sandi Taylor was staying with her mother and father, should have been under twenty-four-hour surveillance.

In summary, this investigation has been a complete fiasco from the beginning. Not to mention, a major embarrassment to the City of Los Angeles.

It's time for a thorough housecleaning in the LAPD. Start is at the top, and work down.

Chief Walton Walker should tender his resignation immediately, followed by a commission selected by the mayor to determine how to put our local law enforcement back where they belong—at the top of the list of the best police departments in the nation.

Chapter 36

Saturday, March 22, Burbank

Arnie arrived at his mother's house a couple of minutes before two. Earlier that day, she'd told him over the phone she and Ray wanted to take him out to dinner that evening.

The truth was, he was tired of eating in restaurants. Besides, he was afraid he would be recognized. This hadn't been a problem so far. Sandy's picture had appeared in newspapers and on television far more than his. A femme fatale acting out a real-life melodrama, is of far greater interest to the public than an innocent, naive insurance man dumb enough to be married to a disreputable seductress.

But Arnie feared this might have changed. Friday's *LA Times* featured his photograph on the front page, along with Sandi's. This morning's paper displayed the two of them again, this time on page three. While driving from the Hilton to his mother's, he switched radio stations in an attempt to learn the local scuttlebutt concerning the latest outrageous news. After tuning in to KMPC, then KRLA, then, finally KFI, an NBC affiliate, he'd heard enough. All three stations offered nonstop chatter concerning the monstrous events of the past couple of days, with the major emphasis today focused on the gross ineptitude of the LAPD. And with constant references to this morning's scathing editorial in *The Times*.

The first thing Arnie noticed upon entering his mother's house in Burbank was a beautiful bouquet of roses in the center of the dining room table.

"My God, Mother, these flowers are beautiful." He smiled, then added, "Do you have a secret admirer I don't know about?"

"Of course not, Arnie. Ray brought these home from work last night because he knows how worried I am about you. He thought this might cheer me up a bit.

"By the way, I have good news for you," she said "Phyllis and Bob stopped by yesterday on their way to Las Vegas. They left the keys to their beach house in Carpenteria. It's right on the ocean, a half hour south of Santa Barbara."

"That's great," he said. "I'll take it. I'll have more privacy there, and I can still drive up to Santa Barbara to dine at Brophy Brothers on the wharf, my favorite fish restaurant in the whole world."

"You'll also save a small fortune on a hotel, which, by the way, leads me to another question," said Gladys. "How much life insurance do you have on Sandi?"

"$200,000."

"$200,000? Jesus, Arnie, that's a lot of money. Will Bear Republic pay, though, in light of the fact she committed suicide?"

"Yes. The so-called suicide clause stipulates that there's no coverage during the first two years of the contract. After that, it's covered.

"I may have had some time to myself since Thursday night," he said, "but I can't say it's done anything to increase my energy level." He stood and stretched for a minute, then headed back toward the guest room to take a nap.

About quarter to five, Arnie got up from his nap and joined his mother in the living room. Ray was home now, and, in his usual gregarious manner, gave his step-son a warm hug, and announced it was cocktail time.

Arnie's stepfather went into the kitchen to prepare a vodka and Fresca for himself and his wife, a ghastly combination in Arnie's mind. Then, a gin and tonic for him, an appropriate drink for a civilized man.

Gladys sat anxiously in the living room glancing at her watch, with an eye on the front door as well. Her insistence upon taking her son out to dinner this evening was pure fiction. She had a surprise in store for Arnie, one she was certain would lift his spirits. At five o' clock on the nose, the doorbell rang.

"Would you mind answering the door, Arnie? I just remembered something I need to tell Ray."

Arnie opened the door, then shouted, "Oh my God! What a surprise. What are you doing here?"

Rolene smiled, handed him a chicken casserole and said, "Take this in to your mother. I've got a couple of side dishes to bring in."

After Arnie hurried into the kitchen and handed the casserole to his mother, he headed outside to help Rolene with the rest of the meal.

While Arnie and Rolene were outside, Gladys couldn't restrain herself from running into the living room to peek through the curtains at the front window. She saw them hold each other in an affectionate, lengthy embrace which included several kisses back and forth. She also noticed Rolene wiping away tears from her cheeks.

After everything was in order in the kitchen, and Rolene had been handed a vodka tonic, the four of them sat down in the living room to visit.

"I'm confused," said Arnie. "since I didn't even know you two knew each other. When, and how, did you two get together?"

Gladys glanced at Rolene. "You start, then I'll jump in when it seems appropriate."

"It all started Thursday night," said Rolene, "when I learned the repulsive facts. First, about Sandi, then a little later on, her mother and father.

"I never went to bed that night, but just sat in my living room with the television on trying to make sense out of all this violence. At seven o' clock Friday morning, I called Judy Isenberg at home and told her to inform Mr. Amalfitano that I would not be in that day, and, in addition, I would be taking the entire next week off. Whether he counts it against my vacation time, or just treats it as a leave of absence, makes no difference to me."

"Did I hear you right?" asked Arnie. "You're taking all of next week off?"

"Yes, Arnie. I need a break. The murders, along with the subsequent negative environment throughout the office, the impact of all this on you and on your career? It's more than I can handle. They can get a temp, or whatever, but I'm not going in."

"It was Rolene who brought me the flowers, Arnie," said Gladys. "We had a hamburger yesterday at Denny's, and a great visit that lasted most of the afternoon. When I invited her over for dinner tonight, she said she'd only accept the invitation if she could prepare the meal in advance, and bring it over after you were already here, Arnie. She wanted to surprise you."

"Well," said Arnie, "she certainly succeeded."

The party broke up a little after ten o' clock. After hugs were given and thanks expressed all around, Arnie said he would follow Rolene home to be sure she arrived safely. He didn't say whether he'd be back.

After they drove away in their separate cars, Ray looked at Gladys. "Do you think that maybe they're moving a little fast? After all, he's very vulnerable right now. I just hope that, well, you know, he doesn't end up getting hurt. He's been hurt enough, not just these past couple of weeks, but his entire life."

"Nobody knows that more than I do, Ray. But I appreciate your concern.

"The fact is, Arnie and Rolene have known each other a long time. And his marriage to Sandi was a disaster almost from the beginning. I've known for years that his feelings for Rolene were, shall we say, more than casual. I don't even think he realized how often he'd somehow manage to bring her into the conversation when it was just the two of us visiting. Now that I've met her, I know why. She's lovely, very bright, and most important of all—she's kind.

"My son is in love, Ray. And she loves him, too. And it's not just a fleeting flirtation. This is for real. Arnie's found a soulmate.

"Trust me—mothers know these things."

Chapter 37

March 22, Saturday Night

As Arnie walked Rolene to her front door, she turned to him and said, "Please come in, we need to talk. Make yourself comfortable in the living room while I put some coffee on."

He sat on the end of the sofa, just as he had on Tuesday night. Five minutes later, after handing him a mug filled to the top, she took her same place on the recliner facing the sofa.

"I've figured out who's behind the murders of your clients, and probably Whit Payne, too," she said.

"That's interesting. When I called Maria for messages the other day, she told me she was pretty sure she knew who was behind the killings, but I told her to save it for later, when we could talk in person. That was right before I discovered Sandi's body in the garage. So, I kind of forgot about it."

"Well, Maria and I have been visiting together about who the real villain is, and we've reached the same conclusion. And I'm positive we're right."

Arnie took a sip of his coffee, but remained silent.

"It's our boss, none other than Dominic Amalfitano himself."

Arnie sat in stunned silence, then shook his head.

"Unbelievable," he said, then sat in silence for a moment. "But I believe it. So, what's the link that connects him to the murders?"

"It's simple. He despises all four of your client-victims. And he doesn't think very much of you, either, which is why he's protecting Kaiser, whom he also dislikes, but who is numero uno in agency production. The big boss has even suggested to me that you're the one the police should be investigating."

"Dom's been on my short list from almost from the beginning," said Arnie, "but I've discounted it time and time again because he has so much more to lose. In fact, he has everything to lose.

The guy will make at least a hundred grand this year, and is well positioned to move up to a much larger agency on Wilshire Boulevard, or New York, or God knows where else. Maybe a senior vice president in San Francisco. And you're well aware that, because of this scandal, Home Office is already threatening to shut down the entire agency and reassign the agents to the Glendale office, and the one about to open in Thousand Oaks. So what does the boss have to gain by designating policyholders for assassination, even ones he hates? It makes no sense.

Arnie leaned forward and looked right into her eyes. "I just remembered something. You won't believe this," he said, "but a wise, charming waitress who's old enough to be our mother, told me in the Hilton cocktail lounge Thursday night the same thing you said a couple of minutes ago. She said that since the police acknowledge these were not random killings, why isn't someone looking into who had it in for the victims. By the way, she had no idea who I am. I'll tell you more about her—Celeste is her name. Please tell me more about how you reached this conclusion."

Rolene disappeared for a couple of minutes, then returned from the kitchen with some notes.

"Okay, the first casualty was Chavez, right?"

Arnie nodded.

"Dennis Chavez. He's the one who, after waiting forever to get a policy approved, ended up with a contract that was heavily surcharged, or, 'rated,' to put it in proper insurance lingo. He stormed into the office one day, demanded to speak to the manager, who—surprise, surprise—was out of the office. He left in a huff and wrote a nasty letter to the home office saying that Bear Republic had ruined his life. That he'd never be able to get a standard policy again anywhere, because it was now on his record."

"I remember," said Arnie. "Amalfitano was furious when the home office called him about the complaint they received from Chavez, who blamed poor service in our agency for all his problems. Of course, it was the folks in San Francisco who bore the responsibility for his rated policy, not us."

Rolene smiled. "Gosh it's nice to see you again, and for just the two of us to be able to be alone."

"I feel the same way," said Arnie. He got up, walked over and planted a big kiss on her lips, then returned to his place at the end of the sofa.

They both took a sip from their respective coffee mugs, then Rolene continued.

"Victim number two was Fred Fukumoto, an engineer with one of the large aerospace companies."

"North American Rockwell," said Arnie.

Rolene crossed her legs, took a deep breath, then resumed: "Fred's the guy who was Kaiser's client, but grew to dislike him so much, he demanded to be assigned to another agent."

"Yeah, you're right again," said Arnie. "That was so many years ago, I forgot all about it. He wrote a letter to the home office, too, a copy of which was sent to Amalfitano, in which he said, and I'm paraphrasing, Bill Kaiser's the most arrogant asshole I've ever known. Any company that hires him as an agent must have their head up their ass. Please, please reassign me to someone else, anyone, or I'll take my business elsewhere."

"I'm surprised you didn't think about how he became your client when he was murdered," she said, her tone soft and sympathetic.

"Now that you mention it, I am too. But he's been my client for so long, and we've always gotten along so well, it never occurred to me that the fact he came to me after leaving Kaiser had anything to do with his murder."

Rolene smiled. "Probably a case of not seeing the forest for the trees. Anyway, I'm now convinced it had everything to do with his death."

They moved on to victim number three, Bill Thompson. His situation was much like that of Dennis Chavez. A rated policy which, in his case, resulted in a personal confrontation with Amalfitano when he barged into the boss's office, late one afternoon.

"Then, the most recent victim, Don Watson, an air-conditioning and refrigeration mechanic. His sin was wandering into the GSO one day after leaving your office and flirting with one of the girls. A week later, he returned, flowers in hand, and asked the lady, Coleen Burns, for a date. She declined."

"You're right again," said Arnie. "Somehow, Amalfitano found out and shouted something like 'we're not running a dating service here.' I forgot what was said, but it wasn't very nice, that's for sure."

"Yeah," said Rolene, "Colleen quit and went to work somewhere else not too long after that incident."

They visited for another couple of hours about the murders, the background music, Arnie's mother and stepfather, and other random topics.

At 12:40 am, Arnie stood and said, "I need to get going. It's later than I thought. Why does time always go so fast when we're together?"

Rolene stood, placed both hands at her waist, smiled and said, "You're not going anywhere, Mr. Taylor."

"I'm not?"

"No, you're not. You've had too much to drink."

It was Arnie's turn to smile. "Too much to drink? I've had two gin and tonics, and that was that was several hours ago at my mother's."

"I'm not talking about alcohol, my dear. I'm talking about all the coffee you've been drinking the last couple of hours."

"Well, you're right about that. I've had enough caffeine to awaken an Egyptian mummy who's been dead three thousand years and is ready to run the one-hundred-yard dash in the Olympics. Which should be sufficient to get me home safe and sound."

"Enough to make you so high, your exuberance will result in a speeding ticket, you mean. Here's the situation. You can't sleep in the guest room because I haven't changed the sheets since the last guy slept here."

"But that was me," said Arnie.

"Are you sure?" she asked. Rolene was cocking her head ever so slightly, her broad grin breaking into a laugh.

Arnie scratched his chin, an obvious pretense that he was giving this last statement serious thought. Knowing where this was going, he could feel his heart rate accelerating.

"Yes, I'm sure."

"Anyway," she continued, "the guest room is off limits so you'll have to sleep with me. Since I have a queen bed, there should be enough room for the two of us.

"Give me about fifteen minutes to take a quick shower, brush my teeth and get in bed, then it's your turn."

Twenty minutes later, Arnie walked into her bedroom, dropped his boxer shorts on the floor adjacent to the bed, and got under the covers. A naked, curvy body moved over to his side of the bed, kissed him, then pressed her breasts against his chest.

At 6:30 that morning, Arnie got out of bed and cast a quick glance at a sleeping Rolene,. He left the room, closed the door behind him, got dressed, and went into the kitchen to start the coffee.

While sitting at the kitchen table, mug in hand, he started internalizing the past several hours. His first attempt with Rolene had failed, which was not only embarrassing, but humiliating. After a little while, she whispered, "Don't worry, Honey. You're just nervous, that's all."

About two hours later, Arnie awoke in a state of sexual excitement. He nudged her, and this time he was able to consummate the act. Three hours later, they did it again.

Chapter 38

Monday, March 24th, Van Nuys City Hall

Ricki Wright was now ready to strike out on her own to fulfill the goal that had prompted her to trail Arnold Taylor in the first place.

Prior to her fortuitous meeting with Arnie at the Red Barn the evening he'd learned of the fourth murder, she had been watching him from a distance for several months. She couldn't devote full time to this project because of her 'day job' as an undercover police officer. She was keeping tabs on him as best she could because, aware of his deep friendship with Mike Slovak back in the 50s, she believed it was more than a remote possibility the two got together from time to time. Ricki was determined to learn if this was true, and, if so, she wanted to discover where the longtime fugitive was hiding out. She would move in and take him, dead or alive. Either way, she would become the biggest star in the Los Angeles Police Department. A household name. A first-class celebrity. Perhaps featured on "60 Minutes" and other top-rated interview shows.

While Ricki was well aware this would end her longstanding friendship with Arnie, she felt that sometimes in life, enduring a personal loss for the greater good is necessary. Business is business. The fact was, she seldom saw him anyway. There would never be a romance. The time for that was long past.

Becoming a Lone Ranger in the hunt for Mike Slovak would also destroy her relationship with Lieutenant Hogan, who had, with considerable reluctance, concluded within a brief period of time that Officer Wright was a model team player. If she was not successful in her endeavor to apprehend Slovak, she would no doubt be fired, possibly accompanied by severe disciplinary action for failure to follow proper department procedures. There was even the possibility she could face legal measures.

In any event, the rewards were worth the effort. The opportunity to realize her long-term fantasy to catch Mike Slovak was real. It was apparent the killing of four of Arnold Taylor's clients was designed to draw Slovak into the action. And thanks to sheer good fortune, she had become an integral part of the investigation. With a little luck and lots of hard work, she could bring down the surviving Crosetti, and Slovak, too.

Ricki's first item of business this morning was to arrange for a second interview with Rolene Ward. Perhaps without even realizing it, Rolene could provide information about Arnie that would be helpful. One thing for sure, she and Arnie had gotten closer since Ricki met with her at Rothbard's Delicatessen. Much closer. Rolene was one of only three people who knew where Arnie was over the past weekend, and she might very well know where he was hiding out this week along the coast.

 She dialed the Bear Republic phone number from her office in Van Nuys, only to learn that Rolene, for personal reasons, would be out of the office for the entire week.

Ricki hung up. You bet your ass she's off for personal reasons. Very personal. She and Arnie are together somewhere along the coast between Newport Beach and Monterey.

Ricki leaned back in the chair behind her desk, placed both hands at the back of her head, and closed her eyes. She was remembering the look on Rolene's face that day over lunch when Ricki asked her what she thought of Arnie Taylor. That was only a week ago. A hundred weeks ago. Since then, the two had connected, their relationship had grown intimate. Boy, had they connected.

This was not good news for Ricki. Rolene was so close to Arnie now, she'd be worthless to Ricki. She was way too close to spill any useful information. Ricki would have to find another source.

Chapter 39

Pismo Beach, Thursday, March 27, 5:00 p.m.

Arnie and Rolene were seated at McClintock's, a popular restaurant on Highway 101 in Pismo Beach. They had a table by the window with a magnificent view of the ocean.

Their fourth full day together, the happy couple drove from Carpenteria that morning all the way to the Hearst Castle, a trip of 150 miles each way. Rolene had suggested on the way up that they stop for lunch at Jocko's, a famous steak restaurant in the tiny town of Nopomo, about 12 miles south of Pismo Beach. Afterwords, Arnie said it was the the best steak sandwich he'd ever had.

"We've been so busy discussing just about everything imaginable," said Arnie, "that I've never asked how you know so much about this area. It's a long way from LA, and there are so many wonderful beach resorts so much closer to home."

"It's simple," she said. "As a kid I use to spend a month or so every summer with my grandmother—my mother's mother— in Fresno. She would always take me here for a week or so, and I developed a love for the central coast that continues to this day."

A leggy, college-age waitress wearing a short skirt approached with a pitcher of water. She pulled a chair over, stood on it, then poured water into their two empty glasses from a height of two feet.

Rolene grinned, then said, "I saw you looking at those legs, Mr. Taylor."

"Well, I couldn't help but notice them, but I was actually comparing her legs with yours. You win by a mile. Of course, I've seen a hell of a lot more of your legs than a brief glimpse I got of hers. In fact, a whole lot more of you, period, than I ever expected to see."

"Good comeback," she said. "You're fast on your feet, or, in this case, fast on your seat."

"Anyway," he said, "back to Fresno. I can't imagine why anyone would want to go there in the summer. I remember our family driving through there three times in the late 40s and early 50s on our way to Yosemite. It was the last stop for gas, and hotter than a four-balled tomcat."

Rolene laughed. "You're right, it's hot there in the summer," she said. "But then, so is the San Fernando Valley. Anyway, my grandmother was Armenian, and she moved there to live with cousins after raising my mom and her two sisters.

"Did you know that Fresno is crawling with Armenians?"

"I've heard that, but, with your blue eyes, fair complexion and light-brown hair, I would never have taken you for being Armenian. What are you, about 25%?"

"Exactly. The rest, English, a little German, Scots-Irish."

They moved on to other topics, then Arnie's face took-on a more serious look.

"So, we're agreed on who is most likely to be the fifth victim targeted?" Asked Arnie.

"Yes," said Rolene. "The most likely suspect at the end of the alphabet is Matt Weinstein."

"Well, he certainly fits the profile, given the reality that Amalfitano can't stand him. And it's all because poor Max use to live across the street from the boss. As neighbors, they had a disagreement or two about, God knows about what."

"You and I both know there's more to it than that," said Rolene. "Amalfitano is extremely anti-Semitic, probably more than anyone I've ever known. We have Judy Isenberg and Eli Lieb in our office only because the home office insisted. I've even heard him refer to Weinstein as a kike, a word I hadn't heard since I was a kid."

"Really? That's ugly. Really ugly," said Arnie. "Matt's a hell of a nice guy."

"And remember," said Arnie, "not a word about this to the police if they interview you again. I no longer have any faith in the LAPD. None. Zero. Zilch. I'm going to handle this on the sly with an old acquaintance, the one man who can bring all this violence to an end."

"I know," said Rolene, "your old friend Mike Slovak. I just hope you know what you're doing. There's way too much at stake for anything to go wrong. And, if anything happens to you, well, I don't know what I'd do. I'd probably suffer a complete nervous breakdown. I've finally found a soul mate. The love of my life. And I don't want anything bad to happen to you."

He leaned across the table, where their lips met in the middle.

"Don't worry, Honey, everything's going to turn out all right," he said.

Chapter 40

Van Nuys City Hall, Friday, April 18, 7:55 AM

Officer Ricki Wright took a quick glance at her watch. Her guest was expected in five minutes.

She mulled over how much had changed in the insurance scandal investigation since she joined the team back on March12th. Lieutenant Frank Hogan had been removed from the case the week following the explosive Los Angeles Times editorial of March 27th, nearly three weeks ago. Everyone else in the department kept their jobs, but somebody had to be the fall guy. He was the obvious victim. The beleaguered lieutenant was currently on unpaid leave, dealing with problems surrounding his alcoholic, drug-addicted wife.

There was a knock on Ricki's door at the top of the hour. Officer Wright got up from behind her desk and said, "Come in."

She then walked around to the front of her desk to greet Maria Tavarez, Arnold Taylor's secretary. The undercover officer had arranged this meeting in darkest secrecy. She had given Ms. Taverez explicit instructions not to say a word to anyone concerning the real reason she would be late to work this morning. Maria had left word with both of her bosses, Michael Wong and Arnold Taylor, that she had a dental appointment.

Officer Wright's meeting with Maria was clandestine as far as her colleagues were concerned as well. Her new boss, Lieutenant David Davenport, was attending a meeting at police headquarters downtown this morning, and his secretary, Rosa Lee Raines, had been out all week with the flu. Ricki had decided that Maria was her last, best hope to obtain information regarding a fifth Taylor client to be targeted on April 24th, just six days away. That ominous date represented exactly forty-five days since the fourth murder. In any case, Ricki was about to find out from Maria what Taylor knew about next Thursday, if anything.

The two ladies engaged in desultory conversation for several minutes, then Officer Wright got to the subject which had been on her mind for six weeks. "Ms. Tavarez, as you know, our meeting today is confidential. By that I mean you are not to discuss with anyone, the fact that you've met with me, that you know me, what we've discussed, or anything else to do with this meeting."

"I understand, Officer," said Maria.

"I'm putting you under oath. Should you violate the confidence of our visit, there could be grave legal consequences."

Maria coughed nervously, then twisted in her chair to get more comfortable.

"I understand."

"This is important, Ms. Tavarez, because, as you know, I'm an undercover police officer. Even other LAPD officers have no knowledge of what I'm working on. This is because there are often leaks from our department that get out to unsavory underworld characters who can do us all great harm. Like kill us. You, me, Mr. Taylor, other innocent people."

Maria Tavarex sat frozen, unsmiling. Officer Wright had just scared the shit out of her, which was her intent.

"Now," said Ricki, "you probably have a pretty good idea why you're here, and what it is I want from you."

"I think so. I think you want to know if I know who Mr. Taylor believes will be targeted next Thursday, the forty-fifth day since the last killing."

"Exactly. Do you know the man's name?"

"Yes. Matt Weinstein."

"And just who is he?" asked Ricki. "What can you tell me about him?"

"Well, he owns a hardware store on Lankershim Boulevard in North Hollywood. It used to be called Yeakel's Hardware, but Mr. Weinstein bought the business a couple of years ago."

Ricki Wright had just hit the jackpot. She managed to suppress a big smile, but it wasn't easy.

"And why does Mr. Taylor think Mr. Weinstein is going to be targeted?"

"Because Mr. Weinstein use to live across the street from Mr. Amalfitano, our agency manager. The two of them didn't get along very well."

"Really? Is that why the others have been murdered? Because Mr. Amalfitano didn't like them?"

"We're pretty sure that's the reason, but we didn't figure this out until recently."

"We? Ms. Tavarez?"

"Yes. Mr. Taylor, Rolene and me."

"Is there anything else about Weinstein that makes him a probable target?" asked Ricki.

"Yes. He's Jewish. Mr. Amalfitano doesn't like Jews. He refers to Mr. Weinstein as 'my ex-neighbor, the kike.'"

"I see," said Officer Wright. "Does anyone else in the agency know Mr. Weinstein is believed to be the next victim?"

Maria Tavarez started to answer, hesitated, then responded to the question.

"Well, like I said, Rolene knows. She's Mr. Amalfitano's secretary."

Ricki smiled. "She's a lot more than that, Ms. Tavarez, isn't she?"

"I'm not sure what you mean," said Maria.

"Rolene and Mr. Taylor are romantically involved, right?"

Maria stared at Officer Wright for a moment. "Yes, they are. But I didn't know anyone else knew about that, other than Mr. Wong, my other boss."

"Ms. Tavarez, I work undercover. I know a lot more than you can imagine. By the way, how's that husky eight-year-old son of yours, Armando? I hear he's a fine young ballplayer. He's sure a handsome kid."

When Maria got up to leave, she was told Ricki would be calling her at the office in exactly one hour. She wanted Matt Weinstein's address. She also reminded Maria that their visit, and the content of their conversation, was not to be shared with anyone. Not Arnie, not her mother, not a living, breathing soul.

Chapter 41

North Hollywood, Thursday, April 24, 1:25 p.m.

Officer Ricki Wright turned right off of Laurel Canyon and headed east on Hartsook Street. Matt Weinstein's house was in the first block on the north side of the street, the second house on her left. This was her third visit to this location since her meeting with Maria. She knew exactly what she was going to do. And when the deed was done, the last Crosetti would be dead, as would Mike Slovak. She would love to take Slovak alive, but was certain that wasn't going to happen. No way.

Ricki drove five miles an hour to the end of the block, looking for any hint that she might not be the first one there for Weinstein's arrival. She then turned right on Ben Avenue, and right again at Otsego. Ricki parked her unmarked car near an alley, one house away from the end of the block. She walked the short distance through the alley to get back to Hartsook.

Officer Wright walked across the front lawn of the house adjacent to the Weinstein's. Along the far side of the house was an alley and a back parking lot for the stores facing Laurel Canyon. With only three small stores facing the busy boulevard, the lot was nearly always free of human or vehicular traffic. .

The undercover officer looked at the front window of the neighbor's house from a distance of perhaps twenty feet to see if she could see inside. The front room appeared to be dark. If no one was home, she would have no trouble breaking the front door lock.

As she headed toward the front door, a woman opened it and said, "Is there something I can do for you? Why are you looking at our house?"

The homeowner's tone was harsh and suspicious. Ricki introduced herself, opened her purse, pulled out her badge. "May I come in? We have something very serious to discuss, something that has nothing to do with you directly."

"How do I know that badge is real, that you are who you say you are?"

After Officer Wright produced her driver's license, complete with photograph. She was invited in.

The neighbor introduced herself as Laura Wheaton. She looked to be in her sixties, perhaps a little older, and when her husband appeared, he looked to be a great deal older than his wife, maybe seventy-five. His name was Charlie.

"Before I explain why I'm here, I need to ask the two of you a question. Have you been following the case of the four murders involving Bear Republic and the agent, Arnold Taylor?"

"Are you kidding?" asked Charlie Wheaton. "That's the biggest local story here in the Valley in years. Of course we've been following it. Who do you think we are, a couple of dodo birds?"

The officer ignored the sarcasm, though she noticed Mr. Wheaton was smiling. "Are you friends with the people next door, the Weinstein's?"

"Yes," said Mrs Wheaton. "We know them real well. Matt and Rose. They're nice neighbors. Why do you ask? Are they in any danger?"

Officer Wright explained that the police suspected Weinstein was targeted to be victim number five, and that she needed to stay in their front room and keep a watch on who was coming and going next door. She also told them the Weinstein's were aware of the danger, that neither of them were home, and that they would not come home until it was safe for them to return.

Charlie and Laura Wheaton both turned ashen. After a moment of silence, Laura said, "I'm puzzled. I'd think there'd be other police officers around.

Are you the only one?"

"Like I said, I work undercover. When Rocky Crosetti appears the moment another undercover officer drives Weinstein's truck into the driveway, we'll be prepared for the assassin. In the meantime, we don't want him to suspect that any law-enforcement officers are in the area. And, by the way, that's why I was staring at your front window. I was trying to determine how difficult, or easy, someone from outside could see into your front room. Since I couldn't see you watching me, Mrs. Wheaton, I now know this is an excellent place for me to hangout until trouble arrives. Then, I will step out on your front porch and take whatever action is necessary to bring this ongoing tragedy to a conclusion. Other officers will be showing up as well."

Ricki was certain Weinstein would not be driving home. That it would be Slovak. That's why she had portrayed Mike Slovak as an undercover officer. At this point Ricki felt the Wheatons knew all they needed to know.

Still shaken, Charlie and Laura excused themselves and went into their den at the back of the house, Charlie mumbling something about fixing himself a highball. Ricki knew this was going to be a long afternoon. It might very well be three hours before the modern version of "The Gunfight at the O.K. Corral" would play out. But it was worth the wait.

A little after 2:30, a stocky, dark-haired man walked from the alley, crossed the street to the Weinstein residence, went to the side gate on the left side of the garage, and opened it. Upon entering the side yard, he closed the gate behind him. The man looked about thirty-five, maybe forty. Ricki thought he resembled Dominic Amalfitano, but she couldn't be certain because he was wearing a straw hat.

Ricki pondered what was going on. This was either the last remaining Crosetti, or someone recruited by him to help kill Slovak after executing Weinstein. Perhaps an ambush was planned. Someone approaches the truck from the street, Slovak gets out of the truck, a mysterious figure behind the gate comes out, and they kill the infamous hit-man in a crossfire thinking they're killing Weinstein. Then, while they stand there wondering where the hell Slovak is, Ricki shoots them both. Three hoodlums dead, including Slovak, and Officer Ricki Wright has choreographed the whole scene. Ricki's pretty face on the front page of tomorrow's *Los Angeles Times*? Hell, this LA gangster shoot-out will be numero uno in tomorrow's *New York Times*.

There was also a possible downside, however, to what she was about to undergo. She would be scorned and ridiculed by her colleagues in the LAPD for taking on this project by herself. For not asking for backup. It would be obvious she wanted to act alone for all the celebrity hood that would follow. The woman undercover cop who killed Mike Slovak and the last Crosetti, thereby saving the life of Matt Weinstein. The gutsy female who ended the drama of the insurance company murders. There would be plenty of jealousy among her peers, but so what? To the greater public throughout the nation, she would be a hero.

At 2:53, a dark-skinned woman emerged from the Weinstein's front door carrying a bucket. Probably Hispanic, she appeared to be the cleaning lady since the bucket contained a broom and various other cleaning products. She opened the door of her red Chevy Maverick parked in front of the house, placed the bucket on the back floor, got inside the vehicle, and drove away.

A couple of dogs suddenly came upon the visitor hiding behind the side gate. He was, in fact, receiving the most unwelcome greeting imaginable. Loud, deafening barks, groans, whining sounds from the dogs, screams and pleas for help coming from the unlucky intruder. The cleaning lady had apparently let the dogs out when she left.

The Wheatons ran into the front room. "Oh my God," Laura shouted, "Someone's gotten into the Weinstein's backyard. It sounds like Gus and Samson are mauling him to death."

"Gus and Samson? What kind of dogs are they?" asked Officer Wright.

"They're pit bulls."

"Well," said the officer, "that's one less gunman I need to worry about. I saw someone go through the side gate into the backyard about a half hour ago. He won't be walking out, that's for sure."

"If that's the case, why didn't he shoot the dogs, for Christ's sake?" asked Charlie.

"They must have caught him by surprise," said Officer Wright. "Perhaps he was leaning back against the outside garage wall taking a little snooze and they were on him before he realized it. Maybe his pistol was in his coat pocket and he couldn't get to it in time. Who knows?"

Several minutes after they heard the last groans from Amalfitano, or whoever he was, the dogs stopped howling and apparently left the narrow area beyond the gate for the larger backyard behind the house.

Pit Bulls? In Ricki's mind, the furtive gangster would have been far better off dying an hour or two later from gunshots than from being the victim of vicious dogs enjoying a midafternoon snack.

At 3:35, Officer Wright observed another man walking down the alley from Otsego Street. She did a double-take. At least from a distance, he looked exactly like the man in the side yard who presumably was out of action. Could there be two Amafitanos? Or was this man a Crosetti who resembled Amalfitano?

The second man stopped twenty feet or so short of Ben Avenue and stood to the side of the alley. He was no longer visible to anyone looking south down the alley from Hartsook, or north from Otsego Street. At 4:10, Laura Wheaton popped her head through the doorway and asked the officer if she would like a Coke, a glass of water, or anything.

Ricki turned her head away from the window for a moment to reply when, suddenly, Mrs. Wheaton pointed toward the alley.

"That's his truck," she said. "That's Matt's truck heading our way through the alley."

Officer Wright turned around and cast a quick glance in that direction. She hadn't looked down the alley since the second gunman had arrived. She was expecting Mike Slovak to be turning off of Laurel Canyon onto Hartsook and driving east. Or coming from the east on Hartsook, but not down the alley from Otsego, coming into view right across the street from the Weinstein residence. Given this new scenario, when Slovak pulled into the Weinstein' driveway and exited the Ford Truck, the gunman in the alley would appear, fire several shots at Slovak, then be killed by Ricki as she unloaded her .38 revolver at Crosetti while standing on the Wheatons front porch.

It was, indeed, Weinstein's '73 Ford F100 pickup. Slovak had decided to drive through the alley, the area most likely to be inhabited by Crosetti, who would also be expecting the target's vehicle to be coming off of Laurel Canyon onto Hartsook.

The two women watched in silence as the driver of the Ford came to a stop fifteen or twenty feet from Hartsook, pointed a gun to his right, and fired two shots. Ricki couldn't see Crosetti, or whoever he was, since he remained out of her view off to the side of the alley. But whoever he was, she was convinced he was now a dead man.

The Ford pickup continued the short distance to Hartsook and stopped. The driver looked both ways on Hartsook, then at the Weinstein house, then even up at the trees across from the house. He then turned left, and headed toward Laurel Canyon, never casting a glance at the Wheaton home where Ricki had a .38 revolver pointed right at his head. As Mike Slovak drove away, Ricki stood and stared and never fired a shot. She dropped her pistol to her side, told Laura Wheaton to call the police at the number on her identification card, then slowly walked out the front door and crossed the street to view Crosetti's dead body in the alley.

Mike Slovak's decision to approach the Weinstein house from the alley instead of pulling into the Weinstein driveway, changed everything. For Rocky Crosetti, and for Ricki Wright.

****

Mike turned left onto Laurel Canyon, then drove three short blocks to Addison Street, turned left and pulled over and parked behind a brand-new Mercury Marquis. A woman was sitting on the driver's side. Mike got into the car and directed his girlfriend to drive to the Riverside Market on the northeast corner of Riverside Drive and Laurel Canyon. They avoided busy streets, then parked in the lot behind the store. While Mike waited in the car, his friend went to a telephone booth and dialed the number of Weinstein's Hardware.

"Mr. Weinstein, you and your wife can go home now. Everything went as planned. Your truck is in the middle of the block on Addison Street between Ben Avenue and Laurel Canyon. Tell Arnie his friend is okay. The important thing is, you're alive, Crosetti's dead, and it's now safe for you to go home."

When his girlfriend returned to the car, Mike said, "Much to my surprise, there was only one man waiting for me. I was certain there would be at least two, maybe three, to put me away. The dumb shit was standing at the side of the alley, obviously unaware of the kind of vehicle Weinstein drove. When my pickup was adjacent to where he was standing, he forced a smile and nodded at me. I then put two bullets in his forehead. There was no question he was the last Crosetti. They all have that same Dago smart-ass look about them. Let's go to the White Oak. I need a drink."

****

At the hardware store, Matt Weinstein and his wife, Rose, exchanged hugs and kisses, then both of them gave Arnie long hugs.

After they left in her car to pick up his truck, Arnie called Rolene at the office with the news. She told him to drive to her house, that she would be leaving work right away. It didn't matter if it wasn't five o' clock. Mr. Amalfitano was apparently away for the afternoon. No one had seen or heard from him since early that morning.

Arnie called his mother to tell her their long nightmare was over. He then walked into the back parking lot, got into his red Gran Torino, and headed for Rolene's house.

Chapter 42

Seven minutes after receiving the call from Mrs. Wheaton, three patrol cars arrived at the scene. Ricki Wright showed her badge to the officers, explaining that she had been following Dominic Amalfitano for a couple of days and, twice, he had driven down this block, stopped, and stared at the house. This being the forty-fifth day since the last murder, she guessed, correctly, that this was going to be the location of the fifth killing.

"Someone needs to open the gate next to the garage and take a look. Someone with a strong stomach," she said. "And be careful. There are a couple of pit bulls in the back." She heard the dogs barking, the sound of two gunshots, then a brief silence.

"Oh my God," said the officer who followed her instructions. "I've never seen anything like this in my life. This poor devil doesn't even have a face anymore."

Soon, an ambulance pulled up, along with two more police cars, and parameds.

Ricki explained what had happened. A man who resembled Dominic Amalfitano arrived, went inside the gate to hide, and was subsequently mauled to death by pit bulls. Then a second man arrived, who looked like the guy who had arrived earlier. His body was in the alley, shot by Mike Slovak, who drove through the alley to get to the Weinstein's home.

Lieutenant Davenport showed up about twenty minutes later. He wanted to talk with Officer Wright alone. They walked onto the front yard of a vacant house across the street from the crime scene. Two of the seven officers at the scene were interviewing the Wheatons. The others, roping off the alley, going into the backyard to determine if there was any more carnage, and other miscellaneous duties germane to mopping up following violent crimes.

"If you had good reason to believe this was the location where the fifth victim would be targeted, why didn't you follow procedures?" asked the lieutenant.

"You know goddamn well you should have passed this information along to me. Why did you hide inside a neighbor's home when we could have had officers all over this area? And how do you know the man driving the Ford Truck was Mike Slovak?"

Lieutenant Davenport' face was within inches of hers, his voice loud enough to be heard half a block away. She stared back at him, backed away, but remained silent. She had to be very careful when giving her version of how she happened to be there with full knowledge that a crime was about to take place. And it was imperative that her story not conflict with what the officers would learn from what she told the Wheatons.

"Well, the truth is, I didn't know who would be driving Mr. Weinstein's truck, but I was pretty sure it wouldn't be him. So I told the Wheatons it would be an undercover police officer. I told them that, knowing it wasn't true, just to ease their minds. Anyway, the man who showed up driving Weinstein's truck was so smooth, so well-prepared, I concluded it was Slovak. But by the time I could process everything, he was gone.

"Why were you 'pretty sure' the driver of Weinstein's truck would not be Mr. Weinstein? How would you know that?"

I just felt that, after all this time, Arnie and Mike Slovak, whom I'm convinced were in touch with one another, had finally figured the whole thing out. And since our own investigation inside Homicide had labeled Mr. Amalfitano as suspect number one, and Lieutenant Hogan had ordered me to put a tail on him, I reached the conclusion that this was the location and Weinstein the target. It turns out I was right.

"As for your other question, I don't have enough confidence in our department anymore to want them around anything as important as this. Remember George Porter? With police all over this place, today's action would have been a fiasco. They would have all gotten away."

"Wrong," said the lieutenant. "With police all over this place, we would have gotten Mike Slovak."

"Remember how the department failed to keep a watch on the Schultz's house, which resulted in their deaths? Or, Sandi Taylor, who was left abandoned by you guys, at the cost of her life, even though you knew the Crosettis had every reason to silence her?

"Maybe it's a good thing Slovak got away. He's killed more bad guys than any ten officers from our homicide department combined."

"I want you to go home Officer Wright, now," said Lieutenant Davenport, while we mop up around here. Tomorrow morning, I want you in my office at 8:00 am sharp. We have a lot to talk about."

As Ricki walked through the alley to her car on Otsego Street, more police arrived, including a mobile lab containing a deputy coroner and a photographer.

Later that evening, she received a phone call from the lieutenant advising her that the meeting the next morning would be at LAPD Headquarters downtown. The meeting, still scheduled for eight o' clock, would be taking place in the office of Deputy Chief Fleming.

As she started downing one Gin and Tonic after another at her mother's house, Ricki Wright knew her career in the Los Angeles Police Department was over. The two bullets fired at Crosetti would no doubt prove to be from Mike Slovak's .38, of that she was certain. But she would be asked again how she knew when and where this would take place, and why didn't she share this information with her colleagues. No way would she put Maria Taverez in jeopardy. She would be pressed to reveal if Arnold Taylor was involved with her in this venture. On this point, she was innocent. She hadn't seen or spoken with him since that night in March at the Red Barn.

At the start of the meeting the next morning, she told her superiors she was resigning from the department, effective immediately. The questions put to her were pretty much as she had guessed in advance. She stuck with her story that she had been following Agency Manager Dominic Amalfitano for a couple of days, and that he had twice driven by the house on Hartsook Street to check it out.

"How did you learn the names of the residents of the Weinstein house?" asked Fleming.

"There's a reverse guide directory in our office. All I had to do was look up the address and the name of the owner would be there," she said sarcastically.

"Anyway, my assignment was to solve the Crosetti case revolving around seven murders and a suicide. I didn't share this information because, as I told Lieutenant Davenport yesterday, I no longer have any confidence in our once-great police department. Mike Slovak's been out there for twenty-eight years, so I doubt you'd want to make me a scapegoat in this matter. If you do, I'll go public, telling the world that the *LA Times* editorial was an understatement. That Mike Slovak's the best officer in the force even though he's not on the payroll. He kills off gang members you cannot seem to find. I'll tell that to the world, and there's plenty else I can say. So it's in the best interest of all of us to let me go quietly."

Ricki Wright was unhappy almost to the point of serious depression. She had joined the LAPD to get Mike Slovak. But when it came right down to it, she couldn't pull the trigger. She had failed. She would now have to move on to something else, somewhere else.

Did she fail to pull the trigger because she was afraid it would end, forever, her cherished friendship with Arnie Taylor that went all the way back to the fifth grade? Maybe. She wasn't sure. Or was it because her disdain for the incompetence of the Los Angeles Police Department was such that she really didn't care if they ever caught the most famous fugitive in the city's history? Perhaps. Or was fame at a national level not worth it if she would always harbor doubts that she had killed a notorious outlaw who, as far as she knew, did more good than bad when it came to society as a whole? She didn't know how she could explain that to anyone's satisfaction, at least not anyone at this meeting.

The truth was, she didn't know why she didn't pull the trigger. But, she knew she was not sorry about it. If given another chance, she would do the same thing again.

She had learned, in a painful way, what philosophers and historians had known for centuries. Life is complicated, and sometimes there just aren't any easy answers.

The Los Angeles Police Department announced that the case of the Bear Republic Insurance Company murders had been solved. There would be no more killings every forty-five days. They avoided taking too much credit for bringing this bizarre case to an end since it was public knowledge that Mike Slovak, not the LAPD, was the reason the Crosetti's were dead. Mike had killed two of the brothers, and most likely would have killed the third, had he not already been mauled to death by pit bulls.

Chapter 43

One day after Ricki Wright resigned from the LAPD, it was announced that lab tests indicated that the two underworld figures killed on Thursday were identical twins. The fact that one of them no longer had a face didn't matter. The photograph on his driver's license proved he looked exactly like the other victim. The name on the license was "Amalfitano, Dominic." It was also announced that the two bullets fired at Rocky Crosetti in the alley were from Mike Slovak's .38.

Ricki Wright finished the semester at Cal State, Northridge, then returned to NYU to work toward a PhD in public administration. She decided she was more suited to academe. Since her name didn't appear in LAPD public announcements, Arnie never learned of her involvement in the case.

Lieutenant Frank Hogan never returned to work at the LAPD. He took early retirement to stay home with his wife. Since he had married her 'for better or for worse,' he decided to stay with her to the end. The truth was, he loved his wife, and he loved his Church. He would do the right thing. When her health improved, he thought he might start a small home security business

Bear Republic decided not to close the Panorama City office. Dominic Amalfitano's replacement arrived on June 1st. A devout Mormon, George Williams was a twenty-year career manager transferred from the company's office in Provo, Utah.

Arnold Taylor resigned from Bear Republic on May 1st. He made a financial arrangement with Michael Wong, who would be taking over his book of business.

Arnie needed time to decide what he wanted to do with the rest of his life. With $200,000 in tax-free life insurance proceeds from Sandi's death, he had plenty of money to live on until he made up his mind. When he sold his Granada Hills home in August for $79,000, he netted another tidy sum, having paid $27, 500 for the house in 1967.

Arnold Taylor and Rolene Ward were married on October 4th, 1975, at the Congregational Church of Northridge, United Church of Christ. There were more than two-hundred people in attendance, including Bill Kaiser and Frank Hogan. Following the ceremony, a reception was held in a private banquet room at the Sportsmen's Lodge in Studio City.

After Rolene sold her house in November, the happy couple moved to Fresno. They paid cash for a house near Woodward Park in the north-central part of the city. Rolene enrolled at Fresno City College for two classes, and would transfer to Fresno State. She wanted to teach English Literature at the high school level. They hoped to start a family.

Arnie had not decided whether he wanted to remain in the life insurance business. He was thinking about becoming a journalist. He was also pondering the idea of writing a novel surrounding the circumstance of his childhood family tragedy. And maybe another one concerning his most recent forty-five days of murder and intrigue. That would occupy him for a while.

Mike Slovak is still at large.

—GARY WAYNE WALKER—